REQUIEM
TALES OF THE UNDEAD
I0740224

EDITED BY LISA MANGUM
WITH WENDY CHRISTENSEN

With an all-new zombie story by *New York Times* best-selling author Jonathan Maberry

Death comes for us all. But for some, it doesn't stay. Mythology and lore is full of undead creatures, and each one has a story to tell—of their life, their death, or their afterlife.

From a haunting melody that leads a ghost to her killer, to a piano that provides salvation during a zombie apocalypse, to a song that grants passage back from death, *Requiem: Tales of the Undead* offers a chilling chorus of monstrous melodies and ghostly harmonies.

These nineteen imaginative stories feature a wide variety of the undead, each woven with a distinct musical element that explores the connection between life, death, and the supernatural. A vampire working in law enforcement learns that "The driver picks the music." A mummy trapped in a corporate cubicle struggles to break free and pursue his own song. Death takes piano lessons. And when a special song is played on a specific gramophone, the dead are allowed to answer three final questions.

These aren't just stories about the undead. They're about what we remember, what we mourn, and the songs that stay with us—long after the last breath fades.

So listen closely. The dead have stories to tell. And they are set to music.

REQUIEM

TALES OF THE UNDEAD

Edited by
LISA MANGUM

With
WENDY CHRISTENSEN

WFP
WORDFIRE PRESS

eBook ISBN: 978-1-68057-819-5

Trade Paperback ISBN: 978-1-68057-820-1

Dust Jacket Hardcover ISBN: 978-1-68057-821-8

Library of Congress Control Number: 202594804

Cover design by **CL Fors**

Kevin J. Anderson, Art Director

Vellum layout by CJ Anaya

Published by
WordFire Press, LLC
PO Box 1840
Monument CO 80132
Kevin J. Anderson & Rebecca Moesta, Publishers
WordFire Press eBook Edition 2026
WordFire Press Trade Paperback Edition 2026
WordFire Press Dust Jacket Hardcover Edition 2026

Printed in the USA
Join our WordFire Press Readers Group for
sneak previews, updates, new projects, and giveaways.
Sign up at wordfirepress.com

CONTENTS

DAYS GONE QUIET
JONATHAN MABERRY

The place hadn't fallen down yet, but it was working on it.

It sagged beneath the weight of all 136 of its years, and it was clear that few of them had been good ones. Even the ivy that clung to the cracked bricks was faded and anemic, the leaves dry and dusty. The trees—two towering oaks and a dozen stately elms—leaned away from the house as if not wanting to play any part in its slow-motion decay.

The house was older than anyone in town. No one really had a clue when it had been built. It was just always there. Families moved into the neighborhood, lingered for a generation or two, and moved on, but the house remained. The place wasn't pretty. Too many of the shingles had fallen over the years and termites had done their usual workmanlike job of making timbers sag. Those shutters that were still on both hinges were missing slats, giving the place a kind of lateral gap-toothed grin that failed to be either charming or spooky. Paint peeled the way paint does, without adding rustic allure. Nothing about the house reached out to fixer-uppers or flippers. It was at the end of an inconvenient street, and even at the reduced price of selling for back taxes was no draw. The current owner always canceled Realtor showings, suggesting a reluctance to sell or perhaps a desire to fade away with the property.

It was big, rambling, drafty, old, and unattractive without the seasonal charisma of looking Halloween ugly. No kids thought it was haunted. No squatters wanted to spend a night there, and no looters even considered breaking in for copper pipes or reclaimed wood. People simply did not think much about it.

It simply was.

It was why Elmer Howard liked it.

Not the house per se ... just its utter lack of appeal.

It suited him because he, too, lacked appeal. He was average height, average weight, average looks. He'd spent his whole life being unexceptional and—in the truest use of the word—unremarkable.

People didn't talk about him either.

There were people he knew, but none of them were friends. He had relatives, but they never called. Not since Elmer's wife, Gina, died. It was as if the last life force in either Elmer or the house had no real desire to move on. Entropy became a defining characteristic of the widower within the walls.

Since Gina died, Elmer only ever got Christmas cards from one aunt in Des Moines, and he knew she bought cards in bulk and sent them to everyone in her address book. Everyone. Her signature was just initials, with no accompanying note. Years back he'd seen identical cards at a cousin's house during a post-funeral luncheon. That dead cousin's card was the same as his. Precisely the same. The aunt hadn't come to the funeral, and Elmer guessed she was still sending cards to that address.

His wife, Gina, was six years in her grave, taken from him by a cancer that showed up during a routine health check and spirited her away within two months. They never had kids. During their marriage, they were very much into one another's company and did everything together. Because they were both—well, *antisocial* wasn't the right word. *Nonsocial* fit better—being together satisfied their needs for company. Quiet folks who enjoyed quiet and didn't feel the need to fill every minute with conversation.

Her ashes were on his mantel, and sometimes—when rainy nights got really long, or snowstorms shut down all ambient noise—he talked with her. Sitting in his beat-up old armchair, feet on a coffee table built from four milk crates and an old door, he chatted as if she were in the other chair. The house was big, and he needed to hear a voice every now and then, even if it was his own. Only once in a very great while did he go crazy enough to think he heard her talking back.

He was strange—he'd be the first to admit that—but he wasn't actually insane. Sometimes he thought he heard laughter too. Or a moan of the kind Gina made while the bone cancer was consuming her. Human sounds, either conjured by his mind or remembered in the aching wooden bones of the house.

The end of the world changed that.

It changed everything.

If the world had been planning on ending, he didn't know about it. Not until much later.

Elmer had a TV but rarely watched it. Nothing he saw on shows or in movies seemed to apply to him. The talking heads on the news never seemed to take people like him into account, and so he discounted them. Seemed fair.

He tried audiobooks, but it felt too much like eavesdropping on someone else's conversation. And he never got the pop culture references.

Mostly Elmer let the house be as quiet as it wanted to be, except for those whispers and moans.

Sometimes he played music. He had a CD player and a lot of CDs. He'd started collecting them back in the days when magazine ads said you could order a dozen for a dollar if you joined a club and didn't bother to read the fine print. He kept buying them, though. That was one thing about himself that he liked—he could listen to just about any kind of music. Sure, he had his preferences. Old jazz, some classical, Kansas City blues. But he had all kinds of rock, hip-hop, rap, pop, country, even polka. Anything to fill the empty corners of the house when silence betrayed him and commonplace noise hit him like screams. At those times he wanted more intentional sounds to push the quiet back. Sometimes, when he felt petulant and perverse, he'd turn the volume up to annoy the mice. Or maybe to entertain the crows in the trees outside.

The only kind of music he didn't like was Christmas stuff. Not since Gina died. The peppy optimism made him sad. And the sad ones, like "Have Yourself a Merry Little Christmas" and "Blue Christmas," made him even sadder.

Loneliness was okay. Sadness wasn't.

Sadness was like being sick. Like having cancer.

Sometimes—not often, but more so since Gina died—he'd get so sad he'd take his father's old shotgun out from under the bed, unroll it from the blanket, oil it, load it, and try not to want to use it. There were close calls. A few really, really close. Times when the music didn't do its job and the house screamed at him that Gina wasn't. Ever. Going. To. Be. There. Again.

But each time, after sitting on the chair hugging the gun to his chest, he'd wrap it up again and put it back. There was some comfort in knowing it was there. Knowing that the exit door was never fully locked.

And that made it okay to keep going.

Keep living.

The thing that changed the course of his need to not *be* was the fear that if he opted out then he would lose the emotions he felt. Lose the memories he had. The thought that death might erase his love for Gina and all his memories of their years together was unbearable.

He lived in opposition to the possibilities offered by that fear.

Most of the time, he wasn't aware that was what he was doing. Moments of clarity and perspective came when they came.

On a cold Thursday morning, he had one of those moments of clarity.

It wasn't the temperature or the slow, sad rain. It wasn't the rustle of damp birds in dripping trees. It wasn't the low rumble of distant thunder. It wasn't even the fact that last night was one of *those* nights. A Gina night.

Last night was very long, with intense wind that made the house moan with too human a timbre.

The wind eased a bit at dawn.

Elmer went out onto the front porch with a thermos of hot coffee and his favorite mug—a gift from his wife on his fortieth birthday that had a Photoshopped picture of him as a baby but with an old man's long white beard. It was chipped now and had a crack around the base of the handle, but it held warmth from Gina.

He wore a heavy sweater over a flannel shirt and sat in his usual seat, pausing only to brush wet leaves from Gina's rocker. Elmer poured himself a cup of coffee, sipped it, nodded, and settled back to watch the rain. Gina and he always liked the rain. She liked big, violent thunderstorms more than he did, but she was always more intense and passionate than he was.

The coffee was good, though a bit thin, representing the last of what he found in the cupboard. He added that to the shopping list in his head for tomorrow. Every other Thursday was a go-to-market day. Not that the day or timing mattered. There were no crowds, but he liked the rhythm of it. A schedule made the world feel like it was still real in those small ways that mattered.

A ragged old crow flapped out of the closest elm and landed on the porch rail. At times, when Elmer had sipped a bit too much Canadian Club, he tried to convince himself that Gina had come back to him as a bird. She always loved birds, especially that particular crow. Once, years back, she found the crow on the front lawn, battered and bloodied by a narrow escape from a neighborhood cat. Gina took it in and nursed it back to health. She hand-fed it, and as trust and health grew, it would come and sit on the porch rail. She'd give it treats, and the crow ate spiders and roaches. When she died, the bird sat in a tree and cawed for days. Then it was gone for nearly a year, returning only a day after the anniversary of her death.

He thought it was her come back *as* the crow. But that thought faded with the alcohol, and the next day, he dismissed the concept as ridiculous. If Gina was going to come back it would be as a songbird. A dark-eyed junco, maybe, or a goldfinch.

The crow, he was sure, was just a crow.

On a whim, he leaned forward and poured a few drops of coffee on the flat porch rail. Steam rose from it, and the crow gave the brown drops an interested look. After a moment, it shuffled sideways and bent down to inspect them. Then, it sipped the coffee. A small taste at first and then all of it.

It raised its head and gave him an expectant look. So, Elmer poured a few more drops. Later, some more.

They were like that for a while. One older man and one ragged-looking older crow, drinking coffee on a rainy Thursday morning.

If the crow knew the world had already ended, he didn't clue Elmer in on the fact.

No, it was the dead man who brought the news.

Elmer had just poured himself a fresh cup and was screwing the lid back on the thermos when the stranger came walking up the street in the general direction of the front porch. It was not a determined walk, though. Kind of crooked, and Elmer thought the guy was drunk.

But the man didn't really look the type. He wore a business

suit. No umbrella, though. But his steps wandered sideways or slantwise depending on how the wind blew. In its way, it was entertaining. It reminded him of the big inflatable tube man outside the gas station near Blue Moose Tavern on Ute Pass Avenue. Except that one had a big smile and the man in the suit wasn't smiling.

As he got closer, it was clear the fellow had no expression at all. Just a slack face and downcast eyes.

Elmer sipped his coffee. He was never the type to wave at passersby, and not only because there were hardly ever any. A wave, however small or merely polite, invited conversation, and Elmer was not a chitchat person. Gina always joked that he wouldn't use two words when no words said it better.

Used to joke.

So, he cupped his cold palms around his warm mug and waited for the man in the suit to realize he'd made a wrong turn and turn back.

The man kept coming closer.

He was forty feet from the scruffy patch of front lawn when Elmer began to realize something was wrong.

The suit hung oddly. Sure, some of it was water weight from the rain ... but there were visible tears in the suit, and some of the dark-blue fabric hung like streamers, revealing the paler lining. The tie was askew, and the white shirt below was a haphazard pattern of indistinct splotches of pastel pink. More like stains than anything intentional.

Then Elmer saw there was a darker pink on the man's hands and on his face. Below his jaw and above his collar, the tone was even darker. Redder.

Elmer set his cup down and stood.

The man jerked to a stop and raised his eyes in Elmer's direction as if startled to see someone sitting on the porch of so dilapidated a house. Those eyes did not squint or blink away the raindrops. Like his face, those eyes lacked any expression. Not even pain.

The fellow simply stood on the grass, his body swaying with the gusts of wind, looking up at Elmer.

"A-are you o-okay?" asked Elmer, stumbling over the words because it had been nearly a full week since he'd spoken aloud. He cleared his throat and repeated the question.

Beside him, the old crow cawed softly.

The man raised his hands toward Elmer—or maybe the crow, or both—and opened his mouth as if to speak. No words came out. Only a low moan.

Elmer tried a third time, raising his voice to make sure he was heard.

"Hey, mister ... you okay? Do you need any help?"

The only reply was another moan. Not loud. But there was something insistent about it. Needful. Weirdly, it was almost the same sound he used to make when Gina took a fresh pie out of the oven.

Elmer went to the top of the stairs. He wanted to be of help even though he didn't like to get involved. With crows, sure. People ... not so much. Even so, he wasn't ever cruel. He never chased the birds or rabbits away from Gina's herb garden, even before it was overgrown.

He came down two steps. "You want to come up on the porch and sit a spell? I can call someone if you need help."

The man's slow walk sped up. Not much, but noticeably. And that moan got a bit louder. More definite ... and definitely hungry.

"Hey now ... what's—?"

The stranger suddenly lunged at Elmer, hands thrust out to try to grab him.

Lunged in an awkward, clumsy slow motion, however.

Those pink-stained fingers clawed at the air, missing Elmer's jacket as he quickly backed up the stairs. The man overbalanced and fell, whacking his forehead on the edge of the bottom step with an audible *thump*. The fall was a bad one, and Elmer felt the solid impact through his shoes, all the way into the soles of his feet.

"Oh no," cried Elmer as he immediately stepped forward to help.

He knelt and began to turn the man over, trying to remember if you were supposed to do that kind of thing after someone fell. As the man turned, Elmer saw the damage the fall had done. There was a four-inch-long gash across his forehead, and a whole flap of skin was pulled up.

Elmer stared at it, aghast and ... confused.

It was a terrible gash, and yet there was not one drop of fresh blood.

Not one.

Nothing.

Just torn skin.

Elmer had time to say "What—?" before the man grabbed him, pulling himself nearly chest to chest. The wounded man's mouth stretched wide, and he leaned forward to try to take a ...

A *bite*.

"Holy crap," cried Elmer as he pushed himself backward and away.

The man flopped onto the ground again. Elmer scuttled backward up the steps like a startled crab, then scrambled to the balls of his feet and fingertips and froze. Staring. His own mouth gaped wide. Eyes wider.

"I—I—" he began, and it took real effort to find his way further along that sentence. "I ... I'll call someone."

Elmer did not have a cell phone. He climbed to his feet, watching with an almost detached fascination as the wounded man began getting up too. That flap of skin flopped down over one eye, and there was still no blood. Despite all the bloodstains on the fellow's face, body, and clothes, there was none in that wound.

It was then that he got a better look at the darker red on the strange man's neck. There was torn flesh there too. Ragged, raw, ugly. Deep, too, but it had clearly stopped bleeding. The blood was wet from the rain, but it wasn't new blood.

A dog attack? A bear?

Or ...?

He had nowhere to go after the "or," so he backed away until he bumped into his door, then he whirled and fled inside, banging the door shut behind him.

The landline telephone was in the kitchen, and he tottered that way, feeling as unsteady as the man had been outside. The phone handset was a firm reality, though, and it felt wonderfully normal in his hand. Even so, his forefinger trembled as he punched in 911 and then put the phone to his ear as it rang.

There was no answer.

No dispatcher. No recorded message from the emergency operator that took calls for the whole county. All he heard were three rising notes and then a mechanical voice told him the "call cannot be completed as dialed."

He hung up and tried again, making sure his finger didn't misdial.

"Your call cannot be completed as dialed."

Elmer stared at the phone.

He licked his lips and called the local police station. Not the emergency number but the one for the office.

"Your call cannot be completed as dialed."

Elmer tried the fire department in hopes of getting an EMT.

"Your call cannot be completed as dialed."

He stared at the handset as if it could provide an answer. Then he thought about last night's rain. Maybe a tree limb had fallen and taken out the lines.

He still had power, though. Were the power and phone lines strung from the same poles? It was one of those things he'd never had a reason to know, and so he didn't.

Behind him there was a soft *click*, and he turned to see the front door open.

The wounded man lumbered inside.

It felt odd that someone so dazed had managed the doorknob, but there it was. Still no blood from that torn forehead. Still nothing registering in the guy's eyes.

The man shambled forward, making that same low moan.

Now Elmer felt he could identify what it meant. It wasn't pain.

No.

It was hunger. It was *exactly* like the moans he gave when the open-oven smell of Gina's pies reached him for the first time. A deep hunger that craved satisfaction.

Elmer hung up. His hand drifted to the knife rack on the kitchen counter.

Something outside caught his eye, and the whole world seemed to jerk to a stop. Beyond the man, past the porch, past the old elms and older oaks, and all the way down to the street, there were more people moving.

Five of them.

More than he had ever seen at one time on his forgotten little lane.

Three women, two men. Dressed for work or for the gym. One was in pajama bottoms and a T-shirt.

All of them moved with that same slow, awkward, clumsy gait. All of them had torn clothes and mussed hair and red stains made pink by the rain.

Elmer stared at them for a very long time. There was a word in his head. What Gina would have called a TV word. Something from movies, not from real life.

Something not supposed to *be* in real life.

Elmer almost said the word, but he was pretty sure it would come out as a laugh. It was an impossible word. A silly word.

And it began with a Z.

It wasn't a word he wanted to say. It was a word he was pretty sure he could not speak aloud without feeling immensely stupid. Or immensely terrified.

All he said was, "Oh my."

The man—the first one, the one already inside the house—moaned again and tried another grab.

It was clumsy. A weak, badly aimed, poorly executed grab. Feeble.

Elmer didn't even need to slap those hands away. A push did it, and it made the man stumble.

He remembered seeing an old black-and-white movie once at a drive-in, back when he was a teenager. The ... *people* ... in that film moved as slowly and awkwardly as this man did. As *these* people did. And yet that movie was about the end of the world.

How, though?

How could people like this outrun, outmaneuver, out-grapple people who weren't sick or ... whatever it was they were? Even though Elmer knew he was no whiz kid, that concept offended logic.

The man grabbed again, and Elmer pushed him again, and the poor guy fell. It took him nearly two minutes to get up. By then, Elmer had closed the door. He peered through the dusty curtains and saw looks of confusion on the faces of the other five. They milled for a few moments, and then simply wandered off.

Elmer fished for a phrase Gina once used about the dog they used to have. They could play with the dog for hours, feed it, walk it, and all that, but if they went out for a drive without the animal, it went crazy. Tore stuff up and wagged itself half to death when they returned.

"Dogs don't have *object permanence*," Gina had said, quoting something from a magazine. "If they can't see something, it just stops existing."

That's what he was seeing now. The five people outside could no longer see him and within seconds seemed to forget all about him.

He leaned against the closed door and looked at the one in the kitchen, who was back on his feet. He was trying to come for him but kept bumping into the fridge, the doorframe, and the edge of the couch.

Elmer ducked behind an armchair and silently counted fifteen Mississippis. Then he peered around the side of the chair.

The man was standing in the middle of the room, looking in the wrong direction.

No object permanence.

Elmer turned and sat down. The chair he'd leaned against had been Gina's. There were a lot of things in the house that were Gina's. He could touch most of them, but he never sat in her armchair. Or her favorite chair at the dinner table. Or her sewing chair. It wasn't about the fact that they were chairs, but they were hers. They belonged to her.

And she was gone. Dead.

In a way, he supposed he was superstitious about sitting in a dead person's chair. Even if it had been Gina's. He had his own chairs. Chairs to be alive in.

Elmer paused and thought about that concept.

He leaned out again and saw the man simply standing. Doing nothing.

Elmer sat for quite a long time, very quietly thinking about a lot of things.

The power went out a week later.

That was fine. Elmer had candles and a good Coleman camp lantern, and he had a little solar-powered generator that Gina bought once after a power outage. It was the size of a briefcase, with cables to attach it to a solar panel he laid out in the backyard.

There was plenty of water from rain, and there would be more when it snowed.

Coffee required going to the neighbors' houses. Food too. But he was careful, and he was quiet.

The evenings were nice.

So were the afternoons.

He sat in his own armchair and listened to the wind. Sometimes the old crow would make some noise on the porch, but Elmer didn't sit out there much. Too easy to be seen. Inside was better.

He had a small fire burning, and a glass of Canadian Club and water resting on his thigh. Another storm was coming. It would be a big one, if the heavy smell of water on the breeze was telling the truth. Elmer wondered what that would do. Would it attract more of them or draw them away? Would they, he wondered, follow the storm path itself? Interesting question, and maybe he'd go out tomorrow and look. Or the day after. Or maybe the day after that.

There was a soft moan, and he turned to the man who sat in Gina's chair. With the power out, the extension cords did a nice job of keeping the fellow there. Snug. Elmer considered him and decided that tomorrow he'd need some fresh duct tape for that gash.

The man looked at him. His mouth opened and closed. It was probably a reflexive kind of biting, but it looked like the guy was speaking.

Quietly.

Comfortably quiet.

It was the same with those other five people. Elmer had gone out and brought them back. Well, let them follow him back. He didn't have to do much, just be visible and snap his fingers a few times to keep them focused.

He still couldn't understand how these slow ones had ended the world.

It was one of those things he knew he would never know. No TV, no radio, no Wi-Fi, no papers.

Which was fine.

Elmer liked the quiet life. He was okay without the rest of the world.

Though, he had to admit, he did like some company. Even if they were what they were. It was nice to have people around.

Quiet people.

Quiet, like him.

He sipped his whisky and smiled, listening to the wind as it rustled in the trees and pushed against the old house. When it gusted, it made the house creak and the old timbers moan. When that happened, the people in their chairs moaned too.

And that was just as much conversation as Elmer wanted.

Mostly, though, they were nice and quiet.

About the Author

Jonathan Maberry is a *New York Times* best-selling author, five-time Bram Stoker Award winner, four-time Scribe Award winner, Inkpot Award winner, and comic book writer. His vampire apocalypse book series, *V-WARS* was a Netflix original series; Alcon Entertainment is developing his YA-post-apocalyptic Rot & Ruin novels for film; and Chad Stahelski, director of *John Wick*, is developing his best-selling Joe Ledger thrillers for TV. Marvel's *Black Panther: Wakanda Forever* was partly based on his work.

He writes in multiple genres including suspense, thriller, horror, science fiction, fantasy, and action, for adults, teens, and middle grade. His novels include the NecroTek series, the Pine Deep Trilogy, the Rot & Ruin series, the Dead of Night series, *Mars One*, the Kagen the Damned series, the Sleepers War series, and others. He's written over 150 short stories, and edited many anthologies including *The X-Files, Aliens, Don't Turn Out the Lights, Nights of the Living Dead* (coedited with George A. Romero), and others. His comics include *Black Panther: DoomWar, Captain America, Pandemica, Highway to Hell, The Punisher,* and *Bad Blood*. He is the president of the International Association of Media Tie-in Writers and the editor of *Weird Tales Magazine*. Jonathan lives in San Diego, California, with his wife, Sara Jo. jonathanmaberry.com

CAME BACK WRONG
MARY PLETSCH

To be fair, Michael was the first to save me. He was the one who'd translated the inscription on the Altar of the Dead. He was the one who'd realized that half of the symbols denoted not words but musical notes—and he'd realized it just in time. Only a few days later, I fell through his arms and plunged down into deep, dark waters.

By the time the paramedics arrived in the museum, I was sitting upright on the Altar of the Dead, dazed and rubbing my left cheek and wholly alive by the definition of modern medical science. They could never have guessed that I came back wrong.

An indeterminate amount of time after my dive into oblivion, I came to on the bank of a river, my left cheek resting on the muddy shoreline, water lapping over my naked body.

Shoving myself up on my hands and knees, I scrabbled up the riverbank and collapsed onto a beige carpet of papery, desiccated grasses that ran from the edge of the river to the crest of the hills behind me. I squinted my eyes shut and pinched my legs in a bid to wake myself from the dream. When I opened my eyes, I was still naked and still lying by a river in the cold gray light of dawn. I slapped myself across the left cheek and felt nothing.

Dead brown reeds protruded from the clear blue water like splintered spires. So clear. So blue. Not a fish in sight. And worse than that—no insects.

I sat by the side of a river and wished for bugs.

A few notes of music wafted on the breeze. I barely noticed because I was too busy dredging my brain for clues as to how I'd gotten here.

I remembered that Michael and I had been in the museum after hours, listening to the recording he'd made of the song inscribed on the Altar of the Dead. He sang with all the talent that had drawn me to him when we first met nearly thirty years ago, when he'd been a grad student with his own band and I'd been a freshman in his audience at the pub.

When the recording was finished, Michael turned to me with a grin and suggested we go out to dinner, then home for a more private celebration. Our twins had recently returned to college, and we had the house to ourselves.

I had a bit of a headache, but I decided to push through the discomfort, because I shared Michael's excitement and wanted to spend the time with him.

I raised my arms to hug him. My right arm encircled his neck. My left arm made it as far as his elbow before dropping back to my side.

Pins and needles. I tried to shake it out. The arm was hard to move; it almost felt as though it wasn't part of my body. I tried again and succeeded only in bringing my forearm to rest against my stomach.

"Becka?" Michael asked with alarm as he released me.

Something's not right emerged from my lips as an unintelligible slur of sound. More pins and needles made my left cheek their pincushion as Michael said, "Becka, your *face*."

I no longer had any sensation below my left elbow. I reached for my phone with my right hand. When I picked it up, the symbols on the screen made no sense.

Numbers. Letters. But I couldn't read them any more than the average person off the street could read the inscriptions on the Altar of the Dead.

Yet I still knew the layout of the numbers on the screen. I poked them awkwardly with my thumb. Bottom right. Top left. Top left again.

9-1-1.

My fingers fumbled, and the phone dropped to the ground. I looked desperately at Michael to pick it up, which he did.

He was talking to the dispatcher on the ... the thing, you know, the talky thing ... when my left leg went numb. I knelt down before I fell down. My mind spun like a hamster's wheel, but my body didn't want to move. I was too tired to be frightened.

My head slumped forward. The rest of my body followed. I caught myself by extending my right arm. I twisted my neck, trying to focus my gaze on Michael, when the Hammer of God landed a blow to the part of the brain where my consciousness lived.

Now I peered into the fog rising off the river and saw first a glimmer of light, then the silhouette of a small boat. As a professor of English I knew damn well what kind of symbol I was looking at. It fit unpleasantly well with my final memory of the world exploding in static except for Michael's eyes.

When I remembered Michael's eyes—blue beacons piercing the encroaching darkness—when I started thinking about Michael, I heard his voice somewhere behind me, calling my name.

"Here!" I shouted back. "Michael, I'm here!"

Relief sluiced over me when he crested the top of a hill. A path made from pebbles spooled away behind him through a thicket of thorns, up the hill and out of sight.

I rushed to him and threw my arms around him. He picked me up and swung me around, crushing my lips in a kiss.

I drew in a breath to ask what had happened.

Michael cut me off and gripped my hands in his. "Sing with me."

Dream logic. The song he started to sing did not surprise me.

So we sang. I didn't understand the words, but I could mimic the syllables. Michael corrected my pronunciation and pitch until I could carry the tune on my own.

"Good," he said, squeezing my hands. "Before we can go home, there are three rules."

Fairy-tale reasoning, I thought.

"First, we must follow the path." Michael lifted his gaze to the lamplight brightening in the fog. The boat was close enough for me to see a hooded figure with its hand on the tiller.

"Second, we must sing as we walk. Can you do that?"

"Sure."

"Becka, the pronunciation is so important." I'd never seen him look so serious, not even on the night he proposed. "You can't afford to get it wrong."

"Huh?"

"No time. Three. Becka, no matter what—don't look back."

I forced a smirk. "I was raised Lutheran. I know what happened when Lot's wife looked back."

I did not know what Lot would have done if his woman had come back wrong.

Later, in the hospital, Michael held my hand and told me how it had felt to lead me out of the underworld, a successful Orpheus striding back into the light of the living with his beloved behind him. "I bet you felt like a princess, right?"

Pain stole my breath. I was able to nod.

I was not able to tell him that his experience was very different from mine.

For me, those stones turned to coals.

For me, that path led into an inferno.

For me, I had to squint against the smoke to keep him in sight while I followed behind him, firewalking out of hell.

The stakes had been real because there was no way I could have slept and dreamed through that much pain.

***

Even when the skin on my feet had blackened and the scent of singed hair and burning flesh rose to my nostrils, I did not dare let my singing turn to screaming. From the corners of my eyes, I could see smoldering corpses littering the sides of the path, curled up like fetuses in wombs of ash, waiting for a rebirth that would not come.

I no longer had consciousness enough to waste on minor matters like how I had gotten here or what I might face next. Existence collapsed into all my love for Michael and my children and my life and surviving just one more step. One more. Just one more step.

And when I stumbled, I stopped counting my steps and started counting my breaths, forcing out a note of the song with each exhalation. I let the heat surround me, permeate me, wrap me in searing hell until the horror of it lost all relevance. After third-degree burns there's no more pain. After the first death there is no other.

I did not know how much farther I had to go. I did not know how far I had come. I could not sense Michael anymore, but I thought of him only.

I breathed in fire and sang out defiance until I stepped through the curtain of light.

I will be forever grateful that I had not known what

awaited me, or I could never have forced the charred stumps of my feet across that final threshold. Had there been pain as I staggered up the hill of coals? I did not yet know what pain was.

Ignorant, I stepped into the light.

Overwhelming brilliance hit me like lightning and lit up my skeleton in an electric apocalypse. I could not inhale. Could not exhale. I heard my heart stop beating.

My body was irrelevant. I could neither feel nor see it, didn't know where it was. My soul hung suspended in a white void, immobilized like a bug in amber.

Torment forges true believers. Pain is the rapture of an incomprehensible God. In the heart of a white-hot sun, I felt agony so far beyond my imagining that it couldn't possibly be *real*.

It could not be borne. Mercifully, it didn't have to be.

My heartbeat echoed like thunder. I winked out like a candle.

* * *

And I woke up on the Altar of the Dead, Michael standing over me, crying with relief because he thought I would be all right.

I would cry later, when I realized I came back wrong.

* * *

Descending to the dead? I should have come back renewed. Reborn. Instead I came back *the way I was before*.

With a time bomb still ticking in my head.

Severe migraine, the doctors said when they released me. At home, Michael helped me to bed and sat beside me.

"We can't tell anyone," I said. "Imagine what would happen if people made a habit of bringing people back from the dead."

"They won't," Michael assured me. "Most people wouldn't believe such a thing was possible, and those who might, well ..." He slowly unbuttoned his shirt to reveal a scar I'd never seen before situated overtop his heart.

I didn't want to ask what he'd done. He read the question on my face and answered it anyway. "To open the gate so the living may pass—the inscription says *blood sacrifice*. I don't think I cut deep enough to … I don't think."

I must've looked horrified. I knew Michael's beliefs had always tended toward the mystical, and given what I'd been through I was reconsidering my atheism, but had Michael really stabbed himself on the off chance that he could bring me back from the dead? Was that love or madness?

Michael must have thought I was about to lecture him about leaving our children without parents, because he said, "I wasn't thinking, okay? I saw you drop and I … I just …" His eyes pleaded with me to understand. "The song says the key willingly given is willingly returned. I'm fine, see?"

His impulsive behavior often frustrated me, but that night I couldn't have been more thankful for his audacity. "I can't believe you took that risk for me."

"I didn't want to be without you." Michael lay down carefully next to me. I tucked my body against his chest, tracing the scar with my fingertips. "I love you, Becka. I swear I'll never let you go."

But I knew he hadn't died. If he'd belonged in the underworld, he would have also faced the fire. Michael had been alive, so he came back right; and I had been dead, so I came back wrong.

The next day, all I wanted was to teach my usual classes, cook my usual supper, and share my usual evening with my husband who, I knew, loved me as much as it was possible for any human being to love another. Life was a gift, and I saw beauty all around me. The journey through hell had been worth it.

The day after that?

It was Saturday. I was tired that morning—the same draggy feeling people get when they first wake up, except that my first cup of coffee didn't have its usual effect. I had a second. A third. Michael laughed and called me "The Caffeinator." I didn't have energy to tease him back. An hour went by. Another. I still felt as drowsy and disoriented as I had when I first got out of bed. My left cheek prickled.

I made brunch, and the smell of bacon felt like a slap in the face. By the time it was cooked, I couldn't eat it. My left cheek stopped prickling and went entirely numb just as the pins and needles sensation started in my left hand. My coffee cup slipped through my fingers and shattered on the floor. I knew I was supposed to do something about that, but what?

Oh. Right. "Can you pass me the thing?"

Michael furrowed his brow.

"You know, the, uh ... the boom."

"What?"

"The sweepy one," I snapped with frustration.

"Becka, what's wrong?"

But I knew full well what was wrong. 9-1-1. While I could still read the numbers on my phone.

Michael helped me to the front door. Slouching on our porch, waiting for the paramedics, I braced myself for the waters of the river. I could remember the tune, but I'd lost half the words. I didn't know if I'd be able to step into the light now that I knew what awaited me there. I might ... I might stay behind. Board the ferryman's boat and cross to the other side.

No. After what Michael had done for me? I was going to come back for him.

But I never made it as far as the river. I was still conscious in the hospital to hear words like *stroke* and *life-altering deficit*.

I went to the ER, and I came back wrong.

I had a terrible feeling that I would be lucky if I were able to return to work part time, but I didn't want to voice it.

Michael told me, "We'll get through this together by focusing on the best."

For the next year we tried to do just that, but of course there were consequences for coming back wrong. I recovered somewhat, though I still had problems moving my left arm and speaking clearly. Migraines ravaged my brain in mimicry of the stroke. Electric pulses of pain illuminated my nervous system. My ability to read fritzed in and out like static on an old-fashioned television.

Michael took on my household chores on bad days, and I loved him for it, but I feared he had begun to look on me as less of a lover, more of a dependent. I went all out for Valentine's Day, ordering some lingerie online.

February 14 was a bad day. Another brutal migraine left me shaky on my feet, easily confused, numb in my left arm. I didn't have the strength to keep our dinner reservation. Michael ate leftover spaghetti in front of the TV while I sat beside him, too nauseated to eat. When he went to put his dishes in the kitchen, I turned off the TV, unbuttoned my top, and greeted him with a smile when he returned.

Michael looked at me blankly. "But you're sick."

I felt taken aback. "I mean, I'm weak and dizzy, yeah, and I'll be better off lying down...."

Michael frowned.

"I know that's not the most exciting," I admitted, "but it's what I can manage today, and ..."

"Let's wait until you feel better, babe."

"I don't know when that'll be," I said with frustration, "and it's been weeks. Can't we make the best of Valentine's? Even if we just cuddle and talk a little?"

"But you're sick. You need to go to bed," Michael murmured distantly, and turned the TV back on.

I stumbled to the bedroom wondering how the man who

wouldn't abandon me in the underworld could be so willing to abandon me now.

I needed him.

It wasn't my fault I came back wrong.

We argued with increasing frequency.

"I don't know how you can say I don't love you," Michael snapped. "I might have *killed myself* to follow you to the underworld!"

"Then how come you haven't been acting like someone who loves me?"

"Because ..." Michael spluttered, "because you came back *wrong*, and it's my fault. Do you know how guilty I feel every time I look at you?"

He couldn't mean that the way it sounded. "You did your best. We did our best together," I said reassuringly.

Michael relaxed, as though he had received absolution.

I continued, because I had more to say. "I'm doing my best too. But I need you, and you're almost never home."

"You can't go anywhere," Michael countered.

"I can when I feel good."

"And what about when you don't feel good? Like, most of the time? That's not often."

"Then stay home with me," I urged.

Michael's eyes became stormy. "It's not fair to ask me to sit around the house. We used to go out, Becka. Parties. Dinners. Vacations. I'm not ready to give that up yet."

"Do you think I'm ready?" I raged. "Do you think I don't want to go?"

Michael sighed. "Just give me some space until you get better—"

"I'm not *going* to get a whole hell of a lot better than this! Why do I have to be alone when I'm scared and in pain?"

I stared at him.

He stared at me.

The distance between us was the width of a river, the distance between the living and the dead.

Surely, he'd see reason. "What am I going to do if it happens again and I can't get to the phone? You saved me once, Michael. I need you with me in case you have to do it again."

Michael cringed. "I never should have brought you back."

His words hit like lightning through my soul.

I'd seen one of my sons get married. I'd published my book and even managed to give panels at conferences, albeit with help from my grad students. I might not have made it on the hiking vacation Michael had planned—he went with a friend instead—but I'd gone on a train trip across Canada with my sister, watching the scenery from the window, exploring the towns along the way on the days that I felt good.

I stammered. Choked. "But I'm happy to be ba—"

He cut me off. "This is no kind of life for you. Becka, I'm so sorry."

"It's not as though it doesn't suck," I said—there was no way to argue the contrary—"but do you really think I'd rather be *dead*?"

Michael looked at me sadly. "If I were you? I would."

Determination circled my heart like wire, holding it together when my horror at Michael's words threatened to burst it apart. "If you think that half a life is worse than no life at all, then I don't know what to tell you."

"I want more than half a life." Michael stormed out the door.

I went to bed and finally dozed off sometime around midnight.

At 1:52 AM the Hammer of God fell on my head a second time.

My phone was plugged in on the other side of the bedroom. Six steps away. I think I made it three.

I woke up naked in the river.

I gasped, thrashed, almost went under. As a matter of principle, I forced myself to start swimming. I knew what lay ahead of me.

Thinking of it made me feel nauseous. God, I didn't want to do this again. I especially didn't want to do it alone.

Michael wasn't coming to rescue me this time. If I wanted out of the underworld, I was going to have to save myself.

I clambered onto the riverbank, singing a song I had never forgotten, but when the path of pebbles unspooled over the summit of the hill and came to a stop in front of my feet, I hesitated. One more step and those stones would erupt in fire, and this time I knew precisely how much it was going to hurt.

"You don't have to," said a voice behind me that was most definitely not Michael.

His—or hers, or theirs, I couldn't tell, but most myths describe this individual as male—his boat had to be right next to the riverbank. His lantern shone behind me, and my shadow fell over the path ahead of me.

"What if I want to?" I said belligerently, keeping my gaze fixed firmly ahead.

"I'm not about to come and *get* you," the hooded figure replied, sounding oddly aggrieved. "I don't ever go to *get* anyone. I find you beings adrift in my river, and I take you to the far shore where you can thrive. I'd certainly never release you onto this bank. There's no future for you here."

"Except the path back to where I came from."

"You'll return to the river eventually."

"Will you take me to the far shore then?"

"If you wish to go. Though I wouldn't recommend staying in the river. Your kind grow odd when you stay in the river too long."

"What if I'd rather come here?"

I heard a sigh. "I have no desire to take you anywhere against your will. You beings tell such cruel stories about me. I simply fail to understand why you would choose what some of your kind call *hell* when you could have *heaven* instead."

"Because of what's on the other side of hell."

"Is that also a heaven?" He sounded curious. "Do you think you can reach it without someone to show you the way?"

"If not," I said, "I'll probably see you in the river."

"You won't," he replied quietly.

I made the connection. "The charred bodies along the path."

"I fear they do not cross the river."

Well, now I knew the score. Having lost my life a second time, I was about to once again risk my soul to …

To … what? Come back as an albatross around the neck of the man I loved?

My children didn't call me an albatross. Neither did my sister. I might have lost a few friends, but I was a hell of a lot closer with the rest. The ones who thought nothing of coming to my place to hang out, clutter and all, even when I was silly with pain medication. I had a new book in progress—slow progress, but to me every page was a victory. A reminder I still had things I wanted to do.

No, I wasn't ready to die. I'd thought enough about dying on the days when I couldn't get out of bed, too weak to get up and in too much pain to sleep. I had discarded the idea every time. By now I knew if I was going to kill myself, to seek the far shore, I would have done so months ago.

"Maybe I will someday," I said, "but not today."

I sang the first word and lowered my left foot to the blazing stones. As the flames rose around me, I thought I heard the voice behind me wish me good fortune. Then pain scoured away my understanding save for a series of small actions: step by step, note by note, climbing to the light.

I had made this pilgrimage before. I could surely survive it again.

Yet this time was even *worse* than the first. I suffered not only the torment of the moment but also the torture of the knowledge of the moments yet to come.

Foreknowledge slowed my footsteps as I approached the curtain of light. This time my love for Michael could not carry me through. Michael was gone. I had followed him through hell, and I had thought he would do the same for me. But his heroism was that of grand, showy gestures and self-aggrandizement, not the heroism of a long, hard slog against the currents of the river.

That heroism was *mine*.

I burned my fear in the fire of a rapturous sun and came back wrong.

The woman who came back from the underworld a second time came back even *wronger*. At least that's what Michael thought when I served him divorce papers.

"You can't look after yourself properly," he protested. "You're my responsibility."

I was prepared to test his thesis. "I don't want to be a *responsibility*. I want to be a partner. A lover. A confidante. I want a life with someone who loves me the way I am *now* instead of the way I used to be." I looked him square in the eye and uttered a truth I'd feared, back when fear had been something I could still feel. "I can look after myself well enough, and you can't stay with me out of guilt."

Michael shook his head. "If I don't, I'm a bad person. What will people think of me if I walk out on you when you're like this?"

And there it was. Michael's reluctance to let me go had little to do with his feelings for me and everything to do with his own self-image. He couldn't bear to see himself as anything less than a hero.

"You walked out on me, emotionally, a long time ago. I don't want to be with you anymore."

I had family. I had friends. I had resources. Oh, I knew it would be hard, but I did not fire walk out of hell to spend the rest of my life in the desiccated husk of a marriage held together by shame instead of affection. I would not trade one underworld for another.

Michael tried a different tack. "Aren't you afraid to be alone?"

"I used to be," I admitted. "But now I know I can *come back wrong* as many times as it takes."

Descending to the dead? Michael should have come back renewed. Reborn. Instead, he came back *the way he was before.*

With cancer slowly growing in his lung.

I hadn't seen him in years when I went to his apartment, mostly at the behest of my children, who'd become concerned with his recent talk of suicide. I almost didn't recognize him.

He seemed diminished. Smaller. A man with a larger-than-life personality had withered into a ravaged stalk as disease took its toll on him one pound at a time.

"Becka. I didn't expect you'd come see me."

"I'm not here to keep you company," I replied. "I'm here because you saved my life, more times than you know, and I owe you for that."

Michael's eyes narrowed. "If you're wondering whether I still know the words and the melody to a certain tune, then yes, I do. Tell the kids I'll see them next Sunday for Easter dinner."

As I expected, Michael fully intended to walk out of the underworld all by himself.

"I'd be amiss if I didn't warn you—"

"Not to hit sour notes."

"What?"

The corner of Michael's mouth lifted in a little smirk. "I'm a better singer than you. I'll come back fine."

Breath left my lungs in a rush. Michael dared suggest the reason I came back the way I did was *because I wasn't a good enough singer*?

I had planned to warn him that walking out of the underworld was a lot easier for the living who weren't supposed to be there than it was for the dead who were. But his arrogance made my temper flare. Instead of warning him about the coals or the corpses or even the electric corona around a white-hot sun, I warned him about what he might find on the other side of that devastating light.

"The cut you make to enter the underworld, that will heal. But the rest of it? Once you walk through that light, you'll come back as you are now," I said softly. "You said you wouldn't want a life like this."

He didn't reply, but his blue eyes sparked with the tiniest flicker of fear.

I had nothing else to say. I turned my back, humming a little tune, and left according to the three rules of fairy tales.

Follow the path. Don't stop singing. Don't look back.

Michael passed away on Good Friday from a self-inflicted stab wound to the heart.

Easter came. Easter went. Michael didn't come back wrong. Michael didn't come back at all.

Decades later. Christmas dinner. I sit at the head of a table of twenty-eight.

My grandchildren. Their partners. Their children. Their children's partners. My great-great-grandchildren. Friends without family of their own. My first great-great-great-granddaughter, lowered gently into my arms.

I'm saddened this is the first year without either of my children with me. They've both gone before me, somewhere across the river.

I'm not ready yet.

Maybe, just maybe, I pass away during the gifts. Or perhaps I simply doze off. Either way, I awaken with memories of the river, hazy through the ever-present fog of a distant pain that no longer seems part of me. These days it's harder to tell the difference between life and death and dream, but I feel joy and love regardless, and that's good enough for me.

I may not be a good singer, but I'm more than good enough. And I have the courage to walk through hell one step at a time.

Oh, I come back, all right.

About the Author

Mary Pletsch attended the first Superstar Writing Seminars in 2010 and learned from the best. In the years since, she has published short stories and novellas in a variety of genres including science fiction, fantasy, and horror. Superstars holds a special place in her heart; it made the difference between writing as a hobby and writing to be published.

HARMONIES IN THE DARK
CAROL HIGHTSHOE

You may know where you are. God may know where you are. But only God can help you if dispatch doesn't know where you are.

It was kind of a joke—a deadly serious one told by the dispatcher who gave us an introduction to radio procedures class during the academy. Most of us nodded knowingly, understanding what they meant. Now I was the one who needed help, and while I knew where I was, I wasn't so sure about God knowing—since He wasn't helping.

Almost fifteen years on the street, and *this* is how I go out?

A call from a regular CI with a request to meet in this old warehouse. Said he had information on a major drug deal going down. Thought it'd be a simple meetup. It always was. Except this time ... it wasn't. My instincts were screaming the second I pulled up. It was too quiet. I thought I was smarter than the setup. Working as a solo unit, no backup. I *should've* known better. Still, I went in like it was nothing. Like I was invincible. I thought my experience would keep me alive.

Turns out, experience doesn't stop bullets. Stupid. *Stupid.*

There was a thunderclap of gunfire: too close and too fast. Then pain. Blinding, blooming in my chest like fire. The first round hit center mass, knocking the wind out of me. We had seen the videos showing how well a ballistic vest worked, but the videos didn't mention how bad it still hurt.

No time to think—I drew my weapon. Dropped it as another round hit. I staggered and fell. The floor was cold. I reached for the radio mic on my shoulder, touched it. A faint click as I pressed. I tried to speak but only a wet gurgle came out. Another click as my hand relaxed.

"Unit five-tom-six, you were unreadable. Say again," came the call from dispatch. One small thing in my favor: I had managed to key the mic long enough for them to identify me. But how quickly would they be able to locate me? I knew the dispatcher was pulling the GPS data for my vehicle. It would be a race.

There was a pause as the dispatcher gave me time to respond.

"Unit five-tom-six, status." The dispatcher's voice was steady, but there was a hint of concern. I knew every officer on duty was listening intently to their radios—waiting—holding their breath—willing me to respond. Cursing the silence they were listening to.

My breathing was becoming agonal, and I tasted copper in my mouth.

I faintly heard the alert tone come over the radio. "Unit five-tom-six, status."

The pause was shorter this time.

"Negative contact with unit five-tom-six," the dispatcher said. This time I heard the quaking in her voice. "All units stand by."

My last breath rattled up my throat, and I could no longer hear the radio, but I heard something else—a new sound. Music.

At first, I thought it was just blood rushing in my ears. But it grew steady, familiar in a strange way I couldn't name. Low at first, and so faint I thought I was imagining it. A low hum winding through the noise of the city, ancient and endless. Low, primordial. I heard not with my ears but deep in my chest, like a heartbeat that wasn't mine. Like wind through hollow bones, twining with the rhythm of the city itself. A song beneath all things. A thread running through the cracks. A presence. A current. Something *old* and *watchful*. Something told me it had always been there. I'd just never listened.

Then came the eyes—golden, flickering, not of this world. Dogs. An entire pack stepped out of the shadows. They were sleek, hairless, regal in a way that made the world around them feel dirty by comparison. Xoloitzcuintli or Xolos; they were the Lantern Dogs. The ones my *abuela* told me stories about. The ones who comforted and guided souls. Golden-eyed, eternal. Sacred. They padded around me, silent and radiant. The song flowed from them and pulsed in time with their steps.

I don't remember standing. I don't even remember breathing.

But suddenly, I was on my feet, staring down at my body like it was a stranger's. The blood pooled beneath me; too dark, too still. My eyes, wide open, had already lost their light. Whatever made me *me* wasn't there anymore. It was here, lingering in the stillness. Stuck between what was and whatever came next.

The Xolos waited nearby. Silent. Watching. Their golden eyes flickered like hooded lanterns. Their song continued, a low hum of mourning wrapped around the ache of memory. They watched me, calm. Waiting.

I should've felt peace. But ...

Not yet, I told the dogs. *I'm not ready.*

I had no blood family left to mourn me, but I had my family behind the badge, and I wanted to stay for them. I didn't feel like my work protecting others was done.

They looked at me with a patience that felt older than time. The song shifted—no longer a lullaby, but a plea. A call to let go.

Red-and-blue strobes cut the night as cruisers pulled up ... too late. The kind of late that leaves nothing but reports and regrets.

"Javi, are you in here?" I heard someone call as several officers rushed through the door, weapons drawn.

"*¡Dios mío!*" Hernández, my last trainee. "Get those paramedics in here," she yelled.

"Get this area secured," someone else ordered as the paramedics pushed their way in.

I wanted to reach out. Tell someone I was okay—or not okay, but *here*. Something. Anything. But I couldn't touch them, couldn't speak.

I backed away. A distant siren rose and fell beyond the walls. Somewhere, a car alarm wailed—a broken scream ignored by the city. Streetlights spilled a dull orange glow through a shattered window, catching dust motes like fading fireflies.

Two of the Xolos stood next to me, their golden eyes unwavering. I wasn't ready, and they knew it. But they weren't going to abandon me. The rest of the pack faded behind us. I glanced back at the scene and saw Hernández staring in my direction. I didn't think she could see me, so maybe it was the Xolos she was seeing. She shook her head slightly then turned to follow the paramedics as they wheeled my body out of the building.

The warehouse disappeared behind me in a slow dissolve. Bricks became blurs. Sirens became echoes. Time slipped its leash. The city didn't stop, but I was no longer moving with it. The Lantern Dogs walked ahead, their golden eyes lighting the way. I followed, not because I knew where we were going, but because it was the only thing that made sense. I didn't need to ask where we were. I already knew; we were somewhere between.

———

We moved through alleys most people avoided even in daylight. Places where the streetlights buzzed but didn't glow. The Xolos padded forward on silent paws, but the melody that both surrounded and came from them never stopped. It was quieter now, a minor key woven through the rustle of garbage, the wheeze of old HVAC units, the breath of the sleeping city.

The Lantern Dogs paused, and I heard a slight change in the song. A single discordant note that didn't fit with the rest of the melody. They stepped closer, and I felt a shift around us as everything blurred.

The young man slumped against a wall next to a dumpster in a dark alley. His breath was ragged, shallow. Too shallow. Syringes lay discarded in the dust like broken promises, and the shadows pressed close, thick with silence. There were still track marks on his arms.

"Overdose," I said, the word rising from instinct. "No one called it in."

One of the dogs lay next to the man. There was something softer about the Xolo—the tilt of his ears, the way he placed his head in the young man's lap. The Xolo appeared to glow softly as the young man stroked the dog's head. The name *Lucero* rose in my mind like a lyric I'd always known but had never sung aloud.

Morning star. Light in the dark. It fit.

The body relaxed as the young man's breathing became more even, then stopped.

Lucero stood and touched his nose to the young man's face.

The man opened his eyes and blinked. He *saw* them. Saw me. He didn't ask where he was. Instead, he asked, "Are you here to take me?"

I hesitated. I wasn't sure how to answer. Instead I asked, "What's your name?"

"Benjamin, but everyone called me Benny."

Lucero sang—a low, warbling hum—and Benny's shoulders relaxed. He leaned his head against the wall. Not in defeat. In peace. His soul separated from his body, lifting like mist in the morning sun. No light show, no burst of angels. Just a soft, gentle release. Like the city finally let him go.

I stood in the alley, staring at the empty shell he'd left behind. A half-smoked cigarette lay with the syringes near his shoe. No one would find him for days, maybe longer. Just another nameless, forgotten person in a city too busy to care. No. No longer nameless. I knew his name, and I would remember it.

Lucero returned to my side. Others materialized quietly around me, their eyes reflecting a sadness too vast for words.

"I didn't do anything," I said, more to myself than to them. "He saw *you*. You were the ones who helped him."

Lucero blinked slowly. The song shifted—mellow, patient. Not a lullaby, not this time. Something steadier. Enduring.

Maybe that was the answer. Maybe just *being* there was what mattered.

"I spent my whole life trying to save people," I whispered, staring at the body. "Most of the time I didn't know if I had succeeded. Now ... I can't save anyone. But I can be here. I can bear witness. I can remember them."

A soft nudge at my hand. Lucero again. His furless skin was warm, like stone that had soaked up the sun. His eyes glowed like embers. Not fire. Not danger. Just the memory of light.

"Is that what you do?" I asked. "You come when they're dying and ... stay? So they don't have to be alone?"

The dogs didn't answer. Not in words. But the song they carried through the streets shifted again, and this time, it carried the faintest thread of harmony.

They weren't just singing for the dead. They also sang for the living and the dying. And they were teaching me the tune.

***

The next place was colder. Not in temperature, but in feeling. The kind of street where laughter never reached and even the wind held its breath.

We found him at an old bus stop. Graffiti covered the back wall and support poles. The metal cover was rusted and cracked. He was curled up like he was trying to disappear. For a moment, I didn't recognize him. Not until he looked up.

Then I froze. "Ramírez?"

He squinted. "No way ... Javier ... Javier Álvarez? Look at you. Still following me around, huh?" The bite in his voice was sharp enough to draw blood.

I stepped closer, slowly. "Wasn't expecting to see you here."

"Yeah, well," he muttered, shifting his back against the support pole. "Not like you didn't help put me on this path."

I didn't answer right away. I didn't have to. We both knew what he meant.

"Dammit, you were my partner. You were supposed to have my back," he finally said flatly.

"I tried," I said. "You blew me off. You were showing up late, sloppy, high as hell—"

"I was dealing with a lot of shit."

"You weren't the only one. You needed help. You wouldn't take it."

He scoffed. "Help. You mean like a suspension and a damn piss test every month? That kind of help?"

"If that's what it took—then yes. But it didn't work, did it?" I stood my ground just like I had that day. "I asked to remain your partner when you came back off suspension. No one else wanted to be your partner—they didn't trust you."

"And you did?" Ramírez's bitter laugh turned into a wracking cough.

Once he caught his breath, I replied. "I don't know." I sat down beside him and waited.

"Sure you don't," he finally said. "You were just a damn stooge IA assigned to report on me. They didn't trust me. You didn't trust me. You were just waiting to find something you could turn me in for."

"You know better than that." I put a hand on his shoulder. "I wanted to make sure you had a fair chance."

"A fair chance." He jerked away from my hand. "Dammit, you were the one who effin' testified against me!"

"Emilio," I said softly. I wasn't here to judge, not in this place, not at this time. "You shot that kid—without justification."

"He was dealing."

I shook my head. "He didn't assault you. He didn't draw a knife like you tried to claim in your statement. You shot him because he wouldn't give you what you wanted."

"You cost me my job and my pension." His voice broke.

"No! You cost yourself. It was your choices that led to that moment and your choices that led you here."

He laughed, but there was no humor in it. "Now here I am, dying alone at a damn bus stop."

The Xolos drew closer, but stayed back. Lucero watched quietly.

"You think I wanted this?" I asked. "That I don't regret how things went down?"

His eyes flicked to the dogs, then back to me. "So what now? You come to finish the job?"

"No," I said quietly. "I came because no one else did." I put my hand back on his shoulder.

He blinked. That took the fight out of him.

Lucero padded forward and sat beside him. Ramírez flinched but didn't pull away.

"I ain't ready," he whispered.

"You don't have to be," I said. "They will wait."

We sat there together in the silence. No more accusations. No more excuses.

Eventually, his shoulders slumped, and he looked at me—really looked.

"You gonna walk with me?"

"For as long as I can."

Lucero's song was softer this time—low and pulsing, like waves lapping at the edge of memory. I stood and held out my hand. Ramírez took it and got to his feet, still unsteady.

The dogs formed a loose circle around us, and we walked. The city blurred again, details dissolving into light and shadow. Street signs faded, colors bled to gray, and the rhythm of traffic grew muffled—like sound beneath water.

I started to feel it too—like something was pulling me forward.

Not dragging, only calling. A pressure in my chest, warm and insistent.

Ramírez noticed. "You feel it, don't you?"

I nodded. "Yeah."

"It's not so bad," he said, voice steadier than before. "Kinda like falling asleep with music on."

We reached a threshold.

There was no glowing portal, no golden gate—just a change in the air. A seam in reality, hidden in plain sight. On this side: shadow and song. On the other: something too vast to name. I couldn't see it clearly, but I *felt* it. Deep and welcoming. Still and eternal.

Ramírez hesitated. "You sure you're not coming?"

I looked down. My feet felt heavy. The melody had shifted again. It no longer pulled at me. It waited.

"I'm not done yet," I said. "There are others out there. Alone. Lost."

Ramírez gave me a sad smile. "Still the cop, huh?"

"Yeah," I said. "Guess I always will be."

He looked past me at the Xolos, then back. "Thanks, Javi. For walking with me."

"Anytime, partner." I nodded. "You code four now?" I asked— *clear, safe, at peace.*

Lucero stepped forward and touched Ramírez's leg with his nose. The song grew fuller, like another voice had joined the chorus.

Ramírez nodded. "Code four, partner." He took one last deep breath, then stepped through the veil. He was gone.

The space he left behind shimmered briefly, then stilled. Lucero looked at me. The other Xolos turned. And we walked back into the city of echoes.

———

Time passed, though I couldn't say how much. Days? Weeks? Months? The city moved on without me. Sirens still screamed, babies still cried, and the lights never stopped flickering. I stopped trying to count. That kind of thinking belonged to the living.

We—me and the Lantern Dogs—kept walking.

The forgotten ones were never far. An old woman whose name had already faded from her own mailbox. A runaway under a loading dock with dreams too big and a heartbeat too slow. A man everyone thought had moved away, but hadn't. Not really.

And then, one night, she found me.

I was standing at the edge of the cemetery, watching the street beyond. The Xolos lingered in the shadows, Lucero among them, golden eyes steady.

She stepped out of a city bus and paused mid-step.

Her silhouette caught my attention first. It was Hernández. She wasn't in uniform. She'd made detective; I could tell by the badge clipped to her belt. She moved differently now. More sure of herself. But her eyes were still the same. Still searching.

She looked right at me. And didn't look *through* me. Her eyes widened. "Javi?"

I didn't speak. Not at first. I didn't know if I *could*.

But then she looked past me and gasped.

"The dogs," she whispered. "I've seen them before. At scenes. Just flashes. Thought I was losing it."

Lucero stepped forward. Hernández knelt, meeting his gaze. "You're not just stories, are you?"

"No," I said, my voice quiet but clear. "They're real."

Her eyes welled up. "So are you."

I stepped closer. The distance between us shimmered like heat off asphalt, but it didn't push her away. She felt it—just enough.

"Why are you still here?" she asked. "Why haven't you crossed?"

I looked down the road—dark, endless, full of lost songs.

"Because someone has to stay," I said. "Not to punish. Not to haunt. Just ... to help. To walk beside the ones no one else sees. To remember their names when the world forgets them. It's what we've always done." I reach toward her badge, then touch my own. "We show up where others don't. That hasn't changed just because I stopped breathing."

Hernández swallowed hard. "And the dogs?"

"They're the melody. They come so no one dies alone," I say. "Not even those the world forgot." I smiled slightly. "I'm just trying to learn the harmony. And ... I bear witness. I remember."

Tears slipped down her cheeks. "Then I'll listen for the song."

I nodded. "And if you ever see someone else like me. Don't look away."

She touched her badge. "Never did."

Lucero gave a soft hum. The other dogs followed, melting into the mist between the streetlights. Lucero looked back at me, tail giving the smallest wag—more felt than seen. I followed.

They say cops run toward the danger. That we are the ones who show up when no one else will. That hasn't changed. I still walk the alleys. I still answer the calls no one else hears. I walk with the Lantern Dogs, and I remember the forgotten.

Not all ghosts haunt. Some of us just keep the watch. So, when the forgotten cry out, someone will know where they are.

About the Author

Born in 1964, Carol grew up in San Antonio, Texas, spent thirty years in Colorado and now calls the tiny town of Brackettville, Texas, home. She has been published in various anthologies and magazines and has published four of the books in her Chaos Reigns Fantasy series.

In addition to her own writing, she is the editor and publisher of the online e-zine *The Lorelei Signal* and is the person behind WolfSinger Publications.

Visit her website at carolhightshoe.com.

BALLAD OF THE RESTLESS LIBRARIAN

AYNSLEY J FRASER

I remembered dying—just a fragment of a memory. A flash of violence. The shadow of a man. And that damn song he was humming. I could still hear it echoing in my head. Loud enough to wake the dead. Loud enough to wake me.

O bury me not on the lone prairie.

I scratched against the suffocating dirt that pressed into my ears, my nose, my mouth. Why was I underground? I needed to escape, and panic seeped into my bones as I gasped mouthfuls of muck. When the crud didn't choke the air from my lungs, my fear vanished. Everything vanished except the melody that drove me to dig for my life.

I must not have been buried more than two feet down, because my fingers broke the topsoil after a few minutes. Scraping clumps of dirt from my face, I sat up coughing and spitting soil.

Where was I? How had I gotten here? Then it returned to me—I'd died. I hadn't been buried alive, or at least I didn't think so. Then why had I woken up? That song persisted, pounding behind my temples.

The night was cold, and moonlight greeted me as I tried to get my bearings in the empty prairie. My open grave lay in the shadow of a dead tree. Its branches were decorated with ropes, both old and new. Just west, the few lights of a town, probably Redemption, flickered across the deserted grassland.

Someone had dragged me up to Hanging Hill, a place where the unjustly killed cannot rest. The dirt that clung to my frozen skin was cursed.

O bury me not on the lone prairie.

The irony wasn't lost on me.

I hadn't died. I'd been murdered.

I threw my head back and howled at the moon, a wretched sound between a roar and a sob. I knew I wasn't the easiest woman to get along with, but I'd caused Redemption no problems, and I had nothing of value worth stealing. But someone had thought to kill me and hide me up at Hanging Hill, where no one went without a cause. They'd cursed me to a death where no peace could be found. I'd be returning the favor.

By some miracle, my glasses had been buried with me, and my sluggish fingers managed to find them. The right lens was cracked. I suspected I no longer needed them, but I put them on anyway.

I would find out who had killed me, and why, but first, I had to dust myself off and walk the miles back to town.

Dawn pushed the moon from the sky by the time I forced my stiff limbs down the hill, across the empty prairie, and toward the buildings of Redemption. I should've been tired a mile in, but I wasn't. Another benefit of my rise from death, perhaps. I'd heard the local warnings about restless walkers—everyone in town had. I'd even foolishly ventured near the ghost town north of us, close enough to get a glimpse of what avoided the daylight there. Given the sunrise hadn't slowed me, I wasn't as far gone as they were, yet. I'd be one of the creatures in those stories before long.

When the dusty frontier town was within reach, I stuck to the long shadows, not ready to face anyone. I'd also need to avoid the horses; the undead always made them uneasy. They knew, before people did, that something wearing a human's face had dragged itself out of the plains. I'd always liked that about them.

I had to make it to the library, my home and book-filled salvation in this misnamed hellhole. Once there, I'd regroup and come up with a real plan.

For now, I had to decide: stroll confidently down Main Street like I hadn't died or sneak like a ghoul in the night? I chose speed over stealth. No one should be out this early unless it was Sunday. But I hadn't heard any church bells.

I hurried as fast as my uncooperative limbs allowed. I caught a tune from a harmonica drifting on the breeze long before I saw its player. Another gift from the Hanging Hill? I'd be paying the price for these powers soon enough.

On the saloon's porch, Sheriff Silas Boone nearly dropped his harmonica when he saw me. What must I have looked like to scare a sun-worn man like him? His voice faltered once before he managed to ask, "Are you all right, Miss Books?"

I hated that nickname, but what else should I have expected in a mostly illiterate town? There were practically no families in Redemption, which made my whole existence here feel pointless. I don't think half of the town's population even knew my name.

Boone and I had never pretended to enjoy each other's company. A gruff man with a habit of gambling despite a paycheck that couldn't keep up and the town's unwanted librarian weren't a good match.

"I asked if you're all right, Miss Books. You look like death warmed over," Boone said, standing, his hand resting on the revolver at his hip.

"You're right about half of that," I snapped. My untested voice had a nasty rasp.

His fingers tensed on the trigger. "Which half?"

"The death half," I answered truthfully.

His eyes widened, and he glanced behind me, probably toward Hanging Hill. I wasn't the first creature to drag itself back into town. We both understood what had happened to me without me needing to say it.

Boone asked, "Who did it?"

"Is Roxie awake?"

I detoured into the saloon. If there was anyone in this godforsaken town I could trust, it was Roxanne Kincaid. Not Boone —he'd put a bullet in me sooner than help.

He followed me. "Miss Books, who murdered you?"

"Roxie!" I yelled, then I kicked her bar for emphasis. The hardwood cracked under the force. I flinched, muttering curses.

Having apparently decided not to shoot me, Boone perched on a barstool, keeping his stare fixed and revolver in hand. For once, I didn't begrudge his displeasure at my presence. Things like me didn't stay human-acting forever.

"Roxie, get down here and bring your shotgun!" I shouted again.

This time, my demand was met with frustrated swearing and slamming doors. Roxie appeared at the railing above the stage. Her usually curly blonde hair was hidden by a bonnet, her makeup stripped away, and she wore only a thin nightgown. I was one of exactly two people in Redemption allowed to see the flirtatious saloon proprietor this undressed. The other one was Boone, for similar reasons to mine.

Tiny towns make for slim pickings for your book club. Thankfully, Roxie had enough personality for two people.

"Why do I need my shotgun? Are we forming a posse?"

"No, but I might need you to put a round of buckshot in me," I answered.

Her eyes narrowed as she took in the full horror of my condition. Thankfully, like the wise woman she was, Roxie went back for her shotgun before joining us downstairs. "Have you seen yourself in a mirror today?"

"No, but I can imagine." I sighed. I didn't want to know, but I couldn't avoid it.

"Let me see your hands." Roxie's voice sharpened, and she lifted the shotgun.

Between Boone's murderous stare and Roxie's fear, I knew it was time to face it.

I'd kept my fingers hidden in my skirts since I first noticed the change. But I needed help. I held out my trembling hands. My well-trimmed nails were gone, replaced with ten perfectly pointed claws, the dirt from Hanging Hill still caked under them.

Boone sucked in a breath. What little color left in his cheeks drained.

"Oh, I'd kill for nails that healthy and long. A little red polish and you'd be big-city worthy." Roxie laughed weakly. She was terrified but still trying to make me feel better.

"You mean you'd die for them," I corrected.

Her smile fell. "So that's what happened to you, Miss Books?"

I finally said it aloud, "Yes. Someone killed me. Recently, I think."

"Very recently," Boone muttered. He reached over the bar and poured himself a drink.

"You were in here yesterday afternoon, do you remember?" Roxie asked.

A flash came back to me: pink feathers on Roxie's headband, two shots of whiskey, laughter.

"We sat over there," I said, turning to point to the table by the stage. "You were telling me a story about a drifter who came through town this week."

"That's right," she nodded. "What else?"

I strained to remember. Someone had been humming ...

That infernal song came down like a hammer into the back of my skull.

O bury me not on the lone prairie.

Pain lanced through my head. I stumbled back with a growl. Two guns cocked in response. I looked at Boone and Roxie over my shoulder. I needed to get my revenge before someone put me down with a bullet, so I tried to soothe them. "I'm still in control."

"Are you sure?" Boone asked, not lowering his revolver.

"Not craving flesh yet. I don't know how long that'll last." I didn't have specific knowledge on timelines. But most of the undead from the prairie eventually ate people.

Boone holstered his weapon. "Then we need to stop wasting time. Go borrow something from Roxie. And you," he said, gesturing at her, "rouge her up enough that no one notices the dead woman walking through town."

"Where are we going?" I asked, sitting heavily at a table. I wasn't tired, but my head ached.

"To find who killed you," Boone announced, and something in his voice made me feel like he already knew the answer.

Following Boone's semblance of a plan, Roxie took me upstairs, bringing her shotgun along. When I undressed, I finally saw the extent of the damage. The back of my blouse was stained a brownish-red along the collar and shoulders. I'd bled ... badly. But my killer had clearly strangled me too. Large, butterfly-patterned bruises winged across my neck.

Roxie couldn't hide her growing horror. While combing dried blood from my hair, she asked, "So who'd you piss off this week?"

"Only everyone with money, or authority, or a penis in Redemption," I answered flatly. My disagreeable nature and college education had never made me many friends. "Do you see any bullet holes?"

"Nope," Roxie said as she tenderly touched a wound on the back of my head.

I felt no pain, but the same melody that had crawled into my soul since waking rang in my ears. I'd taken a significant crack to my skull. That would explain the blood and memory loss.

By the time Roxie finished painting me up like the living, I looked almost human again. I stared longingly into the mirror. Most of my teeth had taken on sharp points. But if I kept my hands in my pockets and smiled with tight lips, only the bright red of my eyes would give me away.

In ten pounds of makeup and Roxie's Sunday best, I looked like myself. She had worked an absolute miracle, but I couldn't stop the doubt that crept in. Roxie had nothing to gain from aiding the monster wearing my face.

"Why are you helping me? I could be a cannibal by next week, hunting you in the night."

"Miss Books," she said with a scowl, "you're literally the only person in town who doesn't owe me money. Even the stable boy's wages are spoken for next month, and Boone's so deep in debt his grandchildren'll still be paying it off. Until you give me no choice, I'd rather not aim my gun at you."

I let out a tense breath. There was no way I could stay here, no matter how this ended. But I'd miss Roxie. Hugging her was too dangerous with my undead affliction.

"Thank you," I muttered.

"Just kill the bastard who did it," Roxie said, turning away, and I heard the faintest sniffle in her voice. She knew when I left, there was no more us. I suppose I'd be getting vengeance for both of us now.

I rejoined Boone.

My human disguise wasn't enough to stem the fear in his gaze as he looked me over top to bottom. No traces of death remained, just a high collar, wide-brimmed hat, and lipstick thick enough to bury my face.

"Where to first?" I asked.

Boone hesitated, then puffed out a breath. "Take me to where you woke up. Maybe there's a clue there."

"There isn't," I shot back. So much for relying on Boone's law enforcement expertise.

He bristled. "All right then, Miss Books. Where should we start?"

I could hear more people stirring outside now, but I headed for the saloon doors. "To the crime scene, obviously."

No one looked at me twice as I stepped into the sunlight. Roxie's efforts had paid off. Only Boone's horse, tied up behind the saloon, reacted by snorting and stomping, its ears pinned.

The sheriff seemed to know where we were going and led us toward the library.

"Do you really not recall anything from yesterday?"

I recounted my fragmented death; I kept the resurrection part to myself.

He nodded. "You're handling all this well. I've seen plenty of monsters out here, some with familiar faces. None half as composed as you."

"Is that how it looks?" I continued without waiting for his answer. "Because I'm not. I'm rage and vengeance wrapped in a petticoat, barely keeping myself in check. Someone in Redemption killed me, and a lady doesn't just get over that."

Silence stretched between us, and Boone struggled to meet my eyes. It was for the best; we'd barely tolerated each other on a good day. He began to hum.

A flicker of something—guilt, or recognition—flashed across Boone's face, and he silenced himself. "Nervous habit," he apologized.

Our awkward tension was pushed aside as we approached my home. The front door was pristine, aside from the usual layer of frontier dust, and the lock was intact. I didn't want to break it down even though my newly undead strength would've made it easy, but my keys hadn't been on me when I awoke.

"Let's try around back," Boone said. He didn't seem eager to throw his shoulder into the solid oak either.

My breath hitched as we rounded the side of the library. I froze mid-step. The back door stood open, and a brownish stain marked the mat and surrounding dirt.

This was where I died.

Boone brushed past me to inspect the door. "The lock isn't broken."

"So?" I asked. Did that mean I opened it myself?

"You got a secret married boyfriend?" Boone stepped over the dried bloodstain, taking the moment to smear my reputation. "Who else would come to the back door except someone who didn't want to be seen?"

I stomped after him, fuming. "No. I'm not looking for anyone else's company."

As I stepped inside, I felt the first rush of warmth I'd had all day despite the sun beating down outside. Dozens of shelves were stacked with wonderful books: geography, history, novels, and old journals. Everything I could get my greedy hands on. My library. My home.

Being dead hadn't changed that.

I had expected the inside to be a wreck, but aside from the bloodstain near the door, it looked untouched. No, that wasn't right. I knew this space, and something was wrong.

"Looks like you were attacked at the door," Boone said, scanning the room. "Probably opened it for a guest who cracked you over the head before dragging you up to Hanging Hill. Otherwise, we'd see signs of a struggle."

There it was—that nagging feeling again. I inhaled deeply and found what was different. The faintest scent of soap.

I opened my mouth to inform Boone, but a second scent caught my attention—ash from the cold iron stove in the reading room. That didn't make sense. I never used it except to warm up people during late-night reading hours on winter Sundays. It shouldn't be dirty.

Boone kept talking, theorizing from the doorway about strangers and unlocked doors.

I ignored him, approaching the stove cautiously and kneeling in front of it. The iron door was cool to the touch, so I opened it. No embers remained, but a half-burned paper was caught between the grate and the brick.

Carefully, I pulled it free. It was a page from my library ledger.

Did I burn this? Why? I *loved* my meticulous records.

It was definitely my handwriting, beautiful and deliberate, impossible to replicate now with these claws.

The visitor's name was burned beyond readability. There might have been an *E* and an *O*, but I couldn't read the rest. They'd requested *The Langford Ledger*, and I'd noted, "He wouldn't take no for an answer."

I knew that journal well, though I had a less kind, unofficial name for it. Regardless, I didn't lend it out. Anyone who wanted to read it had to do so during my working hours. And under my supervision, of course.

I tucked the page into my skirt pocket and crossed the room to the historical shelf, already knowing what I wouldn't find. *The Langford Ledger* was gone. Well, that answered my questions.

O bury me not on the lone prairie.

That damned song rang in my ears again. My hand went to the back of my head, to the cracked spot that ached something fierce. Then it hit me. Not just a memory. *The* memory.

The night I died.

"Good evening, Miss Books, sorry to bother you," Sheriff Boone said, being so polite, especially for coming to my back door so late. "I need to borrow a book from your collection."

"I didn't know you could read, Boone." My wit cut into him before I could stop it. But I'd waved him in anyway, stuffing down my annoyance. I only tolerated Boone because he took care of Roxie. I opened my library ledger and started a fresh page by writing down his name.

"It's called *The Langford Ledger*." Boone grinned.

I knew that hopeful look, and I'd disappoint him the same way I did every fool that came here for that particular book.

"May I ask why?" I inquired, writing the name all the same.

"That's a bit personal. I was hoping I could borrow it for a few weeks," Boone said, keeping up his gracious act.

I sighed in exasperation. "I'm afraid not. That one doesn't leave the library."

"But I need it," he persisted, though his charm had already started to crack.

"I'm sure you think you do," I said while retrieving the journal. "It stays, but you can look at it while you're here." There was no harm in letting Boone see the contents before he left.

His smile turned into a scowl. "I need that book!"

"And I said no." I met his anger with a cold glare before scribbling a note about his insistence. I should have been smart enough to be afraid, but I'd run my mouth instead. "Being Roxie's dog doesn't get you special treatment here. You can return during working hours tomorrow, and if you ask nicely, I'll let you read it in full."

I thought Boone would stalk off, calling me names under his breath like always. But this time, he unleashed his anger on me.

Fear came too late as large, callous hands wrapped around my neck, cutting off my screams. My lungs burned from lack of air, and just before I suffocated, I saw some sense return to his maddened eyes.

Boone released me, hands shaking as we both took deep, needed breaths.

"I'm taking the book," he spat and stuffed *The Langford Ledger* into his jacket as he turned away.

I grabbed his arm, but he lashed out with a vicious swing. I fell back. I don't know what I hit on the way down, but pain exploded at the back of my skull.

The last thing I heard as I faded away was the tune that had summoned me back to life: *O bury me not on the lone prairie.*

Pure rage boiled my frozen blood as the memory burned through me. Last night, Boone murdered me for *The Langford Ledger*. Not even a motivation worth writing about, like love or jealousy. I should have burned that damn journal years ago.

Now he stood at the door, looking at me expectantly. I didn't know what he'd just asked. I scanned the room sorrowfully, realizing this would be the last time I'd set foot in my beloved library. I said a quiet goodbye and resolved to do what came next.

"I think you're right," I said, keeping my voice calm and praying my face matched it. "There isn't anything more to find here. Perhaps we should go with your original plan."

"Finally, you're speaking sense. We'll make it to Hanging Hill by noon." Boone nodded.

Boone's horse refused to take me as a passenger. I made the poor thing nervous every time I glanced at it.

So Boone rode while I walked with my stiff but untiring body. Along the way, he hummed that infernal song. He was like a man possessed by the tune.

I let him hum and sing to his heart's content without complaint the whole way even as his song sent tremors of rage through me.

The sun was high in the sky by the time we reached the foot of Hanging Hill. My makeup had melted off in the heat, but I didn't mind. I didn't need it anymore. Only a narrow path led to the top safely, so Boone joined me on foot and hitched his horse for the ride back. I'd try to remember to let the nervous creature free later.

As we climbed, he muttered darkly, "I hate this place."

"If you've got no sins on your soul, then you've got no reason to be afraid of what's waiting at the top," I said without glancing back.

Boone stumbled, but we both knew he couldn't turn back now, not after suggesting we come all the way out here.

I only had to keep myself together for a little longer. Redemption was far behind us.

No sooner was the dead tree in sight than I heard Boone's revolver cock behind me. He didn't scare me anymore, so I kept walking until I could rest my hands on the tree's rough bark. I looked up at the ropes that had strangled so many guilty souls. I wasn't meant to be one of them, which is why Hanging Hill spat me back out.

"Did you know the legends about this place?" I asked Boone as I looked down at my shallow grave. It was smaller than I remembered.

"Until you showed up this morning, I didn't believe them," he admitted.

I turned to face Boone, and with slow, deliberate movements, I brought my hands to my throat. Since simple actions like undoing a button were beyond the ability of my claws, I ripped open my high collar to display my bruised neck.

Boone's features became marred by guilt and his lingering fear. "What gave me away?"

"That ridiculous song you sing deafeningly loud. It woke me from death and led me toward you all day. But I suspected you from the start. I never said where I came from, and you looked right at Hanging Hill. You knew exactly where I'd died. And, of course, there was the foolish slipup when you declared I'd been killed at home and then dragged to Hanging Hill."

Confusion, then the realization of his own stupidity spread across Boone's face. He hadn't been as sly as he thought.

"But there was something I couldn't figure out. We didn't particularly like each other, but we'd lived in our tenuous peace for years. I never asked Roxie to pick between us, either. So, why'd you do it?" I slowly reached into my skirt and pulled out the burnt ledger page. "Then I found this in my library, my home."

Steadying his shaky revolver, Boone grumbled, "I hate smart women."

Carefully, I opened the ledger page and held it up for him to see. "If you'd listened to this smart woman, I could've saved us the showdown. I call that book *The Fool's Ledger*."

Boone narrowed his eyes at me but gestured for me to continue.

"Jeremiah Langford kept a detailed journal about his search for gold in the hills of California. Supposedly, he struck a massive vein right before cholera got him. His son, Lucas, inherited the journal and followed its directions out west. You know what he found?" I let a sharp-toothed smile spread across my face. "When Lucas sold me that journal, he told me all that's waiting at the end is fool's gold."

"But my debts," mumbled Boone. He didn't loosen his grip on the revolver and fumbled to pull the missing journal from his jacket pocket with his free hand. "This was supposed to get me in the clear."

The truth lay bare between us. I had been murdered, and my killer did it for gold that had never existed. I had died so Boone could play a few more hands of poker. I hadn't been an angel, but I'd deserved better than this.

Rage boiled in my gut and erupted with a banshee's scream.

Bang!

My wail had scared Boone into firing. The bullet slammed into my shoulder, knocking me back into the tree.

"This time when I bury you, you'll stay put."

Bang! Another bullet into my thigh.

Despite Boone's harsh words, he couldn't aim straight with shaky hands.

Good, I wanted him to be afraid. Fool that he was, he thought he could kill me again without a fight.

I smiled as wide as I could, showing off my pointed teeth. The undead don't feel pain. *I* didn't feel pain. Shrugging off his bullets, I straightened up and hissed that damnable song at him, my voice raspy, but strong.

"O bury me not on the lone prairie."

I marched forward. Boone had nowhere to run unless he fancied a fall from Hanging Hill.

"These words came low and mournfully ..."

Bang! This bullet didn't deter me any more than the first two.

"From the pallid lips of a youth ..."

"Stay back," yelled Boone, emptying the last of his bullets into me.

"Who lay on his dying bed at the close of day ..."

When I was close enough to touch him, he swung his revolver down like a hammer. It cracked my cheekbone, but nothing would stop me.

"O bury me not and his voice failed there ..."

I cut off Boone's weak threats by wrapping my hand around his neck, digging in my claws.

"But they took no heed to his dying prayer ..."

I dragged him off his feet toward the dead tree as he fought to free himself.

"In a narrow grave just six by three ..."

He had nearly stopped struggling by the time we reached my former grave.

"They buried him there on the lone prairie ..."

I held him above his soon-to-be resting place and drank in the fear in his eyes.

"O bury me not on the lone prairie ..."

My claws tore the tender flesh of his throat into a bloody mess.

"Where the coyotes howl and the wind blows free ..."

I dropped Boone in the shallow grave and crouched so I could see the life draining from him as he slowly choked on his own blood.

"There's not a man who will search for me ..."

He died in pain having dug his own grave.

"O bury me not on the lone prairie."

I finished the song as Boone's last rite, which was more than he deserved. Satisfaction hummed through my blood. I'd gotten my justice. My vengeance.

No guilt hung over me. This time yesterday, I couldn't have imagined killing a man. That woman had been human, and I wasn't. If I'd been unjust with Boone, then Hanging Hill would send him to find me soon enough.

Where should I go now? There was no Redemption for me

anymore. I looked north toward the ghost town where creatures like me belonged. I walked stiffly in that direction, humming my new favorite tune.

About the Author

Aynsley J Fraser writes supernatural tales of mystery and fantasy featuring sharp-witted heroines. When she's not crafting stories, Aynsley enjoys solving puzzles in escape rooms, adventuring through the world of Pokémon, and rolling dice in tabletop role-playing games. Her stories mix the eerie and the empowering, and she hopes you'll enjoy getting lost in the strange and supernatural right along with her.

A Hymn for the Living

EDWARD J. KNIGHT

Amazing Grace, how sweet the sound ...

I sat in the back pew of the country church and let the tears roll down my cheeks. I shed deep, fat tears that threatened to turn my cotton Woolworth's dress into a sea of sorrow. Through my flooded eyes, I could barely make out the ragged choir of farm kids pressed into service.

My chest ached. My head hurt. My nose ran and forced me to snuffle.

... that saved a wretch like me.

I clutched my daughter's embroidered handkerchief in my hand. The one with the stitched strawberries and their little green leaves. She'd so loved strawberries as a babe. She'd giggled and cooed and then held out her hand asking for more.

Her papa and I had been so happy to dote on her.

I shook with the pain of memory.

I once was lost, but now am found ...

I wiped my eyes and my nose. The handkerchief would wash. It'd been washed so many times it'd grown bare and thin in spots. But then, it was old.

Almost as old as me.

... was blind, but now I see.

I shouldn't've come. Not to this service. Not to this town. Not even back to Kansas. There were too many memories. Too many reminiscences of pain and choices gone wrong.

But this was kin. This was family.

My daughter's daughter's daughter, who'd lived her entire life within thirty miles of where she'd been born. And yet she had been the first woman in my family to vote. The first to drive a car. The first to listen to jazz.

And then had left no children of her own.

'Twas Grace that taught my heart to fear ...

I had to bear witness.

Even if it pained my soul.

There was no one left. Just me. Just me to close out Gladys's life on Earth.

The last time I'd been in a church, I'd asked the minister about the nature of heaven. I asked how we knew what it was like, since none had returned from beyond the veil. He quickly pointed out that Jesus our Savior had. He paled when I quoted him verse after verse to show how little Jesus had said about His time in heaven. He'd grown frustrated and cut me off—just telling me to pray.

I'd prayed plenty. God had never answered.

... and grace my fears relieved.

One of the boys in the choir sang loudly, eyes wide. He was badly off-key but so earnest it actually teased a small smile from me. The half dozen other children swayed and shifted with the uneasiness of youth under the magnifying glass. Such babes. Such beautiful babes. Too many young ones these days were trying to be cool cats listening to jazz. These were purer, as if from an earlier era.

I wiped away my tears and settled back on the hard wooden pew.

The heat of the sanctuary bordered on suffocating. This rural church was too poor for air-conditioning or electric fans. Kansas summer heat was something I did not miss.

Still, a dozen congregants were scattered through pews that had once held a hundred. At least in my day. They'd painted the walls an off-white and then added several murals where once we'd hung paintings imported from distant Kansas City or Saint Louis. I liked the murals better. They depicted a loving Jesus and iconography from the Sermon on the Mount. As cartoonish as the figures were, they all looked happy.

It'd been a long time since I felt happy.

The children's choir helped. I watched the eager boy for the rest of the service. He, at least, still had the look of wonder on his face.

———

The minister stood by the door and exchanged the Peace with the congregants as they shuffled out into the hot sun. A tall, skinny man with a thick crown of shocking white hair, his wrinkled face made him look like one of the dried-apple dolls I'd played with as a girl. Like them, he had a worn and crooked smile.

I hung back, some because I wanted to speak to him alone. More because I needed to get control of the wild racings of my heart and mind. My line, ended. Except for me, and I could birth no more children of my own. What good is immortality without descendants?

But here we were.

I waited until the last of the old ladies who'd known my sweet Gladys had said their farewells to the minister. He turned to me, the final soul in the church. Other than himself of course. He smiled expectantly.

I forced a return smile, approached, and offered my hand.

"Katie Adams," I said. "Gladys was a distant relative."

He clasped his warm, strong hands around mine. "I'm so glad you could come."

"No one should die alone."

"She wasn't completely alone." He released my hand, and I raised a questioning eyebrow. "She was well loved here," he continued. The lack of audience at her funeral belied his kind lie, but I did not call him on it. "She will be missed."

"Did she have close friends?" I asked. My occasional correspondence with Gladys had not always been clear on the point.

"Some. I believe the MacDonalds ..." He pursed his lips as he looked beyond me and thought.

"Could you give me their address?"

"Oh, they're easy to find," he said. "Go down Main Street past that new gasoline filling station and turn right. You'll see the MacDonald home just beyond that."

I nodded.

"But," he continued, "is there something I might be able to help you with?"

"Thank you," I said with as much kindness in my voice as I could muster. "But no." Then, on an impulse, I added, "She was the last of my kin. Perhaps you could pray for her and for me."

His eyes turned serious, as if I'd given him a formal commission.

"I will," he said. "For you, for Gladys, and for all of us."

The church stood on a little rise surrounded by wheat fields that had once been pasture. My Elias had helped raise the roof back when we were young. When I was young. Before the Bushwackers had come and taken him from me.

My heart felt leaden. I still missed him. Even now as my memories of him faded, too jumbled with a century of others laid on top. He was always my Elias, with his wild grin, his strong arms, and his eagerness to help.

On a chain around my neck under my dress, I carried his wedding ring. I reached up and clenched it through the fabric, holding it tight. Touching it brought back the sharper memories, as it always did. I reveled in them as I slowly walked down the path into town.

Elias had wanted to raise sheep, to be a shepherd, even though Kansas was more suited for cattle. "We shall not want," he'd tease, quoting the Bible verse. I would roll my eyes and playfully swat him. He'd laugh and seize me for a kiss.

Elias had been my shepherd. Not the Lord. Elias had laid me down in the green pastures, with our beloved Molly the result. He had led me by the waters as we entered Kansas Territory to find our home.

And then he had been taken from me, leaving me to walk the Valley of Death all alone.

Which I did. One step after another. Just as I walked to town through the muggy heat of a Kansas July.

My thoughts drifted back from the past once I reached the small stretch of businesses that now made the town more than a blip on the map. The general store had a sign hawking radios—"Hear Roosevelt yourself!"—next to another sign offering ice delivered to your door. The neigh of horses mixed with the rattle of a Ford bouncing along the road. The present had turned strange—a crossroads between the settled old ways and the unknown new.

A land I barely recognized.

But I continued on.

A few folks waved their general hellos as I passed the businesses. Not many were out, but enough. Some I recognized from the funeral. My favorite choir boy chased after another with a pointed stick, calling, "Bang, bang, bang!"

I smiled at that.

Ahead, the Ford jalopy turned into the newfangled gasoline filling station. I watched the driver emerge and engage in quiet discussion with the attendant. The driver wiped his brow and pointed to something on the car. They went inside the garage entrance before I reached them, so I turned my attention elsewhere.

I spotted the stables. The paint was worn and faded on the sign. The smell of horses was strong. I heard shuffling as I passed it by but no voices.

I reached a small, plain, single-story house with a little square porch. White posts supported a sloping roof that covered the porch and hinted at the house's large attic. Flowerpots filled with large black-eyed Susans sat at either end of a long wooden bench. The porch was tidy and swept and the front of the house clean of the usual dust and dirt. I took that as a good sign.

As I approached, a woman stepped out of the house. She had long black hair tied back loosely, tired eyes, and wore a smudged apron over a simple skirt and blouse. She put her hands on her hips as she regarded me. I recalled her sitting on the far side of the church with a tall, thin man of commensurate age.

"Hello," I said as I pulled up short. "I'm Katie Adams. I saw you at Gladys's funeral."

"We were there." Her gaze remained wary.

"I'm Gladys's last living kin," I said. "Are you Mrs. MacDonald? I was told you were one of her friends."

"My daughter, perhaps."

"Ah." I could not remember a girl from the service that would have born a resemblance to this woman. "Well ... I have no need of Gladys's remaining possessions. I thought perhaps I might pass them on to her friends."

She looked me up and down again, and then her face softened. "Why don't you come in?"

Mrs. MacDonald led me into a small parlor lit by the sunlight streaming through a large window. Needlepoint adorned the walls, and the room smelled strongly of bleach. My eyes immediately fell on the girl bundled under quilts on an old, upholstered couch. Every part of her was cocooned except for her head.

The girl's ashen hair hung close to her cheeks, her skin pale but her amber eyes lively. They tracked me, and her lips pursed in a curious smile.

"Mary," Mrs. MacDonald said, "this is Katie Adams. She's Miss Gladys's kin."

"I didn't know she had any kin." Mary's voice was high and thin. I placed her age at about ten.

I smiled sweetly. "Distant kin. We used to write letters to each other."

"Oh. I see."

"Mary and Miss Gladys were in the hospital together," Mrs. MacDonald explained. "Mary has tumors in her bones where the blood is made."

My chest froze. Tumors. Mary was far too young for such a weight on her soul.

"It's okay," Mary said. "They don't hurt much."

Much was such a deceptive word.

I forced my jaw to work. "I'm glad. And I'm glad you got to know Miss Gladys."

"She was nice." Mary's face fell. "I'm sorry she died."

"So am I. So are we all. Perhaps you can tell me more about her?" I glanced at Mrs. MacDonald for her permission, and she slowly nodded.

"Mary's father had an appointment at the bank," she said. "But perhaps I could fetch you some water?"

"That'd be mighty nice." I smiled at Mary.

She smiled back.

I settled into the chair across from the couch, and we began to talk.

Mary made me laugh. Despite her pallor. Despite her occasional wince of pain. We sat in the living room, her under her blankets, me with my water, and talked as the sun descended and the shadows from the window grew.

The girl had a knack for turning the innocuous into the hilarious.

She told how Gladys had helped her smuggle rock candy past the nurses. She spun yarns about the older doctor who Mary was sure was sweet on Gladys. I had my deep doubts, but the stories were too good to discourage.

In turn, I shared some of what Gladys had written in her letters. She had not mentioned little Mary by name, and I chose not to mention Gladys's sad musings about the fate of "that dear little girl in the next bed." Instead, I talked about Gladys's love of cats and music.

"She used to make the janitor sing!" Mary blurted with glee.

"Make?" her mother asked from the kitchen where she leaned against the doorjamb and watched.

"Ask. He had a deep voice," she said with a blush. She looked knowingly at me, as if I were part of her secret. "I think she liked him."

"Ah." The doctor. The janitor. Mary was a font of romantic speculation. "So what did he sing?"

"'Sweet Chariot.'"

"That's a good one," I said.

She nodded solemnly before smiling once again. "Sometimes we'd join in. Do you wanna sing?"

It'd been ... I couldn't exactly remember. Just so long since I'd sung. So long.

"Please?"

I smiled. "Yes, let's."

We sang together. "Swing low, sweet chariot ... coming forth to carry me home ..."

We sang and we sang. Mr. MacDonald returned home just as Mary and I finished our tenth song. Tall and worn, he had the creases in his face of someone aged past his years. He wore a faded black suit with a thin black tie like something Doc Holliday would've had. He paused as he entered the parlor, and his eyes darted all around until they settled on his wife. She stood straight and brushed invisible dirt off her skirt.

The last notes trailed off, and Mary swiveled her head to look at her parents.

"You should get some rest now, dear," her mother said. "Your father and I need to speak with Mrs. Adams."

"Okay, Mommy." Mary gave me a winsome smile.

"I'll be here a few days yet," I said with an honest grin. "I'm sure we'll sing some more." I wanted nothing more, to be truthful. I would stay and sing as long as I was allowed.

Mary nodded, nestled under her blankets a bit more, and closed her eyes.

Mrs. MacDonald gestured for me to join them in the kitchen.

———

The kitchen was as clean and tidy as the parlor and porch. The MacDonalds had a new refrigerator, one of those newfangled Westinghouses, but also an old fire-burning stove from the turn of the century. I caught the faint scent of smoke from behind the smell of bleach. Mrs. MacDonald motioned for me to sit at the small square wooden table while she refilled my glass. The water was cold and sweet on my throat.

"How did it go?" she asked her husband.

"Not well." His shoulders sagged before he turned to me with an apologetic smile. We made our introductions, and then he sat across from me. Mrs. MacDonald served him a glass of water and then joined us.

We sat quietly, none of us speaking. My mind jumped hopscotch, though it kept landing on the square of Mary's illness.

At last, Mr. MacDonald cleared his throat. "So ... what can we do for you?"

"I could use some assistance in disposing of Gladys's

possessions," I said, my long-practiced words for this moment. "While she saved a great deal, I have no use of her house nor everything within, other than some family heirlooms."

The MacDonalds exchanged a sideway look. Mr. MacDonald took a sip of water.

"So you wish our help in selling her house?" he asked.

"In a way," I said. My heart had changed, which made my tongue numb. My words were no longer rehearsed. "I thought ... I thought I might sign the deed over to you. You could ... you could use the money for Mary's treatment."

Mrs. MacDonald's eyes brightened and widened, but her husband's neck stiffened.

"We don't need your charity," he said.

"It's not charity." I nodded toward the parlor. "Mary ..." I grimaced and thought back to the letters. "She was a joy to Gladys. The closest thing to a daughter she ever had."

His jaw clenched. His eyes darted back and forth as he thought.

"John ..." Mrs. MacDonald gently placed her hand on his forearm.

"It won't help," he snapped. "The doctors think ... the doctors don't think anything will help."

"Her blood's dying," Mrs. MacDonald patiently explained. "The money would be a blessing, but ..."

"It's just a matter of time," Mr. MacDonald finished.

I took a sip of water.

We sat there as the shadows grew. None of us had anything of significance to say.

I stared at the ceiling of my boardinghouse room, unable to sleep. The stifling heat didn't help. The open window brought in the chirps of crickets and the distant hoot of an owl, but no cooling breeze. Even stripped to my unmentionables and laying atop the rough sheets did not help. I had sweat on my brow and a heavy heart.

It wasn't fair.

That sweet, sweet child would soon meet her Maker. That innocent girl's light snuffed out.

Yet mine never would.

I had been shot in the heart, fallen off cliffs, and been hanged more than once. Yet I healed and went on.

What merciful God would do this?

The psalmist said that goodness and mercy would follow me all the days of my life.

The psalmist lied.

I rolled onto my side and tucked my hands under my lumpy pillow. I stared into the night, but it offered no answers. No respite.

The Lord was not here in my darkness.

My mind sank into despair.

I had begun grieving for Gladys upon receiving the lawyer's letter telling me of her passing. She had died without children, which hurt in my bones. Yet I had foreseen that and her passing for some time. She had chosen to live her life her own way, right through her treatments for the tumor in her breast.

Mary had never had that choice. Her life was to be cut short because her blood was dying.

And my blood never would. It couldn't.

Or ... maybe it could?

I searched my memory for clues, but the jumble of the past was too much. Too many memories. Too many thoughts.

But I didn't need memories. Not when a simple test would do.

The electric light in the boardinghouse kitchen blinded me when I turned it on. The harsh bright white made me wonder about progress. I missed oil lamps with their softer, simpler glow. Likewise, the steel table and cabinet made me yearn for good old-fashioned wood. But the world moved on.

The oak knife block on top of the cabinet offered a range of choices. I chose a small paring knife based on the sharpness of its blade. I actually nicked my thumb testing it, but the cut healed before I could even bring it to my mouth to suck. I snorted softly as I considered where to cut—where to balance the pain against the amount of blood I wished to spill.

In the end, I slit my left wrist.

Pain shot through me as blood gushed over my palm and my fingers, dripping onto the steel table. I clenched my teeth and held my wrist low so that the blood pooled instead of scattering like rain. When my left wrist sealed up and the bleeding stopped, I took a deep breath.

Then I slit my right wrist.

I sucked in my breath. It *hurt*. My eyes watered. I shoved my cut wrist into the blood already spilled. I forced my eyes to remain open as I watched under the sterile electric light.

The old blood flowed back into my wound as I healed. Three dozen heartbeats later, the steel table gleamed without a dot of red.

I rubbed my right wrist and smiled with satisfaction.

Even outside my body, my blood did not die.

Hallelujah. Praise God on high.

Mr. MacDonald regarded me warily after I'd laid out my proposal. The MacDonald kitchen was cool in the morning, and Mrs. MacDonald had been a good hostess and served us coffee. The smell stirred my brain and I smiled. The bitter taste usually suited my mood and might yet again today if Mr. MacDonald did not agree.

"A blood transfusion," he said, repeating my earlier words. "We were told those could be dangerous."

"If you don't have compatible blood types," I said. "Surely the doctors discussed that."

He furrowed his brow and slowly nodded. Next to him, Mrs. MacDonald's eyes brightened.

"My blood is type O," I continued. "It's compatible with everyone. It surely can't hurt, and it might give her more time."

Mr. MacDonald drummed his fingers on the kitchen table. He stared into space. Behind me, the refrigerator hummed, filling the silence. His emotions warred until we heard Mary cough in the parlor.

"She's awake." Mrs. MacDonald jumped to her feet and hurried out.

Mr. MacDonald's eyes narrowed, and he turned his gaze back to me.

"You barely know us," he said. "So why would you do this?"

"It's the best way I know to honor Gladys. By helping her friend enjoy life just a bit more."

He curled his lip in contemplation.

"And it's my Christian duty."

Mary's and Mrs. MacDonald's voices spilled in, too faint to make out words but loud enough to make out Mary's excited tone.

Mrs. MacDonald appeared in the doorway, smiling. "Mary wants to know if you would like to sing with her."

I raised an eyebrow at Mr. MacDonald in a silent question.

He stared back, before answering with a nod.

***

Morning has broken, like the first morning ...

They'd added air-conditioning to the church sometime in the decade since my Gladys had passed. Air-conditioning, cushions for the seats, and a new young minister with the energy of those who had missed the Second War.

Blackbird has spoken, like the first bird ...

I wasn't sure I liked this new hymn. Certainly not played on a record instead of sung by a choir. But the town had shrunk between the war and the young seeking better lives in the cities. Even Mary and her husband, the former choir boy, had moved to Saint Louis. Yet their parents remained.

Praise for the singing!

I clutched Elias's ring under my dress. In the pew ahead, Mary's baby fussed.

Praise for the morning!

Tears formed in my eyes. Such a beautiful, beautiful baby girl. Even if Mary had not insisted, I could not have missed her daughter's christening for the world. Not in the church of her family and mine.

Praise for them springing fresh from the word!

Katherine Gladys MacDonald Reynolds. My goddaughter.

I looked forward to teaching her to sing.

About the Author

Edward J. Knight writes historical fantasy focused on the nature of heroism and the meaning of living. Katie Adams will appear in a forthcoming novel, expected in late 2026. More of his work can be found at edwardjknight.com.

BLOOD AND BADGES
H.T. ASHMEAD

The music—if it could be qualified as such—reverberating from the vehicle thumps in my chest. Not only is its rhythm disconcerting, I worry my sensitive ears will hemorrhage from the assault. I press the button to scan stations.

"Susannah, what're you doing?" Detective Latsis growls.

"Seeking the sonorous sounds of the Italian masters."

"Huh?"

I roll my eyes at the dark-haired detective. "Finding something more conducive to pondering than this chaos you call music. What do you say—rock? That is an apt description, for I wish to smash the sound-producing device with a stone."

He pushes a button labeled number one. The pounding thump returns. "My car, my station."

"Are we not assigned to work together?"

He looks sideways. "Yeah."

"And do you use your income to purchase this carriage?"

His body shifts. "Well, no—"

"Then it does not seem to me that you can claim ownership of this vehicle and therefore full rights to the musical selection."

His jaw ticks, clenching and unclenching. "Fine." He huffs. "We'll take turns."

I parked my car behind a police cruiser, its red-and-blue flashing lights reflecting in the dark windows of the closed storefronts.

With a grin, Susannah switched off my powerful '80s rock, her fangs glinting in the neon lights of the street. Inexperienced rookies. Always excited for the first case. The fact that she was a bloodsucker made it worse.

I tensed to stop the shudder. After all, I'm a professional. Chief had emphasized the honor of being the human in a human-vamp partnership. "Make sure she doesn't lose control," he'd ordered. "Make it work or put her down."

I eyed the woman warily as we climbed out of the car.

At five foot ten, she met me inch for inch. Until she put on those blasted three-inch heels. Her fitted top accentuated her silhouette without revealing too much. The black duster she'd called a pirate coat buttoned at the torso but flared into an open skirt to allow for the practicality of black slacks. If she'd been anyone else, I would've called her style "business sexy."

But she wasn't. She was a vamp.

Complete with speech patterns like she'd lived hundreds of years ago. And the expected pale skin against auburn hair. In the office, men *and* women had eyed the leggy woman when they'd first met her.

Until she smiled.

Then they cringed and suddenly found something very important to do. Somewhere else. As far away as possible.

"Detective." Officer Scott greeted us. My brown eyes were easier to face than Susannah's red ones. The fact that tonight, her eyes gleamed scarlet, indicated it'd been a long time since she'd fed.

"What do you have for us, Officer?" I asked, redirecting everyone's attention back to the task.

He lifted the police tape for us at the mouth of the garbage-infested alleyway between strip malls. Too bad it couldn't hold back the skittering rats as well as it did the handful of gawkers. The street shimmered with reflected lights even though it hadn't rained for weeks. Every third step felt sticky, and I was grateful for the darkness.

"Gunshot victim. Female. Thirties. Homeless man found the body behind the dumpster when digging for dinner."

A pool of blood—a huge temptation for a famished vamp. I felt for the smaller gun with silver bullets in its holster beneath my sport jacket before winding between the putrid dumpsters.

I follow my lover—no, that word is incorrect—*partner* to the poor woman's remains. To distract myself from retching from the repulsive stench, I focus on his steps reverberating against the enclosing brick walls.

The brooding demeanor of this olive-toned, dark-haired man is attractive to the version of myself from two centuries past that I still remember. Though a slightly more recent version of myself can imagine toying with him prior to draining his life blood.

Today, I work alongside him because I tire of running, hiding, and fighting. That lifestyle challenges one for a century or so and adds intensity to a post-life. Then it turns into tedium.

I will never regain the zest of life that mortals experience from not knowing what a day may bring. Each sunrise and sunset becomes another glorious proof of life—another opportunity to love or lose.

But not for me. I am trapped in an eternal limbo from which the only escape represents a void. No afterlife awaits my death, just blackness. Therefore, despite my boredom, I do not succumb to nonexistence.

As much as I tease mortals about their fascination with the talking box, I understand the appeal. It becomes an opportunity to peer through a window at a life they either wish for or are grateful to avoid.

Interacting with humanity elicits much the same fascination for me, only I would accept any one of their lives just for the opportunity to *live* again.

Even if it results in the eventual death that follows. Just as it has for the petite blonde woman before me who has transitioned to her afterlife.

Her eye makeup spreads heavy, her round face sporting a sprinkling of freckles. A breeze channeling through the narrow boulevard ruffles her pixie cut.

The splay of her body makes it difficult to determine her height. Perhaps five foot three. Her gold top shimmers as I circle her. Her white skirt would normally meet the middle of her thigh but now lifts to an unseemly height.

Her arms skew in opposite directions, almost like a ballerina. However, her glassy-eyed stare into the aether indicates the conclusion of her dance. Three manicured nails on her right hand are broken. I study her body for any other details of her death, but truly, I am fortifying myself for the work I must do.

After all these years, I turn off my senses as much as possible to avoid constant enticement. Except when I hunt a meal, which is no longer acceptable per this current arrangement.

However, this is a different kind of hunt, a different kind of prey, and I must allow myself every advantage.

I inhale deeply, a shuddering breath that represents more habit than need. As I never truly die, I never experience how it feels to cease breathing, and my lungs continue to inflate. The intake of air does nothing for me, but the action itself calms my nerves.

Crouching inches from her face, I absorb the girl's floral perfume.

My eyes water as I stifle a cough. I take three normal breaths to clear the overwhelming scent followed by one slow inhale to parse out the undertones. I mentally set her perfume aside and dig deeper. A sweet-smelling soap—her skin looks supple and soft. The tang of hair spray.

And there it is. The bitter iron separate from the rest.

I examine her wound. A crimson flower reminiscent of a liquid poppy blooms across the left side of her golden top. A stream trails down the side of her blouse, curling beneath her and spreading into a puddle.

I fan my fingers wide, flexing them to control their quivers, then curl them into a fist. Extending my smallest finger of my left hand, I dip it into the dark liquid. With a deliberate motion, I lick the lifeblood from my fingertip.

An explosion of ecstasy spreads across my tongue. The metallic bite of iron. The hint of astringency from the B antigens. The sweetness of pheromones unique to this woman. All natural substances.

I savor the flavor, touching my tongue to the roof of my mouth.

Men and women around me retch. But they do not understand. What they see repulses them, yet they demand it for their benefit.

Mortals always are hypocritical.

I swallow, allowing the taste of the victim's blood to dissipate. However, it persists in my mind. My stomach twists into complicated knots. I want nothing more than to ravage her prone body and drain her dry. But that would prove their fears. And Detective Latsis carries that specialized weapon beneath his jacket that he thinks he hides from me.

I clench my fists, my nails engraving half-moons into my palms, and take two shuddering breaths, restraining myself from tasting again. Once is all I truly need. Any more, and it becomes indulgence.

Then I stand. "I am ready."

The vamp rose from her awkward crouch and faced me. Her scarlet eyes blazed with a fierceness that almost caused me to step back. But I didn't make detective because of a weak heart. My hand reached for the extra gun under my arm. Her eyes flicked to it, so I pulled out a notebook and flipped through it.

I'm not sure I fooled her.

Swallowing bile against the vision of her licking—no, relishing—a dead woman's blood, I said, "Let's get started."

Her lithe body darted past me.

"Hey—"

She whirled so fast, I gasped and gripped the handle of the revolver before catching myself. "Do you not want me to track down that woman's killer?"

"Well, yeah, but—"

"Then I must lead." And she raced down the alley.

Men and women stepped aside as she sped past. I lengthened my stride, but I refused to chase after her; she'd just have to learn to slow down.

Susannah lingered at the crossroads, sniffing in each direction. She took three steps down the road to the left, paused, inhaled, then spun 180 degrees and took off to the right.

"Wait up."

But the vamp didn't stop.

I caught up to her three blocks down the street, masking my irritation that she didn't seem winded.

She squatted in a parking lot, surrounded by vehicles of every size, make, and color.

"Here," Susannah said, pointing in the narrow space between a newer Toyota and its neighboring Ram.

"Here what? I don't see anything."

"Nor do I," she replied. "But I smell her."

I scoffed. "That's impossible. She's almost half a mile away."

Susannah glared then spoke deliberately. "More accurately, I smell her blood."

My half-formed sneer fell under her fiery eyes. Those scarlet eyes. I swallowed at the memory of the vamp's blissful look as she'd tasted the victim's blood.

And yet, she hadn't attacked the body. That one taste, as disgusting as it was to watch, was all she'd tried.

Perhaps I should give her a little more credit.

I cleared my throat. "So is this where she came from?"

The vamp shrugged. "Perhaps. I follow the scent of her blood. When blood remains inside a body, it leaves no trace of passage. But this blood lingers after her death. Therefore, the perpetrator has carried the girl's blood to this location—an amount imperceptible to him, but not to me."

I straightened, focused. "If her killer was here …" I scanned the area. A convenience store, clothing shop, bakery. "There." Across the street, a flashing neon sign advertised a bar. A bass line pounded through the night air, a few strains of melody audible when the doors opened.

"Why there?"

I shrugged. "Human nature."

Her delicate eyebrows furrowed. "I do not understand."

How to explain what my instincts and training picked up on as soon as I'd scanned the parking lot? Susannah's discovery confirmed my suspicions. "The victim was dressed up, but the local beat didn't recognize her. So, not a hooker." I noted the vamp's cringe at the word. "Must be enjoying a night out. Not fancy enough for a play or concert, so bar is the most likely scenario. If the killer came back here, it's probably where he parked his car. A logical conclusion would be that he met her at the nearest bar."

I peruse the drinking establishment. The room luminesces with dim-colored lights piercing it in sequence with the pounding beat. Men and women move their bodies in grotesque forms, sometimes together, sometimes apart. At this time of night—or morning—most individuals hang on to each other. Body odor, perfume, and pheromones fester the air. I choke from the onslaught.

Detective Latsis shows the bartender a photo of the girl.

The man nods to a corner table while drying a glass. He raises his voice over the music. "Two women sat there. Her friend tried to get her on the dance floor. She kept taking her by the hand and trying to drag her out. They both were laughing about it though."

"Okay, so she didn't want to dance," Detective Latsis says. "Anyone else keep her company?"

The barkeep scrunches his features. "Not at first. She just watched her friend, sipping her daiquiri. Eventually, some guy walked over. She must have known him because she stood and hugged him."

Detective Latsis makes a note. "I'm surprised you remember all that."

He shrugs. "Better tips for noticing things. Besides, she reminded me of my ex."

"So then what happened?"

"The friend came back, then left with some other guy. Half an hour later, your girl and the first guy were gone."

Detective Latsis gives me a look as though we share a secret. "What did this guy look like?"

"White, medium height, brown hair, button-up shirt, jeans."

"You just described half of the men here."

The bartender grins and shrugs. "Men tip worse."

Detective Latsis slides a card across the bar. "Can I get a copy of your receipts for tonight? And if you think of anything else, give me a call."

I clench my teeth. He does not include me.

I climbed in the car and turned on the radio.

Susannah wagged her finger. "I believe it is my turn to select."

I sighed, already dreading the operatic crap she preferred.

She scanned the stations until she found some dude warbling more than a mating finch. Then she leaned her head against the seat and closed her eyes as I turned the car toward her apartment.

After about a minute, I couldn't stand it any longer even though I'd agreed to let her choose.

I switched the radio off and launched into a question about the case before Susannah could complain. "If our killer was in the parking lot, why couldn't you sniff him out at the bar?"

After several seconds of her smoldering eyes, she answered. "I smell *her* blood. That trail ends in the parking lot."

I mentally snapped my fingers. *That's* what rubbed me wrong about Susannah—she never spoke of the past or in the past tense. But asking why felt too personal, so I filed it away.

"How can you be sure? I mean blood is blood, isn't it?"

She tilted her head and studied me. "My impression is that you are only interested in the results I can produce for you, not the process."

True—at first. But now that I'd asked the question, my curiosity simmered. I met her gaze. "I'll listen if you'd like to explain."

Susannah nodded once. "If it becomes too gruesome, please request I cease." She leaned back into her seat again and stared out the window. "Do you indulge in wine?"

"I'm a beer kind of guy."

Susannah growled low in her throat. "Well, hopefully you will still appreciate the analogy. Each batch of wine has its own flavor. All rieslings have similar flavors, as do all chardonnays, and pinot noirs. But the amount of sun, water, soil conditions, and other factors add subtle undertones that make each batch unique."

"Like fingerprints. They each contain whorls, loops, and arches, but in infinite variety."

She nodded. "Blood is the same. I can tell you the blood type after a single inhale. But with further exposure, I can determine the combination of undertones that make each human's blood unique."

"So what's my blood type?" I asked with a half chuckle.

"B negative." No hesitation.

My eyes widened. "I'm not sure how I feel about that."

"You can put your mind at ease. I would be unable to track you effectively."

"Why not?"

"Because I do not taste you. That is the only way to identify all undertones." She grinned, her scarlet eyes blazing above her ivory fangs.

I cleared my throat and rubbed my stubble. On impulse, I pulled into a hospital parking lot. "Wait here a moment."

———

Twenty minutes later, he returns to the car. "I frighten you, Detective Latsis."

"If I scared that easily, I wouldn't be a cop. And call me John. It's easier." He hands me a paper bag. "Here."

"What is this?"

"Dinner, per the agreement. You looked a little hungry. Thirsty? Man, I don't know the right term." He rubs the back of his neck.

I withdraw three rubbery bags filled with a carmine liquid. I lick my lips, and my stomach convulses. My mouth waters with the memory of the metallic tang on my tongue. But with trembling hands, I replace them in the paper bag then set it in the central storage box of the carriage. I will move them to my icebox once I am home, but for now I must remain focused on my task.

"What's wrong? I saw your eyes, and I thought—"

He fears that ravenous rampage that follows the brightening of vampires' eyes. Those moments that initiate the stories. The slaughters even I find abhorrent.

I place my hand on his forearm. "No. You are observant. But if I feed before we locate this young woman's executioner, it will taint her scent."

His shoulders slump. "Sorry. I didn't know."

"I very much appreciate your consideration on my behalf, John." The last expression of concern with *my* comfort occurs decades, perhaps centuries ago.

John sets his jaw and grips the steering wheel. "Then I guess we need to catch him quickly."

———

By the next morning, we'd identified the victim's friend through receipts. Now we stood in the Latina's modern apartment, her eyes bleary with sleep.

"I'm sorry to tell you, but your friend was killed after you left the bar last night."

"Killed? Amber? That's impossible." She placed trembling fingers over her lips, staring into space. Then the brunette collapsed onto her cream couch in sobs.

I stood, pen poised over my notebook. Once she had calmed some, I asked in a soft voice, "What's Amber's last name? And can you tell us about last night?"

The woman wiped her eyes. "Amber Morris. We went clubbing." Her voice broke and tears started anew.

After a few moments, Susannah sat and placed a hand on the woman's knee. "The bartender says he saw a man talking to her."

"Jimmy. We work with him."

I stiffened. "What can you tell us about him?"

She shrugged. "He's sweet, but awkward. Tries to flirt with every woman on the floor, but he's really bad at it. Oh, Amber! Why did I leave?" Her sobs intensified, her voice muffled behind her hands.

Between sobs, the woman said she'd met a guy who invited her to a party. Amber said she'd hire an Uber, so they'd parted ways at the bar.

I got the guy's name and left my card.

Susannah strode with that same unnerving speed I'd seen before. She pressed the elevator button for the third time when I caught up. "We must speak with this Jimmy next."

"I agree. But as genuine as she seemed, we can't rule the friend out either. We need to confirm her alibi."

"She is not the murderess."

"You can't be certain of that."

The elevator chimed, and the doors opened. Susannah stepped in and faced me. "I can and am. Amber's blood does not touch that apartment. The woman speaks truth. Amber lives in her encounter."

That's ... interesting. I stepped in beside Susannah and pressed the button for the main floor.

The distance to Jimmy's townhome is short, so I endure but a few minutes of John's music.

Flowers grow in lush beds, but only rust-colored gravel fills the space by Jimmy's front door. Small birds twitter from nearby branches. I pull my hat low against the intense sun, grateful for the protective pirate coat. John knocks on the door.

After a few moments, a lanky young man wearing glasses opens the door. He focuses on me and licks his lips. "On a scale of one to ten, you're a nine, and I'm just the one you need."

John tenses then steps forward. "I'm Detective Latsis, and this is my partner. Do you know Amber Morris?"

"Yeah, I work with her. Why do you ask?"

"When did you last see her?"

"Yesterday."

"It is difficult for me to stand in the sun," I say with a honeyed tone. "Might we discuss our business inside your home?" I give him a toothy smile.

Jimmy swallows once, taking half a step back.

John's mouth twitches.

Jimmy regains his composure, then he gestures us inside. "Any knockout is welcome in my house." But his smile stretches no further than his lips.

John opens his notebook. "You say you saw Amber yesterday. What time was that?"

I stroll around the front room, hands clasped behind my back. Everything exudes beige: beige walls, beige couch, beige entertainment table, beige shelves. I hide my tracking by studying a few abstract paintings—the only vibrancy in the room—a photograph of Jimmy and his mother, his DVD collection.

Jimmy informs my partner that he had offered to give Amber a ride home, but she declined.

I step close enough to Jimmy to feel the heat from his body. "I am parched. Might I get a glass of water?"

"Sure." His voice quivers.

I follow him to the door of the kitchen. "Your home is lovely, Jimmy. I know this is terrible timing, but I am considering an abode like this. How many bedchambers does it contain?" I take a sip from the glass, lifting one eyebrow.

"Two."

I lean in. His sweat almost, but not quite, covers the scent I seek. "Might I be allowed to view them?"

Jimmy leads me up the stairs eagerly.

John tries to follow, but I gesture him away.

At the top, I step toward the left, but Jimmy closes the door. "That's my room, and if I'd expected company, I would've cleaned up." He winks, but no spark reaches his eyes.

I utilize a small portion of the charming smile of a hunting vampire; he cannot handle the full force. Nor does it seem necessary with him. "Perhaps the other room?"

He places his hand on the small of my back and steps toward the door on the right. "Right this way."

Such easy quarry.

He murmurs in my ear, "If you'd ever like to stay here, you know, to see if this is the right fit, you're welcome to crash."

I desire to detach his presumptuous limb from his torso, but instead I step into the sleeping space. "Are you as generous with all your female visitors—like Amber?"

His smile fades.

I lean close, dropping my voice to a sultry whisper. "Someone harms her, yet not once do you question us about her. I wonder how she felt to have her life force under another's command. Do you?"

Jimmy's color drains.

I hear the rustle of John's jacket and his tread on the stair. I step back. "You may put away your specialized weapon, Detective Latsis. No threat exists here. Good day, Jimmy." We exit the home.

As we climb into the vehicle, John says, "That was reckless and dangerous."

I press the number two on the radio presets. "My turn, yes?" Then I settle into the seat. "Every predator toys with its prey before the attack, yet always in complete mastery. Amber's scent fills that residence, strongest from his bedroom." I allow the smooth tones from the music box to cleanse me of the filth from Jimmy's townhome. "And now, if you would be so kind as to return me to my residence, I would like to feed. I am starving."

***

"The man admits to seeing the victim the night of the murder?" Judge Nguyen asked.

"Yes," I said.

"And then he says he left the bar before the victim?"

"Yes, sir."

"Do you have any evidence that says otherwise?"

I deflated. "No, the cameras show him leaving about fifteen minutes before the victim. No other cameras along the street."

"And no witnesses?"

I shook my head.

The judge leaned back in his seat, peering over his glasses. "Then I don't know how you expect me to issue a search warrant. The evidence corroborates everything he said, and nothing you've presented suggests differently. I'm sorry, but until you find me something concrete, I'm going to have to deny your warrant." He handed back the sheet of paper.

I took it.

Susannah, who had remained silent, stepped forward. "Honorable Judge Nguyen, am I to understand that we must have the search warrant in order to gather evidence against James Coleman, and yet we must have evidence in order to receive such a warrant?" Her mahogany eyes met his.

He swallowed thickly then nodded. "That's an over-simplification, but basically, yes."

She pursed her lips, tracing his walnut desk with her finger. Then her intense gaze returned to the judge. "Do you know who I am?"

The judge cleared his throat. "I do."

"Then you know of what I am capable."

He pressed deep into his chair, his eyes wide.

Susannah held her palms up. "I apologize. That sounds threatening, but that is not my intent. I wish to clarify the purpose behind my position at the police station. It is true that because of my ... changed nature, I possess certain abilities beyond the scope of a mortal. And because of these specific abilities, I assist the police force in solving crimes in a timelier fashion. You are aware of this arrangement, yes?"

The judge nodded.

Susannah strolled around his office, her gaze directed to the floor. "I thank you, Honorable Judge Nguyen for your faith in me. I will not go so far as to say trust, for that must be earned. I wish to attempt that now. If a trained bloodhound indicates it smells the victim in a residence, would you deny that request?"

"Well, no, but—"

"Then will you please give me the same level of credence as you do a canine?" She stopped pacing and leaned across his desk, palms spread on the dark wood. "I swear on my mother's two-hundred-fifty-year-old grave that James Coleman is responsible for the execution of Amber Morris. The longer you deny us the opportunity to search his dwelling, the more evidence he will destroy that is necessary for a court conviction."

Judge Nguyen leaned away but lifted his chin. "Perhaps the victim was at his place at some other time. I cannot deny basic rights of presumed innocence without justifiable cause."

I placed a hand on Susannah's arm, but she pulled away.

Taking a deep breath, she straightened and faced the judge. "Mortals understand just enough about my kind to be wary. The only way I am capable of smelling *unique* blood is from standing beside the individual or after it leaves a body. Otherwise, I detect something like her perfume or laundry detergent. Yes, it is possible that Amber visits Jimmy's home at some other time. However, I specifically mark her *blood*.

"I am performing as you hope, and yet you continue to set me and this alliance up for failure by distrusting the very information you request I provide." Susannah attempted to keep the pleading out of her voice.

The judge looked from Susannah to me and back. "What's your assessment of the situation, Detective Latsis?"

I studied Susannah's face before answering. "Judge Nguyen, my instincts align with her deduction, or we wouldn't be standing before you now. Her abilities led us to a parking lot, which then led us to the bar. That, in turn, led us to the friend, and the person of interest. I cannot elevate James Coleman's status to a suspect without searching his townhome or workplace." I gestured toward my partner. "Susannah denied herself sustenance in order to maintain her sensitivity in pursuit for the victim."

His eyes narrowed. "Isn't that dangerous?"

I smiled briefly. "Susannah has conducted herself with absolute professionalism. Thanks to her, we have a viable suspect in less than forty-eight hours. I'll admit, I was uncertain about this initiative at first, but I wouldn't mind working alongside her again."

Susannah lifted her chin.

Judge Nguyen looked between us for several moments, his fingers steepled in front of his mouth. "Let me see that warrant again."

I handed him the paper.

As the judge signed it, he said, "I hope you know what you're doing."

"Thank you for defending me," I say as we position ourselves inside the vehicle.

John shrugs one shoulder. "Yeah, well, hopefully after you have a few successful cases under your belt, no one will have to anymore."

I smile.

"Since I chose on the drive here, it's your turn," he says, gesturing to the music box.

I press the first preset. A slow but heavy beat fills the space.

John raises one eyebrow. "I think you pressed the wrong button."

I lean into my seat and close my eyes. "I would like to try something unexpected today."

He sits in pregnant silence. "Why do you never talk as though something has already happened?"

A smile ghosts across my lips, and I sway with the rhythm. "When you are undead, time becomes meaningless. Everything is present. Now." I open my eyes and look at John. "This melody is surprisingly ... beautiful. Haunting."

He chuckles once. "One of my favorites."

"How is this ballad named?"

"'Silent Lucidity.' Now, should we go nail that bastard?" He pulls into the street, lights flashing.

About the Author

H.T. Ashmead writes whatever the muse dictates in the moment. *Usually*, this translates into speculative fiction, both long and short form. No matter the genre, her focus is always Writing That Explores Our Humanity. She has a short story published in both the online literary journal *Inkpot* and the anthologies *Particular Passages: Decked Halls*, *Extraordinary Beasts: Tails and Talons*, and *Win in the End*. Her novel debuts 2026. You can follow her online at htwrites.com, facebook.com/htashmead/, and TikTok @htashmead.

A HAUNTING FUGUE

J.L. SMYSER

There is a bent nail in the wall where our photograph used to hang. Without it, the room feels barren. Lifeless. Everything else has remained the same for years. Our various instruments are displayed, collecting dust. Violins, guitars, and a saxophone hang on the far wall. The piano fills the void in the center. A flute lays slightly askew on the windowsill. The heart rate monitor is next to the metronome. Everything is exactly how it was left when they took you away. It must always be the same. Otherwise, this doesn't work.

The only acceptable change is the odd mirror in the corner by the window. It is full-length, with faded symbols on a frame curled like driftwood. I can't seem to remember how I attained it or when, but every day it draws me back here. It's not myself I care to see in that reflection. I'm trying to see beyond. To my muse. But you are not there. Not yet.

Very well. I will do this all over again.

I sit at the piano bench. The fallboard squeaks as it opens. The instrument is perfectly tuned for the melody I play every day. It must always be the same.

My feet tap a rhythm against a scored floorboard. Hands that once entertained thousands of people now plunk away at single keys. These first gentle tones are a warm greeting. It's not for me. I never play for myself anymore—or anyone else, for that matter. This is only for the mirror. For you. My muse.

Here comes the overture—a melody of a hastening heartbeat. An intensifying allegro. You always loved this song. We used to perform it, and dance to it. And later it drowned out the noise of the machines that kept you alive.

Now, I believe, it may be the only thing that can bring you back.

Bony fingers I hardly recognize as my own now dance across the keys like young lovers. There is no sheet music in front of me. I work off memory alone. The kind of memory that stings at night. I resist increasing the tempo to get to you faster. The song needs to be perfect. Unaltered.

It must always be the same.

Keeping the steady pulse of the music, I glance over my shoulder. An incorporeal silhouette appears in the mirror, for now, a visage of rot and decay. I can never be sure if it is you or another wraith who visits me until your faint humming arises to harmonize with me.

How many years has it been since I first heard this song? Two bars hummed while in line for coffee. I tapped your shoulder to ask the tune's name, not knowing it would be the inspiration for our future opus. Together, we became a passionate duet of true renown and genius that no one else could truly appreciate. Not the fans. Not the critics. And especially not your siblings, who kept ruining everything.

They must never know about this mirror. I will not let them take you away again.

The overture ends and the main melody begins. You join in with a violin formed from ghostly wisps. Your bow glides across spectral strings. With every passing note, you rematerialize, becoming more alive. Through this mirror of undeath, my muse returns.

We performed this song at our first concert. Such a small venue.

Less than fifty people. Together, we enraptured them. The picture that once hung on the wall captured that triumphant moment. I'm sorry I ruined that picture. Why didn't we take more?

But hopefully, you will retain this memory when I bring you back. We can return to how things once were.

I scoot the bench backward a little and use one hand to pull the piano forward an inch. It's the only way to get closer to you. But I am careful not to stop the music. You'll blink out of existence. I can't let that happen again.

When we hit a forte in the song, your flesh has been completely threaded back into existence, and color returns to your dimpled cheeks. You look as young as the day you left me. No, even younger than that. It takes me back to the peak of our career. Playing across the country for weeks at a time. Long, arduous traveling and cramped living arrangements. Our first major fight happened then. What were you so mad about? I can't seem to recall. Probably something we laughed about later.

A bodiless accompaniment of other instruments flows from the mirror along with a cold blast of air that sends a chill down my spine. You are still out of reach. I move the bench, then the piano. It carves another groove into the floorboards, but that is fine. These little movements will not stop the mirror once the music has started.

I miss the days of late-night composing with you sleeping nearby. I could look upon your resting face and find the music. Without you, I can't do that anymore. No more masterpieces. Not even a fledgling spark of inspiration. I need you back. And I will have you back. No one else deserves you like I do.

There is a natural swell as we near the peak of this symphonic power. I know we could touch now. If only we were closer. Timing the music, I tug the piano with a momentarily free hand. Wood shavings peel and curl under the piano feet as I pull and play, and pull and play.

I keep my eyes on the mirror to ensure you're still there. Despite my drawing closer and closer, you don't acknowledge me, just the music. Why do you refuse to look at me? All of this is for us.

I played for you after the diagnosis. I took care of you during your treatments. Of course there would be dissonance during difficult times. I shouldn't have pushed you away, but I was scared. We built our music career from the ground up, and then it was gone overnight. It was our livelihood. Who wouldn't be worried about that?

Impatiently, I kick the bench backward, and it tips over. I play while standing.

It's not like your family cared for you the way I did. During our interlude, they used the money we earned to keep you in a hospital. Who would want to die in a hospital and not at home making music? Making art? Making masterpieces like this one?

One hand plays, the other pulls. Piano feet grind deeper gashes into the floor.

I only wanted the best for us. I fought them. Challenged them with every legal dispute I could muster to bring you home with me for your final coda. You were mine. Not theirs. And I'm sure you would have agreed with me if you could have. But you had already entered your coma at that time.

The music crescendos. Your cold siren smile tempts me closer. I reach, but I'm not quite there. Just a little more. One hand plays, the other pulls.

This is the closest I've come to bringing you back.

You stop playing, and for the first time ever, you look at me with chilling white eyes. The bow evaporates, and you reach toward me. Fingertips emerge from the mirror glass, and we are but an inch apart.

One hand plays, the other ...

The final lurch is too much. The overturned bench trips me. I'm ripped away from the piano during the final cadences. From my prone position, I take hold of the mirror, but you are gone. Once more, it reflects the lifeless room.

Rising to my feet, my exhausted bones creak. I float to the windowsill next to the mirror and grab the flute resting there. I lift it above my head, trembling, poised to strike the mirror. I could shatter it and rid myself of this curse.

Perhaps this is my punishment for keeping you so long after the metronome of your heart stopped. For staving off the rot and stench to create compositions from a decomposing muse until they took you away to be buried.

Hovering in front of the mirror, I try to see beyond, but you are not there. Neither of us are. I swing the flute in a downward arc, but falter before it hits.

You would have wanted me to do what I have done. I know this to be true. Your placid smile, frozen in death, told me how happy you were. You loved me. You will love me again when you return. For that, I will accept any curse. We will compose again. We will enrapture them. We will hang another photograph in that space on the wall. We will never let anyone take you away again.

Though I wonder, as I do every day, if I'll have the strength to try again tomorrow.

I set the flute back down on the windowsill in its original position, still slightly askew. Before I leave, I reposition the piano. The bench too. I make sure it is all exactly the same as it was when I entered the room.

It must always be the same.

About the Author

J.L. Smyser is a teacher, an award-nominated editor, and co-owner of Blue Feathered Quill Publishing. He squeezes in his writing time by scribbling on any scraps of paper or sticky notes, and the cats that use him as furniture are his muses. The curious reader will find his debut short story in the anthology *Chaotic Cupids* by

WordFire Press, and other stories he's written or edited at bfqpub.com.

THE DEVIL'S MUSIC
L. BRIAR

Spring 1930

Strange fruit and Spanish moss hung from an oak as Robert Johnson's train sped past. Even as he sat picking his guitar licks, he caught a whiff of the fruit's sour decay in the breeze. The state fruit of Mississippi was a bitter one. The taste could make a Black man shrink into himself, fearful and broken in the shadows. But for Robert? A crooked smile played on his lips. That fruit's pain fueled his soul, the same as coal fueled the train's race down its tracks.

The nineteen-year-old plucked a few more notes that echoed in his empty boxcar. Rotten wood splintered into his cotton breeches with each jostle of uneven track. His long fingers fumbled on the strings, noising the place. He was outta practice since getting hitched. Hell, if he was being honest, he'd yet to master the guitar he had spent nearly every dime on. Frustrated, Robert lay back and set his guitar aside. It'd do no good dwelling on things he couldn't control. The church taught him that much, even if they frowned on his "devil music."

He let his thoughts drift to Virgina, her embrace as warm as coffee at sunrise. A young slip of a girl with dark, rich skin. Big eyes and a big smile waited for him to come home. *Would the babe in her belly be a boy?* The thought straightened his crooked smile into something honest. He brushed a hand in his pocket and found minted metal—a Hoodoo nickel. Before Virgina had gone to stay with her family, she'd been sure to bewitch him with the coin from her nation sack. A silly tradition. He didn't need anything but the thought of her to keep him happy. It was time to go back, and he was almost there. Almost home.

Fall 1938

Papa Legba felt the twangy melody as his hand brushed the boxcar's floor. With a bladed tongue, he licked the spirit's melody from his hand. It tasted of resonating bronze strings—just a nibble of his prey. Prey that, by all rights, should be in his possession. So why could he find only echoes? In the Mississippi Export Railroad's scrapyard, the boxcar had been left to decay, but Papa had *finally* found Robert's trail. After months of nothing, here was something honest.

"You can't be here, boy," a gruff voice called from behind him.

Papa turned. Behind him stood an imposing man, broad as a barn and thick as a barrel, holding a lantern shining with a dim light. Clubbed ears spoke of too many hits to the head, and his white face was as pale as the moonlight in the night sky. Beside the bruiser was a black-and-tan bloodhound, its hackles raised, a growl low in its throat.

"I've trod many places." Papa pulled the pipe from his lips and smoke curled around his words. "Don't think I'll stop now."

He knew how the man saw him. A Black man bent with age, a hump on his back, whose white hair poked out from under his straw hat and filled out a long, full beard. Weak. Old. Easy prey. Men who underestimated others based on looks didn't last long in Papa's experience.

"The uppity type, eh?" The bruiser unstrapped the baton from his belt. "Good. I'd just been wishing for something to do."

"A wish already? That be in my power to grant." Papa tipped back his hat and fixed his ageless eyes on the pair. The dog whimpered, but the man didn't notice. "Ya sure that's what ya want?"

"What I wish is for you to stop talking to me." The guard's voice dripped with malice as he spat the words at Papa.

"Deal." Papa smiled and nodded.

The bruiser took a swing at him—but hit the empty air. His bloodhound yelped and scurried under the railcars. He whirled around, and Papa materialized again.

Papa's inhuman eyes burned orange.

The man took a step back. "What in the ...?"

With a devilish smile, Papa unsealed the sack on his hip. Shadows poured out of it. Inhuman haints crawled over one another, smoke come to life, their former humanity as twisted as the claws that replaced their fingers. Guttural growls emanated from their fanged mouths as they fell on the guard.

He opened his mouth and choked on his scream as the haints crawled inside filling his mouth and nostrils. The man's bloodshot eyes widened. He coughed. Once. Twice. He bent over, vomiting up black tar into a festering pool on the dirt. The man collapsed into his own filth, twitching in agony.

With a whistle, Papa called the haints to him. He counted their dark spirits one by one as they oozed back into his sack. It wouldn't do to lose one.

Nose crinkled, Papa stepped up to the groaning man. The man's spirit was a neglected thing, rotten as a gutted fish left in the sun. From the mess, Papa plucked a small figure—a doll with clubbed ears and wide eyes. He dropped the figure into the sack at his hip.

The man grasped Papa's bare feet and croaked, "Give it back."

Papa shook his head. A man's gain came at the price of his spirit, and once Papa'd granted a wish, that was that. Regret didn't come into it, but he couldn't tell the soulless man that without breaking their deal. Papa Legba was nothing if not good to his word. So, silently, he stepped away.

This wasn't the prey he wanted, but it would suffice for tonight. Finally, he had a trail, and he'd find the man whose music still haunted this godforsaken land. From under the boxcar, a whimper caught his ear. Striding to the train, he reached a hand underneath. The bloodhound jerked back, but Papa remained still. After a turn, the hound sniffed him. Cautiously, the animal slunk out from the boxcar.

Papa smiled as he patted the dog's head. "No one gets to renege their word."

Summer 1930

Robert Johnson bled upon the graves; his fingers were a mess of practice. He couldn't stop. He never wanted to stop, but the music in his mind wasn't singing on the strings. Leaning against an upright headstone, he let the notes go. His broken melody died quickly, lost among the numerous headstones in disrepair, the wrought iron fence twisting its way through weeds and the leaning willows. He was just noising Beauregard Cemetery's haints at this point. Well, them and Ike.

Ike Zimmerman chuckled from his seat on the ledger gravestone nearby. A bottle of whiskey and guitar lay by his side. At twenty-three, the teacher wasn't much older than his student, but Ike had already made a name for himself in the Southern blues. In his tweed suit and loosened tie, he had a careless air about him. "Your gonna run me crazy with that reckless strum." Ike scratched his forehead, knocking his black hat sat askew. "What you trying to say in all that noise?"

Robert tried not to think about Virgina. He tried not to think of the future he'd never have, and the wife and babe gone to earth. He hid his pain in a smile. "Just trying to wake the dead."

"Christ, ya might do just that. Have you been doing the finger exercises I taught ya?"

"Sure as a cow shits in the field."

"Let's see that hand." Ike's eyes narrowed.

Robert hesitated before setting down his guitar and placing his hand in Ike's palm. His teacher clicked his tongue. "Well, ya done hurt yourself. Gonna have to give it some time to heal."

"I ain't got time for that," Robert snapped. He needed to play.

Ike shook his head. "You're gonna have to make time." He poked Robert's finger with his own.

Pain flared.

"That hurt, ya old bastard!" Robert yanked his hand back and glared at his teacher. He grabbed his guitar and slung the strap over his shoulder. He nicked the whiskey from Ike's side. "I gotta take a walk about."

"You do that. See if you can't find a cure for that attitude." Clicking his tongue, Ike pulled his guitar onto his lap.

In a huff, Robert stormed out of the graveyard. Once past the twisted gate, he took a swig of whiskey and let the liquid burn down his throat. Let it choke the pain as if it could wash him clean like baptism cleaned the soul. Enough might make him forget this world of death and strange fruit.

How he got to the crossroads by the railway tracks, Robert didn't recall. The breeze carried the heat of summer scented with Southern magnolias. His guitar felt heavy as he pulled it off. Maybe here, where no one watched, he could do it. Maybe he could give voice to the pain he'd been pushing down. Robert hesitated as he dared to touch the sorrow in his soul, to try to pluck it away. The melody started as fresh as the breeze's flowers, but soon enough, his fingers fumbled again. His off-pitch notes warbled like a croaking toad.

"I can't even have this one thing?" He roared at the night, spittle flying. "This world takes, and takes, and *takes*. It doesn't matter what I give or how hard I try. Why are you punishing me?"

Only cicadas replied. Enraged, Robert tossed his guitar away. His hands didn't hurt anymore, but something wet trailed down his cheek onto the dirt road.

"He's not fair, is he? This God they give you."

Robert turned around to find an old man with a hunched shoulder and Robert's guitar in his hand.

The man used a cane to step closer. "You don't have to answer to him, ya know? Your roots run deeper than that."

Though the man's eyes were hidden under a wide-brimmed straw hat, Robert knew enough hoodoo to know who stood at the crossroads with him. He licked his lips. "What do you want, Papa Legba?"

The spiritual realm's Gatekeeper grinned wide as he tipped the rim of his hat back. Robert sucked in a breath as the Hoodoo spirit, devil, and savior rested his bright yellow eyes upon him. Papa Legba's tobacco pipe burned like a third eye.

"That's not the question you want me answering. You wanna know if I can do it—if I can give you the gift."

"Can you?" Robert asked.

"If you wish it, my word is good." Papa Legba offered the guitar back to Robert. The young man snatched the instrument. His wish already tickled his tongue. The only devil left was in the details.

Fall 1936

For the first time, a master disc recorded Robert's blues. His guitar's seven strings danced as his fingers flew. Melody? Bass? He didn't even have to think about it as he played both. He ran with it, resonating with each twang as they filled the recording studio. The music in his head *finally* brought to life with flesh and metal in the belly of his guitar. His pain intermixed with desires of what could have been. He'd laid his soul on the line for a wish and seeing it coming to fruition left him breathless.

The San Antonio studio's crusted brown carpet still had hints of red, and its walls were like the pages of some old book, but Robert didn't mind. He hardly saw anything around him. It was just him and his guitar. He'd played for coins on the train tracks. He'd played for the sharecroppers in the juke joints. Today, he played for himself —for the nickel in his pocket. He put his soul into his music.

Robert held his breath as the last note sang. He stretched and teased it out until it grew hoarse and, finally, silent. Only then did he let himself exhale. He looked up.

The man in the recording booth at Vocalion Records had a cigarette hanging three-quarters out of his mouth. Behind his studious glasses, his eyes bulged half-outta his skull.

Robert had forgotten Don was there for a minute.

"Did we get it?"

Don's cigarette fell to the floor, and Robert smiled.

Winter 1938

Papa Legba lost Robert's trail at Carnegie Hall. A Victrola spun a recording of Robert's blues, and the music washed over the audience. *"I got to keep movin', I got to keep movin'."* His voice rang through the immense room. Eyes lit up as his voice and seven-string reached out from the past. They'd come for spirituals, and Robert delivered from beyond the grave.

Standing in the technician's soundbox, Papa ground his teeth. Records with names and images of their musicians lined the walls of the tiny room. There was a type of soul to the blues, but it wasn't the one Papa was after. His prey's trail grew as cold as the man's body at his feet. Some men's hearts couldn't handle the stress of selling their souls. Beside him, the bloodhound sniffed the corpse. With nowhere else to go, she'd followed him since the train tracks.

"Where to now?" Papa asked to no one in particular. In the

shadows, his restless haints growled. The Hoodoo legend picked up the sound technician's doll. The tech had answered Papa's questions about the source of Robert's recording before agreeing to trade his soul for wealth. But he'd never spend a dime. Those unfamiliar with Hoodoo didn't know they could negotiate for time. But Robert had known, and now Papa regretted giving him even a second.

"This can't be the end." Papa twisted the doll in his hand.

He couldn't sense Robert here, but he saw the man's photo on the wall. Papa stalked over to it and glared at Robert's knowing smile. As if Robert knew he'd gotten away again. Papa turned his attention to the record below the picture. A smile crept over Papa's face. The producer was Vocalion Records.

In the concert hall beyond, Papa could hear Robert's melodic voice, *"Hellhound on my trail ..."*

"That's right, Robert." Papa reread the address on the record's label. "I'm coming for your legacy."

Summer 1938

Robert Johnson lay dying with bad whiskey on his breath. His guts twisted up in him like gnarled roots and not just because of the poison he'd unknowingly drank. He'd bartered for eight years, and tonight his time was coming to an end. At least he'd made the most of those years. Made a name for himself in the Delta and built a legacy. He'd idolized all those blues men from the crowd, but now he stood shoulder to shoulder with them. His only regret rested in Crystal Springs, where a bastard son he'd never met slept. He'd given the mother and her family money, down to the last nickel in his pocket. But now he'd die without ever meeting the boy. That chafed at him as he twisted in fever-soaked sheets.

A shadow in the corner of his sickroom caught his eyes.

"'Bout time you showed up." Robert wheezed. His friends had dropped him off at the shotgun house to recover. He could hear their hushed voices downstairs. Robert wondered if they could hear the footsteps of Papa Legba as the Gatekeeper paced over to him.

"If I make a deal, I've a mind to keep it," Papa said and sat in the empty chair next to Robert's sickbed. He took the towel from the water basin and dabbed Robert's forehead. The cool damp stole away some of his fever, but it hardly made Robert feel better. Papa set the towel down. He leaned in close, and Robert felt the tickle of his sickly-sweet breath. "I gave you your music and your legacy. It's time I got mine."

The Gatekeeper flicked open the sack on his belt.

Robert tried to sit up, to get away, but Papa placed a hand on Robert's bare chest. His pulse thundered in his ears. This was it. Shadows grew long as the spirit, devil, and savior held him and … frowned as he reached into nothingness.

"It ain't there, is it?" Robert choked out a soft laugh as he felt bile roil in him.

"How?" Papa hissed, his yellow nails digging into Robert's skin. "It should be here."

"I must have left it …" Robert's eyes grew heavy and his pain distant. "… somewhere along the way."

Nothing and no one called him as he closed them.

No light. No dark. No pain. Outside, the dogs howled.

No spirit passed into the afterlife or Papa would have felt it.

"No. Get back here!" Papa shook the body. Robert's corpse sagged in Papa's hands before he tossed it back to the damp sheets. He stood in disgust and spat at the musician.

"You owe me, Robert. If I can't find your soul. I'll claw back your legacy." Papa whistled, and his haints spilled out of the opened sack, their smoky forms screaming in rage. They slipped through window cracks and floorboards, searching the night for a lost soul.

Winter 1939

Little Claud wished for snow on his eighth birthday, but that was rare beneath the Tennessee line, rarer still in Crystal Springs, Mississippi. Instead, he wished for a dog. When that wish came true in the form of a bloodhound bounding up the porch stairs, Claud about fell out of Grandpa's rocking chair. The dog plopped down next to him, its tongue lolling out.

"Hey, boy." Claud reached out a hand, and the dog brushed against his palm. It left a line of drool that he wiped off on his overalls. "What's your name?"

"She calls herself Bonnie." An old geezer in a wide-brimmed hat all but appeared outta thin air from behind the family's oak tree in front of the farmhouse.

"Oh ... " Claud frowned at the stranger. Grandpa was a preacher, so it wasn't unusual for folks to show up looking for a hand, but this man moved funny. Grandpa moved careful—on account of being so old—but this man had a cat's confidence as if nothing could hurt him.

Bonnie whined, turned over, and exposed her belly. She stared at him expectantly.

Claud swallowed, not wanting to be impolite. "Is she your dog?"

"Naw, she's a stray I picked up along the way," the old geezer said. He limped with his cane to the steps and sat down on the porch next to Claud. "Do you like dogs?"

"Love 'em." Claud's eyes lit up. He scratched Bonnie's belly with both hands. Her foot flapped appreciatively. When Claud stopped, she hopped up and shook herself before sitting next to the old man.

"Dogs are loyal creatures. Honest things. Easy to love." The man brushed a hand behind her ears. "Are you an honest sort, Claud?"

"Sir, my granddad's a preacher." Claud grinned, a gap where his front baby teeth had been. The new ones hadn't grown in just yet. "If I wasn't honest, I'd be reading Bible verse for dinner."

The old man nodded in approval. "That's good to hear. I've been wronged by dishonest men, and I'm hoping you can help me."

Bonnie whined and circled up to Claud. He patted her absentmindedly.

"A man with Vocalion Records told me you're Robert Johnson's son. Ain't that right?"

"I'm not supposed to talk about him." Claud shrunk in his chair. "He played the devil's music."

"Don't worry, it can be our secret," the old man whispered. His words came faster, "Was he ever here? Did he leave anything?"

"I never met him." Claud thought on the man he'd seen from the farmhouse window. A man with a guitar on his back and money in his hands. Grandpa had taken the money but chased the man and guitar away. A string of longing plucked in Claud's soul.

"That can't be right." The old geezer frowned and licked his lips. "You see, I have it on good authority he's been here. I *know* he stood under that oak."

Claud shook his head. "That might be so, but I never spoke to him. Honest."

"Damnation!" The man stood, and the day's shadows drew deeper. "Where are you, Robert?"

"He's dead," Claud said, trying to be helpful. That must have been the wrong answer because the old man's eyes flashed orange in anger.

"Yes, but his legacy lives on." His eyes rested on Claud. For the first time, Claud noticed his eyes caught gold in the afternoon sunlight. "Doesn't it?"

The boy shrugged. Claud didn't like the predatory look in those eyes. He also didn't like how the sack on the old man's hip moved like something was trapped inside it and was trying to get out. He stood up. "I think I hear my grandma calling."

"Before you go, I want to thank you for helping me."

Claud turned away. "Oh, you don't need to do that—"

The old man grabbed Claud's arm. Before he could react, the man spun him back around. "None of that now. I'm a man whose word is good. So, what can I do for you, Claud? Anything in this world you wishin' for?"

He released the boy and put his hand on his hip sack.

Claud stared hard at him. What was he talking about? A wish? Like tossing a coin down a well? Claud couldn't help but glance at the sky with its unhelpful lack of snowy clouds despite his birthday wish. He glanced at Bonnie, who crowded his feet and whined at him for more pats. Finally, his eyes settled on the oak where he'd last seen his father.

"I wish ..." Claud whispered, and Papa Legba leaned in, a hungry look in his eyes. "I wish I could have met my dad."

It wasn't something he'd ever said aloud before, but it was the truth.

The stranger cocked his head to the side, and for a spell, they stood silent on the farmhouse's porch. Only the breeze rustling oak leaves dared make a noise.

Then the old man began to laugh, louder and louder until his whole body shook with it. Claud frowned, but the laugh wasn't a mocking sound. It was more ... resigned.

"Of all the things to wish for, you picked the one thing I can't get at." He wiped a tear from his golden eyes. He muttered something under his breath that Grandpa would have washed his mouth with soap for, and swept off the porch. He glanced back at the boy standing beside the farmhouse door. He shook his head. "You win, kid."

"What did I win?" Claude furrowed his brow in confusion.

"Life." The stranger whistled for his dog.

Bonnie's ears pinned back. She gave the man a sheepish side-eye and stayed at Claud's feet.

Claud gave her some scritches.

The man frowned but nodded. "Life—and a dog, it seems."

Without another word, he turned and walked away.

Alone, save Bonnie, Claud shook his head. "What a strange man."

Out of habit, he stuck a hand in his overall's pocket and checked on the nickel there.

After Grandpa had turned away the man with the guitar, Claud had gone out to the oak tree. There, among the roots and dirt was a minted metal nickel. Claud had slipped the coin into his pocket and kept it as a keepsake. It was the only gift he'd ever gotten from his father. It felt warm to him, like a good luck charm. Sometimes at night, if he held it to his ear, he swore he heard a blues melody. Claud would never tell a soul, but he enjoyed the devil's music.

About the Author

Author L. Briar is a reader, engineer, and foam swordfighter. She is the author of the Uncommon Universe series and a recipient of the 2024 Sidewise award for short form alt-history for her story "A Brother's Oath."

Today, she is the author of over forty-two short stories, and her debut novel and 535 percent overfunded Kickstarter hit, *Gambling on Common Sense: Rationality, Romance, and the Space Between*, is now available.

SONATA IN Z MINOR: A WALKER CHRONICLE

JASON KRISTOPHER

Browning, Montana
Herrera Farmhouse
Z-Day +8 months

He was gone now—Michael.

A city boy with no survival skills except ordering at Le Cirque. I begged him to join us here in Montana when the first outbreak reports surfaced, but he'd dismissed it as media hysteria, bent over his stock ticker while New York crumbled. By Tabitha Greene's last *HealthWatch* broadcast, I knew he hadn't survived.

Charlie and Esteban were gone too. The six-year-old bitten, the father by his own gun. I couldn't blame Esteban. Losing a child is horrific, especially when it's because you turned your back for a heartbeat while trying to protect them ... I can't say I'd have chosen differently.

Maria couldn't forgive him for Charlie's death or his own cowardice. It didn't matter now; my sister was gone too. Montana's winter ice proved treacherous—a sharp axe, a woodpile, and an unexpected walker.

I was a Juilliard piano instructor, for heaven's sake. Not an EMT.

I'd helped bury the boys, but Maria's grave took several days. Despite my iron grip, honed by years of piano, the frozen hard-as-stone Montana soil refused to yield as easily to me as it had to the much-stronger Maria, with all her years of hard farmwork.

I was different, after. My agile, dexterous hands now bore calluses from hauling walker corpses and stacking them, just like the wood I chopped. From defending myself from what life was now. Like Michael, city rat blood ran in my veins, but survival demanded adaptation.

Juilliard taught me discipline; the apocalypse taught me application.

My battered leather journal served me well, rescued from a drawer by chance during my desperate flight from NYC—and from Michael, truth be told. Page after page now filled with notes, musical and tactical, a survival manual and composition book.

The music ... oh, the music!

Melodies surged in my mind whenever I was out there, away from the farmhouse, among the dying and the dead. Early on, the music lingered in memory, but after witnessing too much—*doing* too much—the notes fled unless captured on paper. The journal never left my side.

Sheet metal from the barn reinforced the windows and doors. Food stocks filled the root cellar, enough for a year or more. Solar power, when I could get it, a generator when I couldn't, though even biodiesel was running low. Water came from an old-fashioned, windmill-powered well.

Maria and Esteban had engineered their remote farm for self-sufficiency. They just never planned for the apocalypse.

Z-Day +14 months

Another thing they didn't expect? A massive, once-in-a-century ice storm tearing south from Canada, coating everything with crystalline destruction. Temperatures plunged as hurricane-force winds shattered the thermometer.

My structural reinforcements hadn't held. Winds, ice, and sleet drove the dead through the broken shell of Maria's home. I escaped to the root cellar through the dead with only my pack and Maria's old rifle.

The root cellar was even colder than I'd expected. I huddled against shelves of dwindling resources, long-spoiled rations, and more medical supplies than I could carry or would ever need.

None of it mattered now.

I shuddered and yanked the parka hood tighter, unsure whether it was to block the moans of the dead shuffling through the farmhouse ruins above, or my own whimpers. Blood and filth crusted my hands from the desperate fight to reach the "safety" of the root cellar.

Third movement, second crescendo—C minor, then transitioning to ...

Music flooded my mind during a crisis, my brain's desperate final defense mechanism against a world devoid of sanity. My fingers pressed against my ears, attempting to drown out the howls above.

Shuffling feet thundered overhead, penetrating even the parka's insulation. Something massive crashed, scattering my thoughts. Dust filtered between the floorboards, dancing in the thin beam from my penlight. My journal lay open beside me, a comfort, measures and notes stretched across staff lines like cryptic incantations against madness.

Fortissimo—D minor with a counterpoint in G ... eighth notes accelerating ...

The music assembled within my mind, each note arranged against the backdrop of horror. Out of habit, my fingers dropped to my lap and twitched against my thighs, playing phantom keys while a melody hummed in my throat. Suddenly, the roof collapsed with a thunderous crack, smashing the cellar door open. Blowing snow and freezing wind poured in, along with several walkers tumbling down the stairs.

Time to go.

There was nothing here for me now.

I tossed the journal in the pack, zipping it closed and throwing it on my back as I grabbed the rifle. I smashed through the cellar doors leading to the yard, but the storm's fury swallowed the loud crash. My gloved hand shot up to shield me against the freezing ice granules seeking any exposed skin.

I stopped once and stared back at my shattered fortress. Heartache crushed my chest, twisting my face into a grimace. Though my Catholic faith had long since abandoned me, I whispered a prayer skyward for Maria—devout until the end—and for Esteban, for Charlie, even for Michael.

Then I yanked my hood tighter and plunged into the storm.

Swan Lake, Montana
Swan Lake Luxury Mountain Resort
Z-Day +2 years

The dusty piano beckoned. My entrance into the beautiful instrument's tomb stirred tiny motes into the air, sparkling in the evening sunlight that streamed through the massive window wall. The vaulted lobby with its lofty lodgepole pine ceilings stretched fifty yards to the registration desk, with a restaurant, café, gift shop, and seating areas between. Throw rugs and enormous pass-through fireplaces completed the "Western resort" aesthetic.

In this remote, forgotten sanctuary, a treasure awaited: perhaps the world's last Steinway baby grand. Abandoned and untouched since Z-Day. My hands trembled until I clenched them into fists, over and over. The fallboard opened under my touch—reverent, slow, yet eager—with no way to predict what lay beneath.

The keys gleamed, pristine but for a thin layer of dust, easily wiped clean with the barest pass of the scarf I pulled from my neck.

Seven hundred fifty-four days since I last touched a piano. I should've counted the hours too.

The keys waited, patient, rosy gold in the last rays of the sun—ready for someone to release the melodies and harmonies trapped within the glorious instrument. My breath caught in my chest as my eyes closed and hands descended.

Perfect pitch—both gift and curse throughout my career—made me wince at the discordant middle C.

The note fell more than flat. The note fouled the air like the aftermath of excessive Mexican food. Like the screech of a fork across a dinner plate. A sound that sets your teeth on edge just knowing it exists, much less actually *hearing* it.

A quick glissando confirmed two things. One: This Steinway was so far out of tune it might as well be a tuba. And two: I would spend whatever time needed to resurrect it.

This broken beauty was abandoned and discordant—but unlike the world, *this* I could fix.

I had a sonata to finish. Those notes in the journal demanded life, and what is life without music? Music *embodies* life itself, and now—perhaps *especially* now—this truth mattered more than ever.

With the right tools, I could tune her in a day. I'd done it countless times in walk-ups across New York with makeshift tools when necessary. Scavenging the resort would yield what I needed: a wrench I could modify, some metal rods, a few rubber wedges.

The fallboard closed with a soft, solemn thud.

Then came what I should've been listening for the whole time, given the situational awareness that this brutal world had pounded into me day after relentless day. The sound obscured by my heart's desperate yearning for a sugarplum fairy's dance or a rousing ragtime anthem.

The rattling moan of a walker from a hallway off the lobby.

Damn. Missed one.

I sprang to my feet, belt knife materializing in my hand. Mummified by the dry mountain air, the walker's desiccated feet scraped and shuffled against the marble tile as it lurched toward me from the darkness.

To my surprise, I began humming Ravel's *Boléro*—always an energizing, rousing piece—as I stalked toward the creature. This ghoul would join all the others I'd dispatched. No walking corpse would separate me from the Steinway.

Some things were worth the effort.

Three Weeks Later

Finally!

The clear, resonant, *perfect* A echoed off the high ceilings. My fist pumped skyward in the now-ancient victory gesture, and my body sagged against the black-lacquered wood.

It had taken three weeks of scavenging to gather all the tools I needed. Despite years of abandonment and neglect, the Steinway had weathered the apocalypse with remarkable resilience. That perfect note testified to its survival, my heart resonating in harmony.

But my work had made the last few days ... interesting.

Even before I'd started tuning, I'd prepared for what the noise might draw. Any noise would bring the dead, but sustained playing? Even humming could get you killed in this world.

That's why I'd cleared the lodge.

Seven walkers, roused by the tuning, went to their rest from the main lodge. Some were more difficult than others. One monster's claws caught my jacket until a quick pivot freed me and my knife found its target: the walker's temple.

I wrote the sonata in my head the whole time. A moment later, I realized I was composing while they were *de*-composing, and chuckled.

Michael had detested my gallows humor.

Those poor corpses had testified to a different sort of resilience.

Others remained imprisoned behind doors now locked forever, mummifying in private tombs—the hotel rooms they'd died in.

Nature had asserted dominion here, too, reclaiming the resort. Alpine grasses sprouted from hairline cracks in the marble floor. The air carried a complex blend of pine, mildew, and abandonment—the olfactory signature of vacated human places.

Floor-to-ceiling windows framed spectacular views of Swan Lake below. Lumber—stacked in a supply closet for repairs that would never happen—now barricaded the lower windows against both weather and walkers.

The shining glass panes sent back a tonal vibration with the music, mirroring the notes I played. The exact opposite of sound-dampening material in a studio. No doubt one reason the piano had been positioned in the giant open space of the lobby.

My eyes swept the surroundings one final time. Registration desk, café, restaurant, gift shop—all lay shrouded in darkness despite weak moonlight filtering through clouded windows. All doors remained secure, window barricades intact. I circled to the piano's bench and sat, my boot nudging the emergency pack resting beside Maria's rifle on the floor out of habit. Making sure they were still there, positioned for instant retrieval.

The apocalypse had taught me a lot of things.

My fingers hovered above the ivory, not yet making contact. The first touch would transform abstract memory into tangible reality—reveal whether the musician still existed within me or only a survivor clinging to delusions.

A deep breath filled my lungs as my eyes darted to the journal open on the music desk. The bench creaked and the dried-out leather crackled a little, but the seat held firm as I settled my weight upon it. Preparation complete.

Time to play.

One last performance before the end. Perhaps the last performance by anyone, ever.

I banished the thought and flipped to the first notation page of

Sonata for the End of Days. The obviousness of the title screamed, but who would judge me? No audience would seek me out, no critics would venture forth to some luxury mountain retreat for a has-been pianist.

There was no one left to come looking for me.

Just me and the music. This sonata contained my entire essence, my beating heart, my exhausted soul. Let it culminate now. Not that Esteban's exit strategy tempted me, but life's unpredictability rendered everything temporary.

The first movement emerged hesitantly—a delicate exploration of humanity's losses. Notes spiraled skyward, questioning, pleading with an indifferent universe. My body swayed, muscle memory awakening with each measure. Juilliard's academic precision dissolved beneath the raw emotion pouring through my fingertips.

The music intensified as I thundered into the second movement —darker, heavier chords embodying my months of isolation. Dissonant harmonies crashed against each other, shattering the illusion of order. My fingers struck keys with increasing force, abandoning caution, embracing the luxury of acoustic expression after months of enforced quietude.

The third movement devoured me. A frantic scherzo channeling my desperate flight from the farmhouse, walkers ... everything familiar. The tempo surged beyond my original composition, my hands flying across the keys. Sweat pearled on my forehead, dampening silver-streaked wisps that had escaped from my tight bun.

The final movement erupted—a resolute return to structure amid chaos—and tears streamed down my cheeks. This section had remained unfinished in both journal and mind, constantly evolving, and now my soul surrendered, plunging into music's depths as it hadn't in years.

The melancholy acceptance of a forever-altered world solidified beneath my touch.

The final chord dissolved as my hands dropped into my lap, and my body stilled, eyes closed, as the echo dissipated.

Then came the sound—resounding cracks that shattered silence and ricocheted through the grand space.

Applause!

I whirled on the bench, adrenaline flooding my system as my knife flashed from its sheath, blade gleaming and ready. Still lost in the music, I yielded to the confusion that slammed into me.

Walkers don't clap.

A bearded mountain of a man occupied the café doorway, hands frozen in mid-clap. Behind him, three figures crept from shadow: a rail-thin young man, a teenage girl, and an older woman whose features echoed my mother's.

"Magnificent," the big one rasped, voice sandpapered by disuse. When even a loud cough could bring shuffling death, conversation was a luxury. He tried again. "Absolutely magnificent."

My blade dangled from numb fingers. Two years alone hadn't prepared me to encounter living, breathing humans. Michael's ghost superimposed itself over the bearded stranger, blurring my vision with unexpected tears.

Two years, and still he haunted me.

"Are you—" My vocal cords seized. The knife clattered to the floor as I stumbled upright. "Are you real?"

Later

"You recorded it?" I leaned toward Marcus, fixing on his weather-beaten face above the thick beard.

"Only some." He tapped the small digital recorder. "My last professional tool. Better than anything consumer-grade."

That tap on the recorder—reverent, almost a caress—mirrored how I touched the Steinway, and that devotion sang to me. For him, recording music was as vital as creating it was to me—both of us clinging to purpose in a world that no longer valued either.

"But how—"

"I wish we'd gotten here a little earlier. We came in through the loading dock, and you were already playing. We only caught the last few minutes, and the batteries died before you finished." He shook his head, still surprised. "Thought we were hearing things a few days ago, down at the cabins on the river, but you kept tuning that beauty, and we knew it was no accident. It was too … deliberate. We were almost out of food, so we packed what we had, and here we are."

Candles salvaged from restaurant kitchen drawers cast flickering shadows across the table. Clouds smothered moonlight, leaving the lobby in darkness beyond a small circle of flame.

"I haven't heard anything like that since … before," Riya whispered, knees clutched to her chest. Dangerously long hair—the kind that invites a walker's grasp—curtained startling blue eyes and fell to the worn, filthy MSU sweatshirt hanging over her skeletal frame. "Forgot what it felt like. I had to know where it was coming from."

"The walkers haven't forgotten," Jerome interjected, gesturing toward the windows where gaps in the boards revealed shadows pressed against glass, attracted by the sound. He was a veteran soldier, dour and taciturn like Michael's friends I'd met in New York, and, like those others, he never let go of his weapon. Unlike them, his gun wasn't metaphorical. "We counted thirty-seven on our way in. More arriving all the time." For the third time since we sat, he checked the gun's chamber, ensuring a round nestled ready.

My chest constricted. I laced my fingers together to hide their trembling. "So many … I never expected the sound to travel beyond these walls. I figured it was just the walkers in the main lodge I'd have to deal with. The resort seemed isolated enough! I still don't understand how you heard me so far away."

"As quiet as the world is now, sound carries," Marcus explained. "Something about the acoustics of the surrounding rock formations in these mountains. I'm sure I heard about a study they did—" He waved a hand, dismissing the idea. "Doesn't matter. My studio made a recording here, years ago when the place opened. Nothing like your playing, of course. But if we heard you ..."

"So did they," I finished, sighing.

Eliza's spidery, weathered hands enveloped mine. The former nurse's smile radiated maternal warmth. "Your music is worth protecting. We've been surviving, but your beautiful music reminds us why."

Jerome snorted. "Pretty thoughts don't secure perimeters."

"Neither does despair," Eliza countered, sharp, but not mean.

I pulled my hands away, overwhelmed by so much human contact after prolonged isolation. "The composition isn't complete. There are sections I'm still refining."

Marcus leaned forward, eyes bright with purpose, with a glance at the others. "On our way here, we were talking, and our plan if this place didn't work out was to head to that bunker in Idaho, see if they'd take us in, but now I've got a different idea."

My confusion must have been obvious, since Jerome spoke up, clarifying. "The AEGIS bunker in Idaho. One of ten, built before everything went sideways. My brother was Army Corps of Engineers —helped design the ventilation systems. Said they were self-sufficient for twenty years. Water recycling, hydroponic farms, the works."

"I thought they sealed the bunkers at the end," I said, frowning. "HealthWatch said—"

"You think they'd take us in?" Eliza interrupted, a deliberate redirection.

Jerome fingered the faded military patch on his jacket. "Doubtful, but if they're looking for people with skills—"

"A classical pianist isn't exactly survival-essential." A bitter laugh scraped my throat raw.

"But a sound engineer might be," Marcus countered. "Communications require audio expertise. Way I heard it, cultural preservation was part of the AEGIS mission. Data storage, archiving human knowledge. Your sonata might be more valuable than you think."

"I don't know ..."

"Even if they don't let us in, I'd bet on shelter or resources being nearby. There's a reason they chose that location. Safety, water—who knows? We can't stay here. Too big, too many windows, too many ways in."

He shook his head and smiled. "But that's for after. For now, I have something better. Five, maybe six days northeast of here, in Browning, my radio station has a soundproof studio with professional recording equipment and a piano. It's no Steinway, but if the generators still work—"

"That's a suicide run," Jerome interrupted. "Too many deaders between here and there."

"Maybe," Marcus conceded, and stared back at me. "What's wrong, Camilla?"

I'd ignored most of what they said, focused on just one word. "You said Browning? You're from Browning?" My voice cracked, and I couldn't breathe.

"Yeah, you know it?" He licked his lips.

I took a deep breath, leaning against the table and closing my eyes. "I'm sorry, it's just ... my sister, Maria, and her family are—were—from there. It took me over a month to make it here by myself. I'm not sure I can go back."

"It was rough there for a while. I have a guess what you went through. The storm, right?" When I nodded, he said, "Yeah, me too. Jeanine ..." He paused, swallowed, and continued. "My wife didn't make it either. She was a schoolteacher. A music teacher, matter of fact."

I sighed. "I'm so sorry about your wife, Marcus."

"Thanks. But that goes to show you: Music is vital. It's important. And this sonata—isn't it worth preserving?"

The others said nothing, lost in their own worlds.

"Tell you what," Marcus said, "forget the studio. We'll record it here, in this operatic space. I heard the reverb and tones you were getting, and there's no way it would sound as good at the station. Then you can come with us. We'll go to the bunker, or somewhere else. Find a place to blast your music to whomever we can reach." He thumped the table gently, just to make his point. "We'll show them life is worth living, even now."

I snorted. "I'm not sure I agree with you. Your recorder would preserve my sonata, but my playing it would draw more of them, lots more. I was playing soft before, just in case, and you still heard it down at the river. We might save the music but sacrifice everyone here."

Eliza stirred. "Yeah, but what makes survival worthwhile? If we're just breathing and hiding and killing walkers until our own deaths, what separates us from them?"

"But why? It's just ... I didn't write it for ..." I fumbled to a stop. "I just wrote it to stay sane."

"Exactly!" Marcus exclaimed, nodding. "That's exactly why it's so important! What if this is the last new classical composition ever created? Doesn't that mean something?"

Silence crashed over us, heavy as concrete. My fingers traced the notations in my journal—each one a lifeline through isolation's darkness.

"I can't tell anyone what to do here," Marcus said, sitting back in his chair. "I think it's vital, part of who we are as a species. Maybe it doesn't mean as much to you," he said, gesturing at Jerome. "I get that. But if you're willing, Camilla, I'll stay and record your sonata. For Jeanine."

My heart broke. He just had to say that. "I need to think," I said finally, retreating to the darkened lobby.

Dawn

The eastern sky blazed with reaching fingers of the day's first light. Below the rooftop railing where I stood, walkers swarmed at the building's perimeter, their restless movements creating a macabre dance visible even in the half-light.

Their ranks had doubled overnight.

The journal's worn leather was smooth and supple beneath my fingers as I clutched it tightly. The sonata continued evolving in my head while the forever-changed world stretched out before me. Even the lake's ripples looked musical, somehow.

Footsteps crunched across the rooftop gravel—Eliza's distinctive limping gait unmistakable. She settled beside me at the railing, our breath forming small clouds in the morning chill.

"You've decided," Eliza observed. Not a question.

I nodded. "I'm going to play one last time. The complete work, including the parts I've never performed." Our eyes met. "In this wonderful space, in the morning light."

"Lucky Marcus scrounged extra batteries for his recorder, then. And after?"

"After that, we leave. Together."

Eliza studied me, and I couldn't tell what she was thinking. "You know Marcus's plan is dangerous. That bunker is a long way off."

"Existence is dangerous now." I shrugged, watching a walker stumble over debris. "But you're right: A life without purpose isn't life, it's just prolonged dying."

"Your music matters that much to you?"

I faced her. "Not the music itself. What it represents. I've been alone, but art doesn't exist in a vacuum. It needs to be shared to create connection." I tapped the journal. "These notes mean nothing without someone to hear them. That's what I've been missing—not just the piano, but the audience. The connection. Without that, I've just been composing into the void."

I understood now what had driven me to compose through isolation. Each played note dies at its birth—like life itself, ephemeral and fragile. The sonata captured that transience, that beauty in impermanence. Even if we didn't survive, the music—the act of human creation—would continue beyond us.

Eliza's eyes glistened too. "So one last performance ..."

"One last communion," I corrected. "Then we face whatever comes next, together. We'll try for the bunker. Marcus's recorder will have to do."

Sonata for the End of Days

The walkers pressed against the windows and doors while sunlight poured through a surprising break in the ever-present cloud cover, bathing the entire lobby in warm, golden light. Inside, the others fortified the lobby's weak points. Marcus and Jerome had purged the walkers from those rooms I'd earlier left alone, just as a precaution.

I gazed one final time at the mostly darkened hotel lobby, committing to memory the place where I'd come back to myself and would never see again. It lay shrouded in dust and dry decay, the joy and laughter and pain of human existence encompassed in a microcosm. All abandoned as surely as music, in favor of survival.

Until now.

Michael would have mocked this—risking survival for a performance. But he'd never understood that music wasn't about recognition; it was about connection.

I sat at the piano, journal open, hands steady.

"How long will the full piece take?" Marcus asked as they clustered around the piano.

"About twenty minutes."

Jerome checked his weapon yet again. "I still don't like this, but we've been together this long. When y'all pulled me out of that mud pit, you saved my life. I owe you." He adjusted his pack with a quick shoulder roll, then turned to me. "What if they break through before you finish?"

Our eyes locked. "Then you'll have a very dramatic finale."

A flicker of respect flashed on his face as he nodded once and took a position near the kitchen door. Eliza and Riya waited nearby, keeping an eye out for breaches.

"When Camilla finishes, we leave through the kitchen." Marcus's hand settled on my shoulder, and for a wonder, I didn't flinch. "Ready?"

I knew this would be the performance of my life … I thought it might be the last too. I hoped I was wrong. "I am."

Marcus set his recorder on the piano. "Ready when you are." He pressed record, then strode toward the main windows, his giant fire axe ready to swing at the first sign of walkers breaking through.

My eyes closed as I faced the keys. The first notes rang with newfound confidence—no longer tentative exploration, but assured declaration. The sonata transformed from personal catharsis into communal experience.

The others' reactions—a caught breath, a stifled sob—fed back into my performance, creating a circuit of emotional exchange impossible during isolation. A quick peek, and I saw that even Jerome stood transfixed, perhaps understanding at last why Marcus had insisted on this objectively ridiculous risk. Music filled the space, overwhelming the insistent scratching and thumping from outside.

The third movement transitioned now, not into frantic flight, but into something unexpected. Notes of defiance and resolve intertwined with threads of hope, tenuous but persistent. Each note was born and died in the same breath yet lived on in memory and in Marcus's recorder—proof that humanity's creative spark persisted even as bodies failed.

Movement flickered in my peripheral vision—more walkers converging outside—while glass and wood creaked under intense pressure. The music commanded my full attention, though, flowing from the page through me. Even though I'd only just met the others, I trusted them to have my back if pressed. I didn't know why, exactly.

Who in their right mind would risk their lives for a piece of music?

But no one was in their right mind, not anymore.

The once-incomplete movement flowed through my fingers with renewed confidence. Not resignation, but fierce assertion. The deliberate choice to forge meaning in a world stripped of former significance. The final chord sang into temporary silence, holding the moment in suspension.

Then the glass door of the main lobby shattered with a crash, just as large cracks raced up the window wall on the opposite end of the lobby. Jerome appeared at my side, handing me my pack and rifle. "Time to go."

Journal in my pack, recorder in my zippered jacket pocket, secure and safe. I was ready.

Marcus joined us, his axe dripping bloody ruin onto the wooden floor.

Our eyes met, and I nodded thanks before we bolted through the restaurant for the kitchen. Past the chrome tables, massive refrigerators, and racks of pots and pans, Eliza and Riya held open the rear kitchen entrance, backpacks secured, urgency clear in their wide eyes and short, shallow breaths. The loading dock waited just on the other side for our escape.

At the kitchen doorway, I paused, risking a long glance back at the Steinway.

"Dr. Herrera," Jerome called, his tone commanding. "We need to go!"

"Coming," I whispered.

A crash from the lobby sent vibrations through the floor.

"They've breached the barricades," Riya whispered, clutching Eliza's arm.

Black-and-white keys burned in my memory, forever still, their silence deafening.

Jerome kicked the loading dock's exterior door open, slamming a scrounged pizza tray into the first few waiting walkers, knocking them out of our way. We pushed forward, Marcus and Eliza flanking me as I struggled with the mental fog that came after losing myself in such an intense performance.

Our group's ragged breathing and the crunch of boots on gravel were the soundtrack to our disappearance into the forest, the echoes of civilization's past outpacing the shambling dead.

A profound calm washed over me as my feet pounded the earth. The notes had lived their brief, beautiful lives in that space, died, and yet continued—preserved in Marcus's recorder, in the memories of those who'd heard the sonata. Like the Steinway, its performance a brief, bright note of perfection in a broken world.

Even at the world's end, humanity's creative spark refused extinction.

My hand found the recorder, its weight reassuring. We might not reach the bunker. I might never play another piano. But this proof of our humanity would outlast us.

That's enough. That's everything.

About the Author

Jason Kristopher is the award-winning author terrifying readers with zombies in The Dying of the Light series (including "Sonata in Z Minor"), thrilling them with the upcoming 1940s noir novel *Loco Moco* and the boy-meets-gryphon-meets-robot adventure *When Iron Wakes*. With the love of his life and the dog that rescued him by his side, he plots his next traumatizing stories from Florida beaches. Learn more at jasonkristopher.com.

RIVERS HAVE TEETH
CAITLIN BARBERA

Name?"

"Sonya Eidelman."

The policeman behind the desk paused on hearing her name, then wrote it down in his little book. "Where do you live?" he asked.

Sonya had never been asked that before when she'd come to see Jamie, to walk with him around the corner to the deli where he liked to get coffee. She swallowed, her throat dry. The radio on a side table buzzed softly, the volume too low for her to make out the words but still loud enough to rattle her thoughts around. "In the Lower East Side."

The man behind the desk twitched an eyebrow but didn't make any other comment. "Are you an American citizen?"

She wanted to be angry, but she was too afraid. "Yes, sir."

"How long have you been a citizen?"

"I was born here, sir." Anger surged for a moment, and she couldn't keep from saying, sweetly, "In New York. At Beth Israel Hospital, in 1900. I'm sure you could check, if you need to."

"Hmm." The man looked at her closely for a long moment.

She met his eyes, even as she wanted to look away.

"Who are you here to see?"

"Officer Russell. James Russell. Sir."

The man nodded and wrote something else. "Sit there," he said, pointing to the row of chairs against the wall, next to the awful radio. Then he stood up and walked back into the main part of the station.

Sonya sat on one of the chairs. She adjusted her skirt, smoothed her jacket, fiddled with the clasps of her purse. Waited. The radio buzzed. To settle the pounding in her heart and the churning in her stomach, she whispered to herself in Hebrew, softly enough that she was sure the man behind the desk wouldn't overhear. "The Lord will fight for you, you need only to be still."

Finally, the man returned, Jamie following him.

"Sonya!" Jamie said, smiling, but not meeting her eyes for more than a second without looking away. "What are you doing here?"

"I need to talk to you about Masha," Sonya said, rising from her chair. "They arrested her, but I haven't heard anything else about it. I went to the police station where they took the others, but they said they didn't have any record of her, which is impossible, because I *saw* them, I—"

Jamie seized her arm and pulled her into a corner, away from the front desk.

"What are you doing?" Sonya rubbed at the tender spot created by Jamie's grip.

"Keep your voice down if you're going to talk like that," he said suddenly angrier than she'd ever seen him. "When did this happen? When was she arrested? Why?"

Sonya wrapped her arms around herself. "Last night. We ... We were at a meeting—"

"You were at that *damn* protest meeting."

Sonya flinched away from his tone, the foul language.

He sighed and shook his head. "I'm sorry. I didn't mean to ... I told you, keep your head down. We've all been told to be ready to bust up those anti-war meetings." He gestured toward the door he'd come through. "It's just courting trouble, Sonya."

"Fine, then we were courting trouble," she snapped, suddenly desperate. "But they took her away in the wagon, and no one can tell me where she is now. I don't want to make trouble for you. I wouldn't be here if I knew what else to do."

Jamie sighed and ran his hand through his hair, light brown and streaked with strands of gold.

She'd always thought his hair was so pretty, had always liked to watch him gesturing with his hands as they walked together down the street.

He won't marry you, Miss Eidelman, Masha had said, putting emphasis on their shared last name, but Sonya had just wanted to enjoy his company.

He wouldn't meet her eyes now. He was quiet for a long moment, while Sonya wrung the strap of her purse in both hands. Finally, he said, "I'll look into it."

She breathed out, her shoulders slumping. "Thank you, Jamie. Thank you so much. I knew you'd help."

He gave her a weak smile and turned away without saying goodbye.

As she turned to leave, the radio shifted from talking to music. It was the same rattling drums and snapping, snarling brass she'd heard on every radio and record player for a month.

Over there, over there …

She pushed through the door and out onto the street.

… Send the word, send the word over there.

She had an afternoon shift at the factory, hunched over her sewing machine, attaching the sleeves to cheap shirts. She could do it with her eyes closed; she often found herself doing the work in her dreams. It wasn't enough to stop her from thinking about Masha.

The women around her chattered to each other over the clunks and whirs of the sewing machines, singing along to the commercial jingles on the radio, laughing with one another. A few tried to talk to Sonya, but she could only shake her head. She pushed away her newest complete shirt and flexed her hands, the joints of her fingers aching.

The song on the radio changed, and she found herself gritting her teeth. Of course, it was playing *that song* again. Several of the woman at the machines around her began to sing along. Sonya kept her eyes on her hands and clenched them into fists.

So prepare, say a prayer,
Send the word, send the word to beware ...
She shivered.

The night before, when she and Masha had stood with a milling crowd, waiting for the anti-war meeting to begin, someone had started singing in a mocking voice, "Over there, over there, send the word—"

"Be quiet," another man had snapped. "Don't sing that here!"

"I'll sing what I please!" the first man had shouted back.

Sonya had grasped Masha's sleeve and tried to pull her away from the argument.

Masha hadn't said anything. She had, apparently, said all she needed to say earlier that night when Papa had tried to stop them from leaving the apartment.

"There's no reason for this!" Papa had said, desperately. "This country *wants* this war, and you'll just end up—"

"War makes scapegoats," Masha had cut him off, eyes narrow. "And we all know who those scapegoats will be."

Papa had gone pale, stepping back with his hand against his chest, as though she had wounded him.

She had hesitated, then had strode out the door, and Sonya had followed her.

She had always followed Masha.

Sonya carefully unclenched her fists and bent to her sewing

machine again, trying not to hear the song as it drifted over the women's voices.

The walk in the dark from the Garment District back to her own neighborhood was unexpectedly frightening. She had walked these streets many times before, including at night. She knew each of the buildings that loomed out of the shadows, each of the streets, each of the alleys. She even knew many of the people she saw, bustling here and there. It was busy even after dark.

But she had never made this walk alone. She had always had Masha beside her, waiting for her outside the factory even if they hadn't worked the same shift. Always with a smile, ready to link arms with Sonya, peppering her with questions about her day.

Her sister had been her courage, and now her sister was missing.

Her favorite route home took her a little out of the way, the East River audible on her left for part of the walk. The sound of the water lapping and rippling was usually soothing. But last night, the sounds of the city had been drowned out by the sounds of the protest meeting being broken up by the police, screaming and thuds as batons hit flesh, and tonight, all she could think of was her sister disappearing into the back of the police wagon.

A soft sound ahead, something like a splash, snapped her out of her thoughts. There was no scream, but her head shot up, wondering if someone had fallen in the water.

There was a person standing by the edge of the river, a woman by the looks of it, although she was little more than a shadow against the moonlight. She had long hair that draped over her shoulder as she cocked her head. She lifted her hand as if to wave. The gesture seemed familiar.

"Masha?" Sonya whispered. Her heart leaped and she stumbled forward.

Between one blink and the next, the woman was gone.

Sonya broke into a run, skidding to a stop where she thought the woman had been standing.

There was no one there.

She pressed the heels of her hands into her eyes, frustrated. Just an overheated imagination. Just her own panic and fear. She turned to go, stopping as her eyes caught on something glinting by the riverbank: a clump of wet hair, long and dark. Like her own.

Like Masha's.

The apartment was quiet when she walked in, her shoes in her hand to avoid waking her parents. When she stepped into the sitting room, though, she found her mother, head bowed, sitting in the dark.

"Mama," Sonya whispered. "What are you doing up? It's late."

"I needed to make sure," Mama whispered back in Yiddish. "To make sure you ..." She trailed off, but Sonya could imagine the rest.

To make sure you came home.

"I'm fine, Mama." She turned toward the kitchen, thinking maybe she'd make herself and her mother some tea, something warm to help them sleep.

"You didn't walk back by the river, did you?" Mama asked suddenly, sharply.

"No, of course not," Sonya answered, the way she and Masha always answered. She'd never understood her mother's fear of rivers.

"You can't trust a river," Mama said softly, switching to Russian, her first language. "Full of rusalki."

"There are no rusalki in New York," Sonya said, smiling with difficulty. "You left them all behind in Russia."

Mama shook her head. "Wherever there are women, there are rusalki."

Sonya didn't answer, her mind on the hair she'd seen beside the river and the stories her mother had told her as a child about dead girls in rivers, jumped or thrown in. Dead girls who would take revenge, sink their teeth into the world that had driven them to the water. Sonya had been frightened by those stories as a girl, but Masha had loved them, her eyes bright and hungry as she listened. Sonya had asked her once why tales of rusalki were her favorite.

"I want them to be real," Masha had answered. "Girls never get to fight back."

"But they're dead," Sonya had pointed out. "They have to be dead to get their revenge." Masha had only shrugged.

Dead girls waiting in the water, teeth bared. There was nothing like that in New York.

The next morning, Sonya sat on the edge of her bed and looked at the room she'd shared with her sister. No Masha, sitting on the other bed and singing softly while she brushed her hair. All that remained were the *indications* of her, the things she'd left behind.

Sonya touched the bristles of Masha's hairbrush and the few soft, dark strands caught there. She imagined Masha opening the window curtains, glaring out at the sun and tossing her hair over her shoulder. *All right*, she might say, although not loud enough for their parents in the next room to hear, *all right, you bright bastard, we're up.* Sonya might snort a laugh, and Masha might wink at her. *Here's another day, Sonya, my dear*, she would say.

Without Masha, the sounds of the city seemed so far away. It was too quiet with her gone.

Sonya spent the morning hunched over her sewing machine again, her thoughts wandering to Masha, to Jamie, to hope and to fear. To her vision of the woman beside the water. To the wet hair.

When her workday was done, Sonya walked out of the factory and began the long walk to the precinct where Jamie worked.

He'll have something for me, she repeated in her mind as her feet hit the pavement. *He'll have something. He'll have something.*

Eventually, though, she was too exhausted to accompany the rhythm of her footsteps with anything other than *Masha. Masha. Masha.*

When she made it to the police station, she was near tears. She forced them back and held her head high as she opened the door.

"Miss *Eidelman*," the man behind the desk said, making her name sound like a curse.

"Hello," she said. "I was wondering if I could see—"

"Officer Russell," the man said and waved her toward the chairs with a sharp motion, as if he were slapping her.

She sat down, her purse in her lap, and waited. And waited. She watched out the window as the sun lowered, night pressing in.

Eventually, Jamie burst through the doors. Looking thunderous, he crossed the room to where she sat. He didn't sit or give her a chance to stand before addressing her in a low, clipped voice. "Sonya, you can't come around here so often. People will talk."

You can't trust a river, her mother's voice said in her head. *You can't trust.*

"This isn't ... My sister is *missing*," Sonya said in disbelief.

Jamie's jaw set. "She isn't missing. She was arrested. For breaking the law. We are at *war*."

There was a long silence, and when Sonya spoke again, her voice was smaller than she'd meant it to be. "You said you'd help."

"I said I'd look into it." Jamie's eyes darted, settling on hers only momentarily before twitching away again. "I can't make any promises. The protest was in a different precinct, and I'm ... I can't look like I'm muscling in on someone else's turf. I'll make enemies. This is my *career*."

He went on and on, but Sonya wasn't listening anymore. She was watching his eyes, the way they wouldn't look at her. She felt as though she was watching all of this from very far away. Or through water.

Realization washed over Sonya like a threatening wave. She stood, gesturing with her hand to cut him off.

"You know something!"

He stuttered to a stop. When he finally looked at her, his expression said he wished she were somewhere else.

"Look, procedure is—"

"Is she dead?"

Sonya stared at Jamie, and Jamie stared at the floor, his shiny policeman's shoes shifting against the tile. She was looking at a stranger.

He didn't answer her.

She turned her back on Jamie and walked out of the police station.

———

She was so lost in thought after leaving the station she didn't hear the footsteps behind her until it was too late. She had time to half turn, her heart in her throat, before there were hands on her, dragging her into an alcove at the entrance to a building and shoving her face into the brick. The rough surface scratched along her cheek; she felt her skin tear and the ooze of blood.

There were shouts all around her, terrible words in her ears, and fists in her stomach and ribs that drove her to the ground. *I'm going to die*, she thought from the same underwater place she'd been at in the police station.

"We know your kind." One of the men standing over Sonya shoved her with his foot.

She realized with a shock that forced her back into her body that his shoes were shiny. Policeman's shoes. When Sonya dared look up at him, he spit on her. Somehow that hurt worse than everything else.

"You're poison. We know where you were two nights ago."

"Eidelman," another man said. "That's German. You all pretend you're from Russia, but we know better, you hear me?" A boot hit her in the gut, and the breath rushed from her body, tears squeezing from her eyes.

"Don't go back to the station," came a third voice. "There's nothing for you there."

"Masha," she whispered, because she couldn't scream, couldn't even draw in a full breath.

Her face was wet with tears, snot, and blood. Blows fell until they all blurred together, and pain became her entire world.

Finally, the beating stopped.

One of the men leaned down so close to her his breath brushed her ear, making her stomach turn over. "You don't belong here," he said softly. "We can't have traitors during wartime. Go back to where you belong, or it's just going to get worse for you."

Then they were gone.

She was alive, and part of her wished she wasn't.

She had heard stories from others at the protest meetings, about mobs who would corner men and beat them, police who would stand by and do nothing or join in. Somehow, Sonya had never imagined that it would happen to her.

In the distance, a group of men started singing.

Over there, over there,
Send the word, send the word over there.

Sonja heard her mother's voice in her mind. *Wherever there are women, there are rusalki.* And suddenly she knew exactly where Masha was.

She wasn't sure how long she lay where she'd fallen, in too much pain to move. Her sister was gone; what difference would it make if she never came home? Her parents would lose another child, but they'd already lost their bravest, fiercest child. Sonya's better half.

She remembered a day three months ago when two drunk men had shouted at Sonya and Masha as they had walked home. Sonya had hung her head, avoiding their eyes, while Masha had given them a very unladylike gesture.

When will they stop being angry with us? Sonya had asked, like a child.

Sonya, my dear, they want you to fall and not get up. Never give them what they want.

"Masha," Sonya whispered, then she pushed to her hands and knees. Her face was a slick mess, and her ribs throbbed with every beat of her heart. She put her hands against the brick wall of the alcove, staggered to her feet, and stumbled toward the river.

The East River. Lapping, lapping, ever thirsty. Carrying away everything thrown into its waters.

Almost everything.

There was someone waiting for Sonya when she reached the river. She couldn't see her, but she *knew* she was there.

"You never made it to the police station," Sonya called over the water. "They killed you, and they threw you in the river."

The lapping of the water changed as something swam against the current. The top of a head emerged from the water until eyes appeared just above the surface of the river. Light glinted off dark, wet hair that clung to a pale forehead.

Another dead girl in a river.

"You need my help?"

There was a slight nod, just enough to disturb the water.

Sonya hesitated, but not for long. "Tomorrow night."

The woman's face rose a little higher above the water, just enough that Sonya could see the smile on her lips.

"Goodnight, Masha, my dear," Sonya whispered and turned for home.

Both of her parents were awake when she arrived at their apartment, sitting together in the kitchen holding hands across the table, their faces lined with worry. They sprang to their feet when she walked in. Mama covered her mouth with her hands, her eyes wide and wet. Papa's face went slack with shock.

"What happened to you?" Mama asked.

Sonya didn't answer. It was obvious, wasn't it?

Papa shook his head. "We saw times like this, in Russia. It's too dangerous, Sonya. You can't go out again, you'll have to stay home from work—"

"No." Her voice was soft, but it silenced both of them immediately. They stared at one another for several long moments, then Sonya said, "Tomorrow night, we can start to sit shiva for Masha."

Mama gave a cry and sank back into her chair, covering her eyes with one hand.

Papa bent as though he had been punched in the stomach, but he didn't look away from Sonya. "But the burial ..."

"There won't be one," Sonya answered. "But there's one more thing to do first."

In the silence that followed, she saw her parents' fear for her and their fear *of* her too. She held her head high as she went to her room —the one that was only hers, now.

The next day, she went to work and kept her answers short and vague when anyone asked what had happened to her. She sewed single-mindedly, her attention focused, her swollen eyes stinging and blurring but her hands remembering the work. There was nothing to think about, now. Her course was decided.

As soon as her shift was over, she walked out into the evening to the police station. Not Jamie's station, but the one where they had taken the arrested protestors that night. She pushed open the door and ran to the desk, startling the officer behind it. She let her face reflect the anguish she felt.

"Please, you have to send someone, I found my sister's body by the river!" With bruises and scratches all over her face, she must have looked like a madwoman. Good. She raised her voice so it could be heard in the rooms beyond. "Do you hear me? I found my sister's body! You recognize me, don't you? You know who I am?" She was shouting now.

"Miss Eidelman," the man behind the desk answered, and she was gratified to hear he, too, was speaking loudly, unsettled by her insistence. "Yes, I remember you, but you need to calm down—"

"I found her! By the East River. Just over there," she said, frantically gesturing. "You have to send someone now!"

The man behind the desk held his hands up, placatingly. She could hear muffled voices coming from other rooms, footsteps. She couldn't stay any longer.

"You'll need to wait for an officer to take a statement," the man began, but she was already rushing back to the doors.

"No, I have to get back to her. Send someone!" She was outside before anyone entered the reception area from the back rooms. If the discovery of Masha Eidelman's body would be a problem for anyone in that building, they'd have to come find her at the river.

She ran through the streets, ignoring the pain in her body, a grin on her face that made people step away from her.

And then the river was ahead of her, the evening's darkness falling across it. Lapping, lapping, ever thirsty. She tucked herself into a narrow alley between two buildings near the water's edge, the sound of the water filling her mind.

By the river was Masha.

At home, there was only a room with one side empty, forever. There was only part of a set. But here, for a while, the sisters would be together again: Sonya-and-Masha, Masha-and-Sonya.

She didn't have to wait long. She heard their voices before she saw the swing of their flashlight beams.

"Are we going to have to search the whole riverbank?" one man groused.

"If that's what it takes!" another man snapped. "What do you think is going to happen if the Jews in the Lower East Side see that body?"

"We've got to find that Eidelman woman," another man said, nervously.

For a second night in a row, Sonya heard angry men's voices in the darkness, but this time she wasn't afraid. She heard the sound of the water change, something approaching through the current, and she grinned. There was the wet slap of bare hands and feet as someone climbed from the water onto the bank of the river. A shout from one of the men.

And then there were screams—short, sharp things that cut off quickly. Wet, tearing sounds, crunching and breaking sounds, the pattering of sprays and drops of something hitting the ground.

Sonya waited until the noises stopped, then she stepped out from where she had hidden. There were six lumps on the ground, collapsed forms she didn't look at too closely. The moonlight reflected off pools surrounding each one.

The figure of a woman stood at the water's edge, limned by the moonlight. She raised a hand in a familiar wave, then vanished into the water.

Sonya made her way to the riverbank, to where the light glinted off something left behind: a lock of hair, long and dark like her own, wet with river water. She bent and picked it up.

"Goodbye, Masha, my dear," she whispered. "Until next time." She worked her fingers through the hair, untangling each strand until it was straight, then wrapped it around her wrist.

"With the staff that is in my hands, I will strike the water of the Nile," she whispered to herself, in the Hebrew she'd been taught at her sister's side in their synagogue. "And it will be changed into blood."

As she turned for home, she whistled the tune that had been on every radio and record player for a month as she recited the lyrics in her mind.

So prepare, say a prayer,
Send the word, send the word to beware …
She smiled out at the city then—a smile that showed her teeth.

About the Author

Caitlin Barbera is a lifelong lover of reading and writing science fiction and fantasy. Her first story was about a girl velociraptor going on an adventure and fighting androids. She is currently a student in the Genre Fiction concentration of the Graduate Program in Creative Writing at Western Colorado University. A native of Colorado, she lives in the Denver metro area with her spouse, child, and dog, and she spends much of her time coming up with more story ideas than she could possibly write in a lifetime. She has been published in anthologies from WordFire Press, Inkd Publishing, Raconteur Press, and Knight Writing Press.

She can be found at caitlinbarberawrites.wordpress.com.

SYMPHONY FOR SOLO STRINGS
AARON CANTON

Adira's music was so good that even the ghosts danced.

Rachel watched the paper charms dangling from the ceiling, each one swaying in time with the dybbuk spirit within it, as Adira drew a bright melody from her violin. The music grew more complex as she played, first adding trills and ornamentation to accentuate the melody, then introducing another voice to contrast with it, but the main theme remained clear through the tapestry of sound. Skilled spiccato bowing produced bouncing staccato notes that kept the sonata energetic and spritely despite its depth. And through it all, the ghosts in the charms twisted and wriggled about, buoyed by what might have been the first music they'd heard since their passings.

When Adira finally lowered her violin, her frizzy brown hair was matted down with sweat and her pale skin was flushed. Outside, people chattered and horses clopped down the streets of Prague's Jewish quarter, but the noises sounded muffled in Rachel's ears.

"Well?" Adira asked. "Which one?"

Most of the charms had stopped moving, but one continued to shift despite the stagnant air in the dingy office. Rachel watched that charm for another few seconds as she considered what to say. She was a couple inches taller than the girl with the violin, her black hair was tied in a sleek bun, and she wore a conservative, almost utilitarian top and skirt which sharply contrasted with Adira's brightly colored dress. Her right hand clutched a silver medallion shaped like the characters for *chai*, the Hebrew word for "life."

"None of them," she told Adira at last. "You don't need dangerous shortcuts like this; you're already great. Just keep practicing—"

"No, Rachel, you promised!" Adira put her violin down and clasped her hands together. "And besides, it's easy for you to say that when you already got into Prague Conservatory. But being 'great' isn't enough for that. I'll have to be perfect to pass the audition, and you know I can't do it without help."

Rachel opened her mouth but couldn't find an answer, and she ultimately turned away from her friend's desperate gaze. Then the office's inner door opened and an older woman entered. Miss Halperin's gray hair and thin glasses gave her an almost owlish expression; a few hexagram talismans, each made of a different precious metal, dangled from the sash wrapped around her waist.

The woman gave a slight smile. "I heard your music stop, dear. Have you decided?"

Adira turned to Rachel with a determined expression. "Well?"

After a long moment, Rachel sighed and pointed to the charm that had kept dancing after Adira had stopped playing. "That one felt the music best."

Halperin's grin widened. "An excellent choice," she told them as she reached up and took the talisman in her thin fingers. "The spirit of Deborah Adler, a true virtuoso of the violin. They say her music could charm the Vltava River itself into reversing course."

Rachel gripped her medallion tighter, focused, and saw the faint outline of a stringy-haired woman superimposed over the charm Halperin had grabbed. "I've never heard of her."

"You wouldn't have. She gave few performances. But that first show ..." Halperin pulled a yellowed scrap of newspaper from her desk and passed it to Rachel; it was a glowing review of Adler's debut concert. "Her single violin sounded like a full symphony. I assure you, she'll be an excellent tutor for your friend. And yourself, though I'm afraid she's limited to the violin and couldn't help with your ... arcane pursuits."

Rachel frowned. She hadn't brought her own violin, she'd only identified herself to Halperin as "Adira's friend," and her medallion was hidden in her palm. "You know me?"

"I met your mother before she passed."

Rachel's eyes widened; her mother, Judith, had been skilled in magic and had dealt with various curses, ghouls, and other mystical problems that had occasionally troubled Prague. She'd also taught Rachel all she'd known about spells and amulets, which was why Rachel was here: Now that illness had taken her mother, there was nobody in the city to keep an eye on dangerous dybbuks—and witches—besides Rachel herself.

"I learned about her family as well," Halperin continued. "Congratulations for getting into Prague Conservatory, by the way; you must be quite the prodigy. But even prodigies often need help transitioning from school recitals and family picnics to *real* performances."

Rachel scowled. "What's wrong with performing for family? Mine had a party just last week when my cousin got married, and they liked my music fine." Her faster pieces had been especially popular, and her relatives had loved dancing to them.

"Of course," Halperin soothed. "I'm just saying that even prodigies need help to reach their full potential."

Rachel grimaced. Then she grabbed a stick of charcoal and a scrap of paper from Halperin's desk, sketched a six-pointed star inside a circle and added a few symbols at each of the star's points to make a Seal of Solomon, and held the paper aloft while muttering an incantation. The charm containing Adler's spirit tore from Halperin's hand and launched itself across the room.

"I don't need help," Rachel said as the others stared. "With magic *or* music. I'm just here to keep you honest."

Adira gasped, but Halperin only chuckled. "I understand," she said. "We witches have such nasty reputations. But I assure both of you: I deal fairly with my clients. I wouldn't stay in business if I didn't."

She fetched the charm while Rachel watched the spirit within it. The ghostly figure stared at Adira with an expression that was half hopeful and half desperate, but when her eyes met Rachel's, the dybbuk flinched like she thought Rachel might attack her charm again.

Then Adira asked, "What are you offering?"

"I will let Miss Adler possess you so she may teach you all she knows." Adira's eyes widened at that and Rachel tensed. Then Halperin added, "Her tutelage will enable you to become the greatest musician you can possibly be. And once you're satisfied you are at the peak of your musical skills, you may return her. In exchange, you will provide an equal term of service after your death."

"So I'd tutor people like she's tutoring me?" Adira asked, and Halperin nodded. "Is Miss Adler happy doing this?"

"Certainly." Halperin beamed. "You see, she wishes she'd held more concerts when she was alive so that more people would have remembered her music after she died, like people did with Paganini and Mozart. In you, she'll have another chance. After all, if she starts you on a path that leads to concert tours, widespread acclaim, and children all over the world practicing the music she taught you, is that not a fine legacy too?"

Rachel looked at the ghostly figure again and saw excitement in Adler's face. Then she turned to Adira and sighed before nodding. "I think Adler's fine with it. But if *you* aren't sure—"

Adira waved Rachel off. "I *am* sure," she said, fire in her gaze. "I'll do it."

Halperin smiled. And inside the charm, Adler did too.

The music Rachel heard when she next climbed the steep stairs to Adira's room was even more gorgeous than before. Adira's shading was so well-balanced that the smallest details were audible, including trills so faint and fast that Rachel knew she'd be hard-pressed to replicate them in her own music. The notes also shifted around the beat instead of following it with metronomic precision. The difficult technique would sound sloppy if it failed, but it didn't, and the subtle variances made the music seem gloriously alive.

She opened the door to Adira's room and saw her standing in front of a music stand. When Rachel touched her chai medallion and focused, she could see Adler's ghostly form superimposed over Adira's body. The dybbuk's face was relaxed in a gentle smile. After a moment, though, she looked at Rachel and tensed.

"Rachel!" Adira's face lit up.

"Haven't seen you in a few days." Rachel sat down. "You've been practicing?"

Adira nodded. "Miss Adler's great at keeping me on task, and it's really helping me. I think I'm almost good enough for the audition. I might even be better than you!"

"Keep dreaming," Rachel joked, though her heart wasn't in it. "Was that all you? Or was …"

Rachel trailed off, and Adler frowned at the implication, but Adira just chuckled. "She wasn't using me like a puppet or anything like that. She's training me, not playing for me. And she's a great teacher. In fact, want to borrow her when I'm done? I'm sure you could learn a few tricks from her."

"No way." Rachel couldn't help remembering her mother's warnings about dybbuks. "Not a chance."

Adira grimaced. "Everyone needs help sometimes. It's not something to be ashamed of. Even you wouldn't be a prodigy if I hadn't bailed you out when we were little. Remember how you kept sleeping through your lessons, so I tutored you to help you catch up?"

Rachel blushed. It was true she hadn't been a good student in grade school. It hadn't seemed worth it to drive herself crazy trying to become a virtuoso; she'd just wanted to make people happy with her music, and her friends and family already liked her performances, so why exhaust herself with endless practicing? But Adira had convinced her that it'd be even more fun entertaining the huge audiences that only an elite musician could command, and eventually, Rachel took her music more seriously.

"I'm grateful," Rachel said at last. "And that's why I'm helping you even though my mother warned me not to mess with spirits. But I still don't think it's a good idea."

Adira thought for a moment before asking, "How about this? If I let Miss Adler possess you for a few minutes so she can show how useful she is, will you stop complaining?"

Rachel opened her mouth to refuse but caught herself. If she tried Adler out and proved the ghost wasn't that helpful, maybe Adira would listen when Rachel again advised her to practice normally. And her mother *had* taught her how to bind dybbuks. If she was careful, she should be fine.

"Ten minutes," Rachel said at last. "That's all. Chalk, please."

Adira grinned and handed Rachel the chalk she used to keep her violin's pegs from slipping. "Thank you! I swear, you won't regret this."

Rachel chalked a large Seal of Solomon on the floor and then stepped into its center. "If she tries to take my body anywhere without my permission, the seal will stop her. Got it, Adler?"

The dybbuk nodded.

As Rachel took Adira's violin and bow, a cold and clammy feeling settled into her. Adler's soft voice sounded in her mind moments later. "Play whatever you like."

Rachel shuddered. The warm excitement she usually felt when preparing for a concert was missing, and she was tempted to jump out of the seal and let it strip Adler from her body right away. Instead, she raised the violin and ran through one of the technical exercises she'd played during her audition for Prague Conservatory. Adler's presence was a silent weight in Rachel's mind as she sailed through rapid arpeggios, nailed several tricky chords which contorted her hand, and then slowed into a few delicately shaded bars which released the tension of the final notes.

"Not bad," the dybbuk said. And then Rachel's hand shifted her bow so as to start the piece again. Rachel tried to gasp, but her body was out of her control, and she couldn't stop Adler from moving it as she pleased. "But your arpeggios are slightly fast. You need to slow down the last few notes in each one, like this."

And Rachel's body repeated the performance.

Rachel could feel how the bow moved in her hand, how it responded to the pressure of the strings, even how her wrist flicked upward when Adler added some crisp staccato notes. This wasn't a teacher simply telling her what to do; it was as if Adler was transmitting the movements directly into her body. And when Adler finished and Rachel could move on her own, she found it was simpler than she'd have imagined to repeat what her hands and arms had done moments ago.

Adler took control again to fix another couple small details, and Rachel's next attempt at the piece was virtually perfect.

Adira flashed a huge grin as Rachel finally lowered her bow and violin. "See?" she asked. "Miss Adler is amazing!"

"Sure," Rachel admitted. "She is. But ..." She frowned. "Has she asked you to play any of her own pieces?"

"No, why?"

"Because Halperin told us Adler had wanted to leave a musical legacy but didn't. If she was a recent prodigy, we'd have heard of her, so she must have passed a long time ago. She's had plenty of time to think about music since she became a dybbuk; it's a little weird that she hasn't asked you to play whatever music she's thought up since she died."

The cold sensation returned as Adler spoke through her mouth. "I can't compose," the dybbuk said in a sorrowful tone. "I tried for years after Miss Halperin brought me into her charm, but even though I remember all the pieces I played when I was alive, I can't come up with anything new. Miss Halperin says only living creatures can create new things."

Adira winced. "I'm so sorry. I wish I could help."

"You are!" Adler insisted through Rachel's mouth. "Even if I couldn't build my legacy before I died, I can help you build yours. That matters." But her voice trailed off, like she wasn't sure if it mattered enough.

Adira took back the violin, and Rachel gasped as the dybbuk's presence left her. Moments later, Adira opened her mouth, but Rachel could see it was Adler who was speaking. "If you want my help after the audition, just ask Miss Halperin. You're a great musician, Rachel. I'd love to teach you."

Rachel almost snapped that she didn't need help, caught herself, and said instead, "I'm not making a deal with a witch."

"Very well." Adler inclined Adira's head. "In that case, we need to get back to practicing." Adira took over and asked, "Can you come back later?"

Rachel was silent for a moment longer before she silently withdrew.

"Thank you for agreeing to play even though you've already been accepted," Dean Ondrej told Rachel as they walked past the dressing rooms behind Prague Conservatory's biggest auditorium. He stepped around a few violinists who were tuning up or rushing through one last practice session, then added, "I wish we didn't have to make auditions open to the public, but it's in our school charter, and ... well, let's just say it goes better when the first performance impresses the crowd. It makes them more tolerant in case anyone underperforms later."

"I'm happy to help." Rachel gave kind smiles to some violinists who waved at her as well as a few who shot her envious looks. It was true she'd already qualified while they were still fighting for the last few spots, but that was no reason to be rude. "Do you know if Adira Neuhaus is here yet? I'd like to say hello before the audition." She'd dropped by Adira's home on the way over, but Adira's mother had said her daughter had already left.

Ondrej glanced at the roster he was holding and shook his head.

"All right," Rachel said as she tried not to worry about that. "I'll go get ready."

In what seemed like no time at all, the musicians were all seated in the auditorium's front row, and Rachel glanced at the open seat next to her where Adira should have been. At last, she saw the other girl hurry through the auditorium's door, but by then Dean Ondrej was walking onstage to welcome the audience, and Rachel had no time to greet her friend before she was called up to the stage too. She had to settle for flashing a reassuring smile in Adira's direction before raising her violin and looking out over the audience. Ondrej finished his speech, the crowd waited expectantly, and Rachel began.

Her piece was "The Harmonic Labyrinth" by Pietro Locatelli, an infamously difficult work, which Rachel had practiced for many weeks before she'd mastered it just in time for her own audition. It opened with a fierce melody that raced over Rachel's violin in a rising river of sound. Harmonic elements came next, including trills in multiple voices and massive chords that added more depth even as they twisted her hand. And as the complexity and richness of the music increased, the river of music became an ocean that surged toward the audience under the guidance of Rachel's bow.

The piece grew even more difficult as Rachel played. The melody twisted around itself, threatening to collapse into an incoherent mess, and the thick ornamentation risked crowding out the melodic line.

But Rachel had refused to let herself stop practicing until she knew she could give her audience the performance they deserved. Now she nailed each interval, keeping the notes separated and distinct, and she shaded and amplified precise sequences to help the listeners focus on the most important parts. The music flowed in an overwhelming wave, but despite its complexity, every element was clear.

Rachel slowed down as the last few measures of the piece approached. She took her time on those phrases and gently dammed the ocean of sound until the river became a thin stream with a single melodic line. The music fell away to almost nothing, though Rachel maintained the clarity and strength of the original theme. When she reached the very last notes, she held them until they decayed into silence, contrasting with the rapid music that had preceded them and also giving a sense of finality and closure to the piece. Only then did she lower her bow to a perfectly silent room—at which point the applause began.

A wave of pure joy swept over Rachel as she heard the claps and saw the delight in her listeners' faces, and for a moment, there were no dybbuks or witches, just the music she'd played and the impression it had left on all who had heard it. She was smiling brilliantly as she returned to her seat and glanced at Adira, who shot a tense look at her just as Ondrej called the other girl's name. Rachel settled back while Adira rushed to the stage and raised her own violin.

To begin the exact same piece: "The Harmonic Labyrinth" by Locatelli.

Rachel stared as Adira's bow sailed over her violin to produce a familiar theme, and then she gaped as she heard new harmonies and ornaments which weren't in the original piece. The timing, the phrasing, and the precision of each note were just as good as Rachel's if not better. Moreover, there was a remarkable casualness to Adira's performance; while it wasn't sloppy, the music felt freer and livelier than when Rachel had played, like this variant of "Labyrinth" was being improvised on the spot.

Rachel fumbled for her medallion, but when she touched it, she saw Adler wasn't controlling Adira. The dybbuk was standing back and listening with an almost sorrowful expression. That was odd, but Rachel couldn't focus on it. Adira was playing like a virtuoso on her own.

The river of music pouring from Adira's violin became a mighty sea, one with arpeggios so fast the notes blended like solid waves of gorgeous sound. Rachel felt like she might drown in the notes. That finally ended as the ocean receded into a single stream which was still deeper and richer than anything Rachel had played. And when Adira finished the last note, the room didn't remain silent for even a moment. People jumped to their feet and blasted a massive wave of applause at the grinning musician.

It didn't matter, Rachel tried to tell herself as she forced her hands together in what could charitably be called a clap. It didn't matter that Adira had surpassed her.

But she couldn't make herself believe it.

"You want to train with Miss Adler?" Adira chuckled. "But you told me she was just a shortcut, remember? You said a real musician wouldn't need spirits and could just practice on her own."

Rachel clutched her violin case so her hands wouldn't shake. The last few days had been agony, sleepless nights followed by endless hours struggling to play "Labyrinth" like Adira had and failing every time. She could no longer pretend she hadn't fallen behind.

"Just a few hours each night, when you're sleeping," Rachel forced herself to say. "Please."

Adira drummed her fingers on her desk for a few moments before flashing a smile. "You'll need to sign a contract. Halperin won't let me loan Miss Adler out unless she gets paid. Miss Adler, can you possess me for a minute and write one?"

The contract Adler wrote looked like the one Rachel had seen

Adira sign, with identical terms: training until Rachel was satisfied she was the best she could be, paired with an equal term of contractual service to Halperin as a dybbuk after death. Rachel knew her mother would be horrified at what she was about to do, but that didn't matter. She had to reclaim her chance at musical greatness before she ran out of time, like it had for Adler.

A thought struck Rachel. "I want to talk to Adler first."

Adira's body hesitated for a moment before nodding, and when Rachel touched her chai medallion, she saw Adler was still possessing the other girl.

"Halperin told us you were great," Rachel told the dybbuk, "but she only showed us one of your reviews, and she said you didn't play many concerts. Even if you didn't perform that often, surely you had more than one good performance. Yet it's like you quit music and gave up building your legacy after your debut. What happened?"

Adler paused again, then said, "Nothing bad. It's just that I still had more to learn, so my dybbuk made me stop playing concerts so I could focus on my daily exercises. You're a violinist; you understand."

"Sure, but *only* doing exercises and never actually playing for anyone?" Rachel asked. "That sounds awful. The whole point of being a musician is to make people happy with your music. If nobody hears you play, then why ..."

Rachel trailed off as she thought back to her first recitals. When she'd compared the little school auditoriums she'd played in against the great concert halls she'd dreamed of, the events had almost felt silly. But she'd seen the smiles on her parents' faces when she'd played, and on the faces of the other listeners, too, and that had made her notes sound all the sweeter. Because the great thing about being a violinist wasn't winning auditions or being the best: It was delighting people with music.

And if the deal on offer was to let a dybbuk train her so much that she never had time to perform, it wasn't worth it, no matter how good she got. In fact, it wasn't worth it to anyone, including

Halperin. After all, people would surely give back their spirits as soon as they realized the problem. So why—

A chill swept through Rachel as she understood. She thought of her mother, who had warned her about witches and dybbuks so many times, and then she spoke. "Adler," she managed, "could Adira return you right now if she wanted?"

Silence filled the room.

"She couldn't, could she?" Rachel continued. "Because the deal was to keep you until Adira's satisfied she's as good as she could be, and every musician knows they could always be better—so nobody can ever get rid of you. She's stuck with you, and you won't let her play for other people under her current contract, meaning she'll need to renegotiate if she wants to perform. I'm guessing Halperin will demand Adira serve her for, what, decades for each concert? Centuries?"

Neither Adira nor Adler responded right away. Adira's body quavered like she was terrified and upset, while Adler stared at the floor, ashamed. At last, the dybbuk sighed. "Correct," Adler murmured. "That's how Miss Halperin works. And in exchange for the few concerts she allowed me, I'm hers for ... for eternity, essentially."

Rachel gasped before addressing Adira. "Why didn't you tell me? I could have tried to exorcise her from you!"

"Exorcism wouldn't help me!" Adira snapped, all amity gone from her face and her voice. "I still need Miss Adler's tutoring so I can sound great when I perform. Music doesn't come as easily to the rest of us as it comes to you these days, Rachel. We can't all be prodigies!"

"But you can't perform if Adler's possessing you! Unless you're crazy enough to serve Halperin for centuries—"

Rachel froze as she realized what must have happened.

"Adira," she whispered, "did you make some kind of side deal with Halperin? Where you can play concerts without paying anything if you got her *my* soul instead?" Adira gulped but didn't answer, so Rachel continued. "Is that why Adler let you do the audition? So I'd be jealous and make a deal? Halperin said she'd been watching me; was this some plot to get me up on her ceiling with her other dybbuks?"

"Yes."

It wasn't Adira that had spoken but Adler. The ghost was still looking down in shame, but her soft words were clear as they flowed through Adira's mouth. "You know magic, so you'd make a powerful dybbuk, but Miss Halperin knew your mother had warned you about her. So she went through Adira. Since Adira already resented you for surpassing her, it was easy to convince her."

Adira started to shake her head, but Rachel saw the ghostly form of Adler stop her. Then the dybbuk added, "I'm sorry. I didn't want to hurt you, but I couldn't disobey Miss Halperin, not while there was any chance you might make a deal."

"It wasn't worth it, was it?" Rachel asked the dybbuk while Adira strained against Adler.

The ghost closed her eyes. "I'd give anything to take it back," she whispered. "I hate dangling in that shop, thinking of all the music I could have created if I hadn't let another dybbuk control me when I was alive. Notes just drop out of my head whenever I try to compose anything new. Even the adaptation of that Locatelli piece—Adira composed the new harmonies and ornaments, and I just taught her how to play them." She looked like she wanted to cry. "I can't create anything."

Silence stretched between the two girls as Rachel considered. Then she said, "If your one concert was that popular, someone will have made sheet music. I'll find it and play it." She managed a smile. "Your music *will* be heard."

Adler's mouth dropped for a moment before the ghost returned Rachel's smile. "Thank you," she said. "Rachel, *thank you*."

Rachel nodded, then took her violin case and moved toward the door.

Adler called, "Adira wants to talk to you. Some of her concerts that I've canceled were really important to her, but she doesn't want to pay for them with centuries on Miss Halperin's ceiling. She wants to apologize and beg you to help her."

A wave of exhaustion swept through Rachel. "I'll check my mother's notes, and when I find a way to save you both, I'll do it," she promised. "But until then … Adira got what she wanted. She'll be the best violinist in Prague, even if nobody'll hear her for a while. And I'm not signing myself over to Halperin just to pay her debt."

Rachel glanced at the anguished-looking Adira and shook her head. "Have fun practicing," she said, and left.

A few blocks later, Rachel petered to a halt on a random sidewalk.

Even with her mother's notes, she knew it would take months if not years to design a spell that could rescue Adler and Adira from a witch of Halperin's capabilities. And after it was all over, then what? How could she and Adira ever be friends again after what Adira had tried to do to her—and after Rachel, despite her studies in both magic and music, had so catastrophically failed to protect Adira?

"What now?" she whispered as she grasped for any last remnants of strength. "What do I do now?"

Her gaze fell on her violin case before moving to the people around her. There were several businessmen walking home from work, plus shoppers hurrying to get back from the market in time for dinner. They were simply a bunch of people going about their lives—

—who were ready for a living musician to play them something beautiful.

Rachel took her violin out and held it quietly for a few moments. She was still alive, so she could still create a song, a spell, or a legacy, anything which drew from the life she lived to brighten the lives of those around her. And she needed to create something right now, before she began her magical research or hunted for sheet music of Adler's only performance.

Her emotions washed over her, and she brought her bow to the strings and played, sending a clear, bittersweet melody through the streets of Prague.

About the Author

Aaron Canton specializes in fantasy and science fiction stories as well as written content for games and other interactive works. He's written and sold over 150 short stories to Eduland, an edulit company, and over sixteen stories to Tellest, an online fantasy universe. In addition to freelance projects, he also writes his own intellectual property, and his stories have been published in *Mothership Zeta*, *Futurstica*, and the *Fantastic Schools* anthology series.

After completing his graduate studies in electrical engineering and then spending a few years as an itinerant postdoc in Singapore, he settled in Salt Lake City, where he still resides.

A complete list of his publications is available on his website at aaroncanton.wordpress.com.

THE FINAL LESSON
KAT FARROW

Marjorie Croft shooed her well-fed tabby, Perry, off the top of her upright piano. A discordant chord sounded as he bounced off the keys. Tutting, she finished dusting.

A wedding gift from her dearly departed husband, the fifty-five-year-old piano stood along the far wall of her front room. It was a comfortable space, with upholstered armchairs, a plush, crimson love seat, and more plants than most sane people would stuff into such a small area. In it, she'd taught many students over the years, from four-year-olds to seventy-year-olds, who were taking lessons either to please a parent, or finally, for themselves.

Death, however, had definitely been a first.

Marjorie had nearly fainted, or rather died on the spot, the first time she'd opened the door and saw the ridiculously tall figure, draped in the blackest black she'd ever seen. But after she'd gotten ahold of herself, she'd informed Death she was expecting a student in half an hour and asked what it wanted. She'd been extremely surprised by the answer.

Her time had come, but Death had a request and was willing to make a deal.

Over the past few centuries, Death had lingered around churches and music halls, marveling at the beauty and structure of certain pieces of music.

When Death had come for Marjorie's husband, Fred, it had found her playing "Lacrimosa" from Mozart's Requiem in D Minor in her grief. It had been a favorite of Fred's, and she had played the short piece over and over as her tears fell.

Death had been touched. Whenever it was in the neighborhood, so to speak, it would stop by to see what she was playing and discovered she was a piano teacher.

At first, Marjorie wasn't sure about the arrangement Death offered—more time in exchange for lessons. She missed Fred dearly, but loved teaching her students. And, well, Death would certainly be a challenge. So, she invited Death in for a little trial.

For something that had been around for eons, Death was rather awkward dealing with someone in their home when not "on duty." It took her several minutes to convince Death to leave its scythe in the entryway. For a moment, she thought she'd have to physically wrench it away. She explained Death couldn't possibly play while holding it, and she didn't want her cats to accidentally hurt themselves trying to investigate it. Apparently, Death had a soft spot for cats and finally relented.

Marjorie sat on the cushioned stool next to the piano and tapped the piano bench. Once Death got situated, she asked if it had ever played before. It had tried a few organs at deserted churches but always seemed to get interrupted, and it liked the sound of a piano slightly better.

Marjorie gently patted the piano and told Death to give it a try. She wanted to know where they would be starting from if she agreed to the deal.

Hesitantly, Death placed fingers on the keys and pressed a few notes. Its fingers slipped a bit, and the tick of bone on ivory was distracting. But after a few chords and an attempt at a tune Marjorie only slightly recognized, she agreed they'd give it a go.

She asked how much Death would be able to practice and just how often would it be coming. She didn't want Death showing up when her other pupils were there, or they might never come back. They agreed on a date and time, and Marjorie sent Death on its way.

At Death's first lesson, she went over the homework Death would have: a few scales and a few short songs, including "Chopsticks" and "Twinkle, Twinkle, Little Star." Then she had practiced them with Death until it seemed to get the hang of the melodies. It had given her an odd tilt of its head when she'd suggested "Mary Had a Little Lamb" for some reason, but she said they needed to start somewhere, and she wanted Death to become more comfortable with the keyboard. She told it their agreement depended upon how well it did next time.

Three months later, Death returned.

Death was a quick learner. It had even added a few simple songs to those Marjorie had originally assigned. She was pleased and asked Death what its goal was. When it told her "Lacrimosa" from Mozart's Requiem in D Minor, she blushed a little, before working out a plan to build Death's skills.

Every three months, Death came for a lesson. Every lesson built new skills, and Marjorie was always impressed by Death's improvements. But the tapping of bone on ivory was a constant irritant she'd never had to deal with before with any other student. Sure, a few had overly long nails, but you couldn't exactly ask Death to trim its fingertips ... and it wouldn't have helped.

At the fifth lesson, she offered a pair of gloves. They didn't fit. Death had extremely long fingers ... or at least they seemed so, since they didn't have flesh and tendons in the way.

The sixth lesson, she offered an extra-large pair, which fit its fingers better but were so loose around the palm and wrists that they kept slipping forward toward the keys.

By the seventh lesson, Marjorie had gotten out her knitting needles. She hadn't knitted in over thirty years, and the gloves were definitely a prototype. They weren't awful, but the gauge wasn't tight enough to keep Death's fingertips from poking through the loops.

Next, she tried a thick, canvas gardening pair. It was almost right but didn't have the right stretch for the octaves. And admittedly, Death had quite the span.

Death took that pair with it when it left and said it would try to see if it could find something like them. At the next lesson, the gloves Death brought were, well, not something Marjorie wanted touching her treasured piano. There was an air about them that seemed— wrong. It made her worry for the next student to use the piano.

Death took the gloves back with some reluctance, and Marjorie apologized profusely. It's not like you want to get on the bad side of Death.

They tried all-leather gloves next. But something made from what was once flesh started to decay in short order when pressed against Death's bones. They'd practically disintegrated by the next lesson.

It was all very trying, especially because Death's playing had improved by leaps and bounds. It could do every Hammond scale in the book in no time flat. And, after the seventh lesson, shorter classical pieces had come fairly easily.

It had taken a while for Death to get the *feel* of the music right. Marjorie wasn't quite sure how to explain it. Death loved music. It could *hear* the feel of it, but when Marjorie convinced Death to let her record a session so they could listen to it together, she thought Death was actually going to cry. It took quite some consoling while Death sat, petting her cats. Marjorie had drunk three cups of tea before Death agreed it was still early days and it could learn to at least mimic the feeling with enough practice.

Lessons continued, along with new combinations of gloves. But nothing worked just right. Her cats, Annabelle and Perry, had grown to look forward to Death's visits. Standoffish at first, the cats had warmed up to the lanky guest in black robes after their "consoling" lesson, and now demanded a few pets before it sat down at the piano. Death didn't seem to mind.

It was the day of their sixteenth lesson, when Marjorie's front door creaked open, and she welcomed her last student of the day.

Death nodded in greeting and stepped over the threshold.

Marjorie smiled. "I've been expecting you." She offered to take its scythe, and stuck it into the umbrella stand, careful to keep the point away from her favorite scarf hanging on the nearby coat hook.

"How has your practice gone?"

Although the hood hid any possible expression, Marjorie had learned to read Death's body language the same as she had for any of her introverted students.

"You *have* been practicing, haven't you?"

The hood nodded rather quickly. It was not the response she had expected. Death definitely had the air of someone not ready for their lesson.

"Well then, shall we get started?"

The two moved into the piano room, Death conscientiously ducking its tall form below the beaded archway. Annabelle and Perry meowed in cheerful greeting.

Marjorie sat on the cushioned stool and tapped the piano bench. Death had paused to pet the cats and seemed reluctant to stop.

Marjorie tapped the bench again. "Come along. Show me what you've got this time."

Death gave Annabelle a final pat before it turned, shoulders drooping, and stepped over to the piano. As Death settled on the bench, Marjorie tugged the arm of its robe.

"I've got something for you before we start." She gave Death a wink and reached behind her to pull a cloth-wrapped package from a basket on the floor.

"I know we've tried quite a few things, but I think these should finally do the trick." She unwrapped the paisley cloth to reveal a pair of cherry-red knit gloves. Each of the extremely long fingers had leather pads attached, and the base of the skinny palm had a Velcro tightening strap.

"When we tried the cloth, or even the heavy knit ones, they just didn't cut it. These will still give you the stretch of the knit, but with the added leather pads, the clinking of your bones on the keys should be a thing of the past, and they should grip nicely."

Death took the gloves in its bony hands and clutched them tightly to its chest.

"I know you probably would have preferred them in black, but honestly, I would never have found black yarn as black as your robes. Would you like some help getting them on?"

Reluctantly, Death handed the gloves back to Marjorie and let her attach them. Death splayed its fingers, wriggled them, and formed a fist. They were a very good fit, and Death nodded with appreciation.

"Shall we get started?"

Death lightly placed leather-padded bone upon the yellowing ivory. It did a few scales to get used to the gloves, Marjorie nodding in approval, then began playing "Lacrimosa" from Mozart's Requiem in D Minor.

Marjorie closed her eyes, listening, a smile creeping upon her face. There was no tapping now, and she was glad she'd given her latest idea a chance.

The previous lesson, Death almost had it. "Lacrimosa" was memorized—Death was actually very good at memorizing—and the timing was nearly perfect.

Today ... well, today it simply was perfect.

The song came to an end, and Death dropped its hands to its lap.

Marjorie leaned over and softly patted Death's shoulder. "Again."

Death nodded and began again.

Marjorie closed her eyes and breathed the music in. It really was perfect. Better than her rendition, and she had played it hundreds and hundreds of times.

She smiled at the last chord, but an ache was forming in her chest.

"That's why you were reluctant to play, isn't it?"

Death nodded.

"Our agreement's concluded, yes?"

Death nodded again.

"All right. I understand." Marjorie gazed around her cozy room with a sad smile on her face. "I've appreciated the extra time you gave me. It gave me a chance to settle affairs. I've been able to visit with my children and grandchildren, and I've taught twenty-two students, other than you. And really, you've been my best and most rewarding student."

Death dropped its head and turned away.

"I do worry about the cats, though. My granddaughter said she would take care of them if anything happened, but I think she was just saying that so I wouldn't worry." She hesitated. "Do you know of a good home for them? They both really like you, and you seem quite fond of them, so I'm sure you would make a good choice."

Death turned to look at the two furry beasts. Annabelle was curled on a shelf and started purring the moment she saw Death look at her. Perry was busy bathing on the love seat, but looked up and slowly blinked at Death.

Death turned back to Marjorie, and its hood dipped in agreement.

"Good. I'm glad that's taken care of." She patted Death's arm again. "Is it all right if I sit in my armchair?"

Death nodded, and she went to her armchair near the window. As soon as she settled, Perry came over and hopped onto her lap.

She petted him absently, taking a final look at her piano room. "I don't really know how this works. Do I need to do anything?"

Death shook its head as it rose and moved beside her.

"You really do play beautifully," Marjorie said. "I've enjoyed helping you achieve your goal. I hope you play often and learn more songs."

Death nodded, and with infinite care, gently placed a cherry-red gloved hand on top of Marjorie's head.

Thank you.

About the Author

Kat Farrow is a genre-hopping author of varied speculative fiction and children's tales. A recovering librarian turned full-time storyweaver, her work has appeared in several anthologies and her award-winning debut novel, *Bobbin and the Magic Thief*, was released in 2023. She lives in northern Utah with her cats and an ever-growing to-be-written list. More at loreweaver.com.

PILI KOKO
LEHUA PARKER

The last time I see Papa Keola alive he's already dead. He's lying in our family room in a rented hospital bed. His broad shoulders that had carried me turtle-back beyond the breakers at Keikikai Beach stick out like bird bones from his chest. His big coconut-twisting hands and lūʻau feet are blue like they've been dipped in ink. Weirdest of all is his face, swollen like bread dough on a Sunday afternoon.

He doesn't look anything like the grandpa I know. *My* Papa Keola would sit in the backyard under the plumeria tree waiting for me to come home from school. Most afternoons he'd be there with his ʻukulele, strumming the chords to "Little Grass Shack" and "Pineapple Princess."

"Eh, Ahe," he'd call, winking and slapping the bench next to him. "Come sit with me, and I'll teach you. Everybody needs a kanikapila song in their back pocket, plus one more for hana hou." When I'd sit, he'd wrap his arm around me and position the ʻukulele between us, his fingers giant next to mine on the fretboard. "This is C," he'd say, positioning my hand. "And this is G7. Strum like this: down-down-up-up-down! Good!" We'd practice until my fingers were sore, then

I'd beg him to play. He'd smile and close his eyes, his ʻukulele pick dancing across the strings like rain on a hot sidewalk, his calloused fingers too fast to follow.

But last Christmas Papa Keola started to cough. Then he got thin and tired, with purple bruises under his eyes and ashy hollows in his cheeks.

"Shh," Mom scolded us. "Kulekule! Papa had a treatment today. Go outside so he can rest."

A month ago, Papa Keola moved into a room at Lauele Hospital. We brought him baked manapua with red char siu, steaming chow mein, and cans of frozen POG wrapped in layers of paper towels and tinfoil to keep them cold. He was too tired to play his ʻukulele, so he and I watched *Let's Go Fishing* or sumo wrestling as we snacked on stale kakimochi from the vending machine.

But one day last week, Mom told the nurses, "No. Pau already." She untethered Papa from the beeping machines and brought him home to a rented bed in the family room, not the one he shares with Tūtū Kari in their room. Mom tries to make Tūtū sleep in her own bed—she needs her rest, Mom says—but I know Tūtū sneaks out to lay by Papa in the moonlight.

Last night, Papa Keola motioned me up on his bed, wrapped me in his arms, and pulled my forehead to his, nose to nose. He whispered, his hā rising from his lips to my lungs. "Ahe, my moʻopuna. No worry, Ahe. Papa's gonna be fine. And even if you no can see me, I still going be there for you. Always. We're pili koko. Blood. Never forget."

Now as I stand in a corner of the living room surrounded by ʻohana, all eyes on the bed in the middle of the room, I don't think that's a promise Papa Keola can keep. It's the kind of thing grown-ups tell kids to protect them from the truth.

But I already know.

It's suffocating in the house. All the windows are open, but too many people press close. Aunty Doreen's perfume is working overtime, strong enough to gag a cat, but not enough to cover the faint smells of Papa's urine and sweat. Tears roll down Mom's cheeks, but she ignores them. Like everyone else, her attention is locked on Papa's breath as his hā travels to and from his lungs, rising like an ocean swell in his chest.

It sounds like he's drowning.

Tūtū sits in a chair next to Papa Keola, holding his hand and wiping his face with a damp dishcloth. Like a thunderclap from a clear blue sky, her sudden voice booms over the muffled weeping. "Outside," she announces, standing up. "Papa wants to be outside."

Uncle Albert and Uncle Joe exchange glances.

"Under the plumeria tree," Tūtū says. Everyone holds their breath, except for Papa who continues to wheeze like a kettle on the stove. "Now!" Tūtū shoos, her hands flapping like church fans in August.

Mom jumps up and throws the lānai doors open. Cousins grab the pūne'e couch and carry it out to the backyard, placing it next to the bench under the plumeria tree. My sisters Lisa and 'Ewa grab pillows and bedding and make a nest on the pūne'e. When they're done, Big Uncle removes the heavy blankets from Papa Keola, baring his legs and tattoos.

Uncle Albert steps forward. "Let me help," he says.

Big Uncle shakes his head. "He weighs nothing now. Go help Mom."

Uncle Albert turns and takes Tūtū by the arm and leads her outside to the bench.

When the way is clear, Big Uncle leans down and gingerly slides his arms behind Papa Keola's shoulders and under his knees. "One last time, Pops," he whispers. "You'll see the sun, feel the wind. You'll know the way home."

In and out, the breath pulled from the world into Papa Keola's body is held longer and longer, the loudest sound in the universe.

When Papa Keola is at last lying under the plumeria tree, a canopy of yellow and white blossoms swaying above, his body eases.

Tūtū says, "Everybody hold hands. E pule kakou."

As we bow our heads to pray, I whisper to Mom, "Shouldn't Papa be in the hospital?"

She shakes her head and wipes her eyes. "No, Ahe. There's nothing they can do. It's better this way."

Aunty Lena is singing "Aloha ʻOe" for the second time when the ocean in Papa Keola's chest rises no more.

At the funeral, there's a casket draped in lei and a church filled with people with sad eyes and casserole dishes. There's a hole in the ground and a dirt mound covered with artificial turf that will be rolled up and put away once the hole is filled. At home, after the pastor leaves, there's lots of laughter and *remember the time* and more smiles as stories ebb and flow, waves coming home to sand.

Somewhere around midnight, tired of the noise, of being told I look just like him, of not knowing where to sit or what to say, I walk into the backyard and stand under the plumeria tree. As I look at stars through the branches, I spak something moving high in the treetop. I shade my eyes and peer closer.

Eyes wide, I don't know what to do when I recognize Papa's swollen face sneering down at me, his gigantic head bobbling on a too-thin neck. His twisted and scrawny body is perched like a mynah bird on a branch, and when he stands, I can see he's wearing only a ragged malo. His tattoo lines of shark's teeth and kalo across his chest and arms are blurred beyond recognition. I draw breath to scream, but my throat closes like a big blue hand grips it tight.

"Ahe," says a voice like the rusted hinge on the back gate. "You're mine, Ahe. I'll never let you go."

"Go away, Papa!" I squeak, the sound flat-tire weak.

His broken glass laughter shreds my ears. "That's right. I'm Papa. You can't make me leave, Ahe. We're pili koko. Come join me in the tree."

"No!"

He leaps from branch to branch, tumbling through the tree until I feel his fetid breath on my cheek. "Ahe. My moʻopuna. We'll be together forever, just like I promised."

"No," I shout and shove with all my might. The next thing I know, I'm on the ground, the sunlight warm on my face, a ti leaf clutched in my hand.

After that, I see Papa constantly. His tiny body with its swollen head leers at me from the back of the school bus. He watches me eat my lunch in the cafeteria, licking his yellow rotted teeth with a swollen black tongue. He hovers over my bed when I try to sleep, cackling nonsense.

Worse is when he whispers in my ear.

The Chang girl thinks you're ugly, he says. *I can tell.*

Nobody wanted you on their team. They just picked you because they feel sorry for you.

Why bother? Even your teacher knows you're stupid.

You think that's good? Look at Lisa's. It's way better.

You know 'Ewa is the favorite, right?

You're a waste of space.

They'd be better off without you.

Everyone would be happier.

You'd be happier.

Come join me in the tree.

I stop eating. I stop sleeping. When I look in the bathroom mirror all I see are Papa's dying bruises under my eyes and in the hollows of my cheeks. *Go away, Papa*, I pray, but no one's listening.

Come join me in the tree.

Aunty Nora notices first. "Hey, sis," she says to Mom, "Ahe—"

Mom holds up a hand. "Ahe's fine. We all grieve differently, Nora. Ahe will figure it out."

Aunty raises an eyebrow at Mom. "How are you doing?"

"I'm dealing. I'm fine. I just wish Ahe—" Mom sighs.

"It's hard," says Aunty Nora delicately. "You want me to—"

"Leave it, Nora. Ahe's fine. We're all fine."

The next day Aunty Nora brings chocolate dobosh cupcakes and kūlolo, my very favorites and frowns when I don't eat. "Ahe," she says, "are you all right?"

"Yes, Aunty. I'm fine."

She tips her head to the side. "You can tell me, you know."

"You're such a tilly," Papa growls, hovering near the ceiling. "Look how you're making Aunty worry over nothing."

I swallow the lump in my throat like a ball of rice after a fish bone. "It's fine. Everything's fine," I say, giving her a hug.

Behind her Papa floats over to the table. He sticks his fingers up his nose, then drags them through the kūlolo. My stomach twists. Papa laughs. He climbs on the table and lifts his malo, dragging his saggy ʻōkole across the chocolate frosting.

Aunty Nora feels me tense and pulls me close. "What is it?"

"Nothing," I stammer.

"Loser," sings Papa, licking his fingers. "Everything would be better without you. Your mom wouldn't have to worry if you weren't around."

A blue hand tightens, strangling my heart.

Aunty rubs my shoulders. "You miss Papa Keola so much," she says with a sad, slow smile. "You two had such a special bond." She tips my chin until I look in her kind eyes. Like sunbeams, the light and aloha I remember from Papa Keola pierces the fog I feel around me.

I think of how Papa Keola stood firm in the shore break and taught me how to hold my breath and grab for sand when the big waves came. How he held me up to put the Christmas star on the tree, and how we had hot fudge Mondays, Tuesdays, and Fridays because ice cream was for every day, not just Sundays. How he'd sneak me buttered rum-flavored Life Savers at church when the pastor droned too long, and how he told me stories about Maui and the sun and great ocean sharks and fire that lived underground.

My eyes well.

Yes, I missed *my* Papa Keola with an ache worse than a sore tooth. It was endless and niggling and—

Bobble-head Papa bounces over Aunty's shoulder. "Boo!" he shouts.

I burst into tears.

Aunty holds me tight. "It's okay, Ahe. Let it out."

"Yeah, Ahe," whispers Papa, "Let it out, crybaby. Tell her. They'll put you in a house for crazy people. We'll have lots of fun then!"

I gasp and pull away, wiping my face on my shirt.

Aunty Nora reaches into her bag. "This is for you," she says and drops an ʻukulele pick into my hand. "Papa wanted you to have it."

The minute the koa wood pick touches my palm, I feel peace. I turn it over and over, the smooth shape soothing my soul, the sharp edge lancing the darkness. For the first time since I saw Papa in the plumeria tree, I can breathe.

Aunty Nora closes her hand over mine. "That's the pick Papa made when he was a kid—you know his uncle taught him ʻukulele and slack-key guitar? He wanted you to have one of his ʻukuleles too. I'll bring it bumbye."

I nod, unable to speak.

She squeezes my hand one last time before letting go. "Ahe, an ʻukulele pick is small and easy to carry. Keep it with you to remember the good times. There's no need to be sad. Pili koko. Our ancestors are never far away."

I slip the koa wood pick into my pocket and nod again.

Aunty shakes her finger at me, grinning, and turns me toward the table with a little shove. "Now eat!"

I look to see where Papa is lurking, but he's gone. At the table, there's no mark in the frosting; the kūlolo is untouched. I force myself to take one bite—oh, so ʻono—then devour the rest.

It's the best food ever.

The rest of the day, whenever I feel anxious, I touch the ʻukulele pick in my pocket and feel calm and peace.

I don't see Papa again until bedtime. He pops into the misty edges of the bathroom mirror as I brush my teeth.

"Miss me?" he smirks. "Loser. You ate all the kūlolo. What a pig. Big Uncle didn't even get any."

I drop my toothbrush and step back. Tears threaten, so I suck my lip tight.

"Oh, baby's gonna cry," he wails, mocking me with gnarled fists rubbing black-hole eyes. He tsks. "Such a sensitive waste of space. In the tree there are no feelings, Ahe."

He's right. I'm too sensitive. Maybe things would be better in the tree.

His face fills the mirror as a pilau grin fissures his face like a rotten mango. "Face it, Ahe. We're all worm food. It's the best thing about you."

Tears fall. "Why do you say things like that? I thought you loved me! I missed you so much! I wanted to see you, but now I don't—not anymore! Go away!"

He slithers through the mirror, an eel through the reef. "Who am I?" he giggles, his breath like hot tar in August.

I flinch.

"Who am I?!"

"Papa!" I groan.

"That's right," he sneers. "Papa. I told you we'd always be together. Blood. You can't get rid of me!"

I run to my room and scramble for the pants I'd left on the floor. Like smoke, he drifts after me. "What are you doing?" he says. I ignore him and keep digging in my pocket. "Stop that!"

Wrong one! I switch to the other pocket.

"I said stop!"

Got it!

I hold up the ʻukulele pick to his face, brandishing it like a cross. "Go away, Papa! You were never like this before. The Papa Keola I knew was kind—you're cruel!"

The ground trembles as a conch shell blows in the distance. I turn and run for the backyard and don't stop until I'm standing beneath the plumeria tree.

The grass is thin and dry, scratchy against my bare feet. Dead plumerias litter the ground, the sickly-sweet smell nauseating in the cool night air. I look back to the house as the earth shakes, shakes, shakes, but no one else comes out—Mom, Tūtū, and the rest must have gone out the front. Plumeria flowers fall about me like sugarcane ash. I wrap an arm around the tree and hold the ʻukulele pick tight. I close my eyes and think of my grandfather, my true grandfather.

I think of his joy when Big Uncle brought him ʻopihi plucked fresh from the rocks and the way his face scrunched when he laughed. I think of his footsteps down the hallway in the middle of the night as he peeked into our rooms, and how he'd listen patiently to ʻEwa's endless stories. I think of the sound of his voice like water over the reef, and how he'd close one eye when I sang off-key. "Eh," he'd tease, "you sure you Hawaiian?"

When I open my eyes, *my* Papa Keola is standing before me.

He's young and strong, tall and proud. A feather cloak stretches across the mountains of his shoulders and falls in waves against his tree trunk legs. In one hand he holds a long spear with a marlin bill lashed to the tip. His tattoo lines are sharp and clear, his malo crisp and ʻehu-tinged in the moonlight. He smiles, his eyes squinting with delight.

"Ahe," his voice like water on parched land, "who am I?"

"Papa," I breath. "You're my Papa Keola."

"No!" shrieks the creature with the too-big head and twisted body. "Ahe's mine! Ahe chose me! Pili koko!"

Papa Keola's eyes narrow. "Is this true, Ahe?"

"No!" I shout at the creature in the top of the tree. "You're not my Papa! I don't want you around!"

The ground heaves and rolls like breakers against the shore. I clutch the tree with both arms, but Papa Keola, *my* Papa Keola, throws his arms wide, tossing his cloak over his shoulders. Bringing his spear forward, he crouches in a warrior's attack. "You heard Ahe. Be gone, foul creature! Trouble Ahe no more!"

The creature rears its ugly head and hisses. "By what authority?"

Papa Keola looks at me and nods.

I swallow hard and find my voice. "Mine!" I shout. "Leave and never come back!"

The creature howls, his head splitting like a melon and running down his withered body, dividing and folding onto itself until there is nothing left but the faint stench of rotten eggs.

The earth stills.

I turn to Papa Keola.

He stands relaxed in the moonlight. "Maika'i, Ahe," he says. "Well done. Never forget, the living always trump the dead. The unliving cannot hurt you or remain in your presence unless you let them."

"I don't understand. I told it to go! Many times!"

"No," he says gently. "You told *me* to go. You prayed for *Papa Keola* to stay away. You didn't see clearly, but now you do."

"But you said you'd always be with me."

Papa Keola kneels and leans on his spear so he can look me in the eye. "I did say that. And I am. But that creature was not me."

"Why? Why did it come?"

"You fed it with your fear and sadness. For creatures like that, those feelings are the most delicious and delightful food on earth. Your feelings, Ahe, the things it made you ashamed of, are especially powerful. They are intoxicating. It would never have left you alone until you made it."

I hold out the 'ukulele pick. "This. It was afraid of this. This pick is powerful. Is that why you left it for me?"

Papa Keola laughs. "It's an old piece of wood, Ahe, nothing more. But it reminded you of who I really am, and that was enough to chase the darkness away. Use it, save it, lose it—the 'ukulele pick doesn't matter. What matters is that you remember how this feels."

I put my hand to my belly in wonder. "Bubbles and light," I say, "like a full belly with a calm heart. Aloha! Papa Keola, this feels like aloha."

"'Ae, Ahe, it does."

The conch shell sounds again in the distance. When I look to the mountains, I see torches lining the ridges. "You have to go," I say.

Papa Keola nods. "One last thing, Ahe. Your eyes are open now, but I don't want you dwelling on this. Ancestors are always with you, cheering you on and defending you when necessary, but it's your life to lead. Live it!" Papa Keola stands, gathers his cloak, and hefts his spear. "I'll see you soon, Ahe." He winks. "But not too soon."

"Wait! Can I give you a hug?"

He laughs. "Every time you strum an ʻukulele, you'll feel my arms wrap around you. Aloha e Ahe!"

The wind rises and blows the last plumerias from the tree as the torches on the mountains blink out and Papa Keola slips into the night.

"Aloha ʻoe, Papa Keola," I sigh.

"Ahe!" calls Mom as she runs through the lānai door. "Thank goodness! We couldn't find you! Why did you run to the backyard? Are you okay?"

"I'm fine," I say and laugh because this time I mean it.

Mom cocks her head at me. "Are you sure you didn't hit your head or something?"

"No."

She narrows her eyes and feels my forehead.

"Really, Mom, I'm fine."

She clucks her tongue. "If you say so."

In my hand, the ʻukulele pick presses against my palm. I rub it between my fingers. "Hey, Mom," I say, "you think we could stop by Aunty Nora's tomorrow? I want to play Papa Keola's ʻukulele."

About the Author

Lehua Parker writes speculative fiction for kids and adults often set in her native Hawaiʻi. Her published works include the award-winning Niuhi Shark Saga trilogy and *Sharks in an Inland Sea*. Her short stories have appeared in *Va: Stories by Women of the Moana*, *Bamboo Ridge*, and *Dialogue*, and her works performed by the Honolulu Theatre for Youth. An advocate of authentic indigenous voices in media and a Kamehameha Schools graduate, she is a frequent speaker at conferences, symposiums, and schools. When the right project wanders by, she's also a freelance editor and book coach. Connect with her at LehuaParker.com.

WRAPPED UP IN WORK
MIKE STRICKLAND

NOW

I'm surrounded by desolation. Muted light oozes from overhead. The walls that box me in have the color and texture of sharkskin. A persistent buzz drowns out murmuring voices. An acrid smell from the cup before me stings my nostrils. Everything is shades of gray.

The gloom weighs heavier on me every day. Hope—what little I remember of that distant emotion—died ages ago.

I rest my fingers on the ivory keys, imagining myself dispelling the gloom with the bright notes of a sonata. But I'm not sure I've ever heard the sound of music in this hellhole. And the only sound these keys can make is the clickety-clack of chopsticks on bones.

"Marvin, staff meeting in five!" Brenda's pearly whites reflect the fluorescents with such intensity that it hurts my eyes. I feel my migraine turn another screw tighter. But Brenda, like time, is inexorable, irresistible. And after all, I need a paycheck. My mom beat that message into me so deeply it's part of my DNA.

"Okay, I'll be right there," I mumble, taking a quick swig of the sludge in my cup before standing. I inventory myself before leaving my cubicle. Clear head? I take a deep breath, and then slowly let it out. Check. Enthusiasm? *Teamwork makes the dream work, Marvin!* Fake smile? I start stretching my cheeks before I remember that no one will see me smile under my wrappings. As ready as I can muster myself, I shamble past the tomb-like cubicles toward the conference room.

It wasn't always this way.

THEN

My first day at Anubis Technologies was one of those memories that popped with the gauzy vibrance of Kodachrome while all the days after it faded like cheap color copies.

Even before I walked into the office building, I took in the bright green palm fronds waving in front of the giant red logo that evoked tropical Christmas vibes. The sun warmed my clean-shaven cheeks, promising a sunburn if I dallied too long. The scent of plumeria blooms made me feel like I was about to enter a spa.

Inside, Brenda was already waiting for me, chatting with Lorna at reception. Big blue eyes and big red hair. Big personality too. She left no doubt that this was going to be the first day of the rest of my life.

"Marvin, welcome! We're so happy to have you, and I hope you'll be just as happy to be here." She led me to the interior office suite, where a warren of cubicles stretched the length of the building. The bright overheads matched my perky attitude.

My interviews had been conducted in a small meeting room off the lobby, so this was the first view of a place that I would come to know better than my music studio at home. And dread more than my dentist's office.

NOW

"The light-green line on the graph represents new adds, and the dark green is new upgrades. You can see how we moved the needle."

At least, that's what I think Ed is saying. Every other word is muffled by the wrappings over his mouth, which he hasn't bothered to push out of the way for our benefit. I'd have to lean closer to know for sure what he's saying, but that would mean I cared enough to listen.

I lean back in the chair, Naugahyde protesting, and idly pull at the gauze-like strips around my left arm. This is a fidget habit I should break, because it's gross to leave bits of myself around the office. Even now, I notice stray threads starting to fray from the fabric. My anal-retentive nature longs for the scissors back at my desk to set things right.

"Marvin, do you have those churn numbers?" Brenda's lyrical voice pulls my attention back to the meeting.

"Churn numbers?" I ask, no trace of the embarrassment I would have felt on that rosy first day by being called out. I have no idea what numbers she's asking for.

Ed chimes in. "You said you were going to get me last month's twenty-five to fifty-four cancels before the meeting. But I didn't hear back from you."

Thanks, Ed. I'll just find a cozy spot to curl up here under this bus.

"Oh, right. Got 'em right here." I open my laptop and make small talk while I tap on my keyboard, pretending to look up the data. "Thirty-four thousand and change," I say, pulling the number out of my ... imagination.

"Thanks, Marvin." Brenda's dimples wink at me as sweetly as they did that first day. She eats this stuff up. There's no trace of linen wrappings anywhere on *her* body.

THEN

I slipped a pod into the slot and pressed a button. A loamy bouquet filled my nostrils as the cup began to fill. The espresso was brewed instantly, but I didn't dare call it instant coffee. This machine was top of the line, one of the perks Brenda had mentioned during my job interview. And damn, it was good. I'd never been to Italy—unless Little Italy counts—and I'd never had the country's signature drink until now. I didn't think my first day at Anubis could have gotten better, until the caffeine hit my bloodstream. I felt like I could do anything!

Then Ed shuffled up to the coffee machine and reached for the stack of pods. His arm—both arms, I noticed—was covered by strips of what looked like gauze or linen bandages. I stepped back to make room for him.

"Good morning. I'm Marvin. First day."

He gave me a bleary once-over. The ragged ends of more linen poked out of his collar. "Morning. Name's Ed. Analytics."

"What happened to your arms?" The words were out of my mouth before it occurred to me that maybe he didn't want to talk about his private medical issues.

"What do you mean?" He extended both arms and rotated them.

"The bandages."

"What bandages? You okay, kid?" He shook his balding head and grabbed his coffee, lurching away without waiting for an answer. Which was fine, because I didn't have one anyway. If wrapping himself in linen was just part of his everyday outfit, who was I to question his fashion sense? It's not like I had any experience with corporate workplaces, other than what I'd seen in sitcoms and movies. And if those were any indication, then Ed and his quirky wrappings were run of the mill.

NOW

I pick at the guitar strings, trying to coax out the tune I hold in my mind. But the muse is stubborn these days. And my music is flatter, more so every day since I started working at Anubis. The quality of what I write isn't worse—or better. Just ... lacking.

The stupid linen wrappings don't help. They keep falling over my fingers, causing me to hit sour notes, but every time I rip them off, they reappear minutes later. There's a small but growing pile of them in the corner. I blame them for interrupting my creative flow, but deep down, I know it's lack of inspiration that's holding me back.

My mom's voice speaks to me again in the back of my mind. My anti-muse, as I like to call her. *You need a stable job, steady income. Your music is good, honey, but you just need to do that on the side.*

She's right—or, at least I think she's right, because I've never known differently—I don't want to end up living in my car. The idea of devoting myself full-time to my music thrills me, but it also scares the hell out of me. How would I pay my rent?

I look at the half-filled sheet of music on the easel in front of me, seeing it for what it is: a page of pointless scribbles. I reach out both hands and crush it into a ball. Then I bang my fists on the side of the guitar. Again. And again. And again.

Finally, I rest my face in my hand. It's Sunday night, and all I have to show for the weekend of artistic effort is eight measures of derivative drivel. As my thoughts turn to the week of corporate life to come, I hear a rustling as the wrappings around my wrists wind themselves even tighter.

THEN

Animations danced to tinny sound effects as my computer booted up for the first time. I was a kid playing with a new toy on Christmas morning. Sure, I'd used computers before, but this somehow felt more real—my first day at my first job, and this computer was *mine*. I basked under the fluorescent lights shining on me. Hard lumps in the office chair dug into my backside, but they felt like the thumbs of a massage therapist. The espresso still coursed through my veins. An on-screen message prompted me to type in my name and pick an avatar. I thrilled at the mundane task, feeling pride of ownership over my newfound responsibilities.

I'd just closed the last setup screen when Brenda appeared at my cubicle. "How's it going? Getting all logged on and settled?"

"Yes, I think I'm ready to go. When do you want me to start working on my first social media post?"

She gave me a look I wasn't sure how to interpret. "Yeah, about that. Unfortunately, we just had to let Hailey go, and she was working on some deliverables that are mission-critical. Let's put a pin in the social media stuff and get you going on Hailey's report. If you can help us close the loop on that, it would be a huge help."

I was ready for anything. It felt good to be needed on my first day. Being needed meant job security. I jumped into Hailey's spreadsheet like it was a best-selling novel.

NOW

I move Hailey's old spreadsheet to the trash, mentally doing the same with the memory it conjured. I can't believe the file was still on my computer desktop after all these years. With so many icons cluttering the screen, I guess I shouldn't be surprised.

The funereal bell tone announcing a new email calls attention to my inbox.

ALL-HANDS MEETING—RESTRUCTURING PLAN.

Oh joy, another reorg. What will it be this time? Merging the Procurement team with Accounting? Acquisition of some no-name company? New org structure because some newly minted vice president wants to put their personal stamp on things?

I open the email and start reading. My heart sinks deeper into my stomach with every buzzword. *Optimization. Rightsizing for the future.*

Outsourcing. Realignment to market conditions. Reduction in force. This isn't just another reorg. This one is probably going to hit me directly. Or, if not me, many others. So much for job security.

Another layer of linen unfurls across my forehead. I push it out of my eyes, trying to parse meaning out of what I'm reading. But the email announcement uses a lot of words to say very little. I hope the all-hands meeting will shed some light, but I remind myself that the word "hope" doesn't get much use here.

I walk over to Ed's cubicle. He loves his job, so maybe some of his optimism will rub off on me. "Did you see the email?"

"Turnaround strategy." He's got the email pulled up on his screen, reading. As I watch, more layers of wrappings curl around his arms. *"Enabling our future ..."* Jargon dribbles out of his mouth like drool.

"So? Should we be worried?"

He finally looks at me, naked fear in his eyes. This is an Ed I've never seen. "I just bought a new car." Barely a whisper. Then he looks down, turning his arms over, as if seeing the wrappings for the first time. "What the hell is this?" His voice is considerably louder.

"What is what?"

"This!" he shouts, ripping off the wrappings. A growing snowdrift of linen collects around his feet while more wrappings snake around his arms. "Who did this? It's not funny!"

"But Ed—" I'm about to remind him that he's been wearing those bandages for as long as I've been working here, but then I remember he's never acknowledged them. Until now.

THEN

I strode toward my cubicle, tiny espresso cup in hand. Brenda was right about that machine. It became my morning ritual from day one. As I sat and waited for my computer to boot up, I took a sip. It tasted like Monday—which for me meant excitement and anticipation. Was I fresh and unspoiled? Or dumb and naive? Like everything in life, it was a matter of perspective. And also like life, perspective was always changing.

That was certainly true of that first day of my second week on the job. The cup of espresso barely lasted long enough for me to open my email and see what the day had in store. I grabbed the cup and headed back to the break room for a refill, deciding to take the long way around to see more of the office.

Brenda had given me the nickel tour, but everything about that first day was a blur. Now, as I walked past the rows of cubicles, I noticed for the first time how identical they all looked. It wouldn't be hard to get lost in this maze. The only visible differences were the nameplates on each workstation. I stole glances inside the cubicles as I passed, and the sameness continued. There were small personal touches—a framed family photo here, a child's crayon sketch there—but otherwise it was the same standard-issue office setup.

Until I turned a corner and saw the mummy sitting in the next cube over. I stopped, mouth agape. The person hunched in their chair, staring at a spreadsheet on their computer monitor. Mounds of file folders towered unsteadily on both sides of the desk. A faded certificate was tacked to the corkboard wall: Employee of the Month. Dated ten years ago. Halloween was still two months away, but they were swaddled head to toe in strips of linen, as if they'd walked straight out of the Valley of the Kings.

The person finally swiveled in their chair, noticing my presence. I closed my mouth, but it was impossible to hide the fact that I was staring. I mean, of course I was staring—*the person was dressed like a mummy*.

"Can I help you?" The voice, muffled by the wrappings, could have been a man's or woman's.

"I, um ..."

The person—mummy—saw the cup in my hand. "Looking for the break room? It's back that way." They pointed down the hallway.

I mumbled a thank-you and scurried back the way I'd come. And then I noticed for the first time that half of the cubicles I'd passed also had mummies typing away at their workstations.

NOW

I close the browser window that displays the website for next week's open mic event. My latest song isn't ready for the public. Or maybe I'm not. I haven't finished a new composition in ages—at least, something I consider *finished* enough to play for anyone. Yes, that "Best New Artist" award still hangs on my wall at home, but get serious, Marvin. That was ninth grade. I've got a real job now.

Speaking of which, it's time for me to do some work instead of surfing the internet. I click over to my email inbox and a warning message immediately appears. *Unable to retrieve email. Please check your connection and try again.* I close and reopen the application. Same result. I notice the VPN is also disconnected, presenting a similar message. I restart the computer and walk over to Ed's cubicle while it boots up.

His face and entire upper torso are now completely covered in linen wrappings. I'm not sure how he can even see his monitor. "Hey, Ed, are you able to connect to email or anything?"

Pulling linen away from his eyes to look at me, he mutters something that sounds like "yes."

I give up on further conversation and return to my desk. My email app is back up, showing the same error message. Time for my favorite activity—a call to the IT help desk.

I'm ready for the IT tech's first question. "Have you tried turning it off—"

"—and on again? Yes."

"Okay, just a moment while I check your account permissions." A moment later, she adds, "Oh." A pause.

"What is it?" I ask.

"You're going to need to talk to your supervisor."

"What do you mean?"

"I'm sorry, that's all I can tell you. Have a nice day."

I put down the phone and stare at my monitor. A sudden flush of dread runs through me. And then, as if on cue, Brenda appears at my cubicle.

"Marvin, can you join me in the conference room, please?" She's not smiling. I'm not sure I've ever seen Brenda without a smile.

As I follow her down the hall, I notice something poking out of her blouse. A strip of familiar, yellowed linen. Something I've never seen on Brenda. That, and the HR representative waiting for us in the conference room, tells me all I need to know about what's coming next.

THEN

Six months in and I still wasn't used to the sight of mummies hobbling around the office. But only a few of them returned my stares with scowls that said *what are you staring at?* like they knew what they looked like and were embarrassed. The rest seemed oblivious to their conditions. I made the mistake once of asking someone about their mummy wrappings. Like Ed on my first day, they looked at me like I was crazy.

Apparently I'd done such a good job taking over Hailey's report that I now spent most days mired in spreadsheets. So much for the social media engagement I thought I'd been hired to do. Brenda kept saying we'd "circle back" to that, but it must have been a really big circle.

I had to admit, the pay and benefits were good. My mom kept bragging about me on the socials, more than she ever did about my music. As if a steady job were the pinnacle of ambition. But something kept nagging at me, even as those direct deposits kept dropping into my bank account. Was this all there was?

Strangely enough, I saw the first sign in the studio, not in the office. I'd just recorded my latest song and played it back. There was nothing wrong with it—the number was as finished as anything else I'd composed—but it lacked substance. Soul. Meaning. It was something that would play in an elevator, not a jazz bar.

When I picked up the guitar to play the song through again, I saw it: a thin strand of linen wrapped around my wrist.

NOW

I'm out on the street—literally and figuratively. Standing at the curb, gazing back at the facade of the Anubis Technologies building, I let it sink in. I'm unemployed. Laid off, downsized, made redundant —the letter they gave me called it a "future-focused adjustment." I wonder how my mom will phrase it in her inevitable social media post.

When I was in that room, Brenda handing down my sentence as new linen wrappings spread across her body like weeds, I felt the expected things: shame, fear, uncertainty. But then a melody for a new song erupted in my head like a supernova, shattering the darkness. The muse, so long silenced, suddenly drowned out everything else with her voice. I even managed a smile for Brenda on my way out.

Ed emerges from the building, carrying a cardboard box. He got the ax too, I guess—or maybe I should say he was freed. He's leaving a trail of linen pieces behind him.

I feel a sudden warmth, as if the sun has just emerged from behind a cloud. But the sun shines on me from a cloudless, blue sky. I look at my arms—the linen wrappings that had mummified me for so long are gone. No shred of them is left anywhere on my body.

I stretch and start walking, whistling the new tune as I turn my back on the office building. It's time to get to work.

About the Author

Mike Strickland is an award-winning speculative fiction author whose work has appeared or is forthcoming in the best-selling anthology *Writers of the Future* (Vol. 42), *Cast of Wonders, Amazing Stories, Cosmic Daffodil*, and elsewhere. He lives in Colorado and writes about the writing craft at www.strick.land.

Until recently, Mike had more corporate layoffs to his name than published short stories. This story is dedicated to all creatives whose muses have withered under fluorescent lights.

THE DUST WON'T SETTLE
'TIL THE BONES DO
VICTORIA RIVERA

Amity Pike did not have time to deal with dinosaur mischief today. Her megaraptor bucked and reared against his reins as she tried to mount the saddle on his back. The sun was low and lighting up the reddish sands at an angle that made them look like molten copper, reminding her that the hour was late.

"Fangor, if you don't behave, I swear to the gods—" She planted one foot, making a show of her dinoleather riding boots as if to say, *Keep this up and your hide is next.*

The megaraptor snorted once but settled down.

"That's it …" Amity patted his scaly rump. She got her foot back into the stirrup, swung her leg over, and nudged the raptor with her heels.

With her hair whipping around her shoulders, she rode across the wildlands between sandstone buttes until she spotted Sauraptor Flats on the horizon, with corrals along the outskirts leading up to rows of wooden buildings.

Amity arrived at the meetinghouse during the first hymn of the sunset sermon. The music came through the window glass as she hitched Fangor, words muddled with the pump organ's chords.

> *O gods whose bounty we possess,*
> *Let us bear your holy brand.*
> *Mark us with the iron no less,*
> *That we may be deserving of this land.*
> *Ye have refined us on our path,*
> *And made us toil to bitter ends.*
> *We know it not to be of wrath,*
> *For only in the fire can we be cleansed.*

Amity's father, the pastor, wouldn't be pleased when he saw her come in late wearing riding trousers and a dusty blouse, but at least she was here. That would cut the severity of the inevitable reprimand by half.

For now, Pastor Pike cast a scornful glare at Amity as she slipped into a pew at the back.

"I would like to discuss the advent of this 'sky rock,'" he told the congregation, "which Magnus Kane and other great dinocattle barons have imported to many settlements from the southern continent. Some say it is divine, that our Three Lords have thrown the rocks from the heavens. Others would call it 'science,' and say it is the debris from celestial bodies outside our world. I say unto you that this strange material that affects the reptiles is a similitude of the faith we have brought from the lands of our heritage. As the rock has the power to help tame reptilian beasts, the faith in our Lords is how we put right the wild natures of the uncivilized peoples."

Amity clenched her jaw. The way her father put Magnus Kane on a pedestal was bad enough—that man as good as owned Sauraptor Flats and never let anyone forget it—but mention of the "uncivilized" made her fingers twitch against the revolver in her holster.

If her father only knew who she'd been with earlier.

"Our own people are in peril as well," he went on. "The vices we face are a plague upon humankind."

He was, of course, referring to the gambling hall on the dusty strip and to the Crimson Crest, a parlor for a more carnal sort of entertainment.

Fixating on the wood grain of the pew in front of her, Amity could only think how she'd rarely heard of a plague that humankind hadn't made worse. After all, it was *people* who were hunting dromaeosaurs to near extinction, which had caused an overpopulation of the horned toads that the dromaeosaurs preyed upon. It was *people* who were depleting local water resources with irrigation to force alfalfa growth in this barren place. And it was *people* who were polluting so much of what little water was left in an effort to extract gold from Pamparaptor Peak. Whenever nature decided to take its revenge, Amity would hardly blame it for doing so.

As for vices, well, that was a matter of opinion, wasn't it? The pastor talked of "wicked behavior," but pride was wickedness too. And it sure took a lot of pride for one people to try to force their language and their customs on another people, all for the sake of "civilization"—which was also a matter of opinion.

A screeching roar wrenched her from her thoughts.

She jerked her gaze to the window, where a blue baryonyx widened its jaws behind the glass.

The spinosaurian features were evident—the elongated snout, the extensive arms and claws—although it was probably one-third of a spinosaur's weight and had no spines down its back at all.

The baryonyx rammed its head forward and shattered the glass. The congregation shrieked, scrambling into corners and ducking behind pews.

An arrow sank into the back of the dinosaur's skull.

Amity's heart skipped a beat.

Four black microraptor feathers comprised the arrow's fletching —shield cut, attached close to the nock. A signature of the Scaleskin tribe. The rough Anglon translation of the tribe's name alluded to its people's strength but didn't capture the scope of their precision.

She darted to the window where the baryonyx still thrashed, its irises bloodred. The arrow jutted up like a slim, feather-tipped horn but seemed to have no effect.

Outside, two dark-skinned young men rode up on green megaraptors, wielding compact wooden bows. Brothers. Their chests were bare, and they wore tanned dinoleather pants.

Amity ducked as the baryonyx snapped its jaws.

"Get away from there!" her father demanded.

She obeyed, but only to bolt for the doors, drawing her revolver.

Rounding the side of the building, she aimed at the dinosaur's temple and fired.

The baryonyx only flinched, then roared with all its might and turned on Amity, charging her with dripping fangs.

"Amity!" shouted the younger of the two brothers.

Talon's familiar voice gave Amity the strength to hold her hand steady as she raised the revolver and fired again.

And again.

And again.

She exhausted all six rounds, but the baryonyx didn't stop. Putting all her energy into her legs, Amity sprinted down the dusty strip, where oil lamps flickered from inside the other buildings and cast an orange glow under her feet.

Talon and his brother, Red Fang, pursued the baryonyx on raptorback, footfalls thundering behind. They launched arrow after arrow, obsidian points sinking into reptilian flesh.

Townsfolk abandoned their carts and carriages to scurry along the boardwalks, seeking shelter.

The baryonyx veered toward a group of gunslingers who had drawn their revolvers and begun to shoot.

Amity skidded to a stop, hands on her knees. *Why won't it die?*

She glanced around at the carts full of wares and supplies that littered the street. There were sacks of flour and sugar, jarred preserves, hay bales, bolts of cloth, and—

Dynamite.

One of the miners must have left it.

She pried open one of the crates marked "High Explosives—Dangerous" and grabbed a bundle of the rust-red sticks.

Talon rode up to her, panting, his muscled arms gripping the reins of his megaraptor. He reached down and pulled her up onto its back behind him.

When the gunslingers ran out of ammo, the baryonyx charged them, catching one man between its teeth and chomping down. The man cried out as blood spurted from his shoulders.

Red Fang shot several more arrows to distract the monster, but they may as well have been hornet stings for all the good they did.

The sheriff arrived on the scene and threw a lasso, roping the creature by the neck. Her deputy did the same, which inspired a couple of dinocowboys to pitch in, too, with all four now working to control it.

Talon looked to the few townsfolk who dared to watch from behind barrels or posts. "Matches!" he demanded. "I need matches!"

A man in a bowler hat stepped out and tossed a pack from his waistcoat pocket.

Talon caught it in one hand.

Amity drew a knife from Talon's belt, tore a dynamite stick free from the bundle, and cut down the long fuse. She passed the stick to Talon, who struck a match, lit the fuse, and rode right up to the baryonyx still fighting the ropes.

The dynamite fuse sparked and hissed.

Talon flung the dynamite into the dinosaur's open mouth. The roaring went silent—and then a violent blast rocked the street.

The dinosaur's head burst into a mess of fiery brains and blood and chunks of bone.

Talon's megaraptor staggered and squealed beneath the wave of heat and energy, but Talon and Amity managed to stay upright on its back.

As if in slow motion, the large, headless body of the baryonyx collapsed, forcing a cloud of dust up from under it.

Amity held tight to Talon's waist, her cheek pressed against his back as the street went quiet and the townsfolk emerged from hiding. Talon clutched her forearm.

A splatter of dark gore painted the street.

The silence turned to a clamor, with dozens of new people coming to the blast site, including some of the meetinghouse congregation.

When Pastor Pike came forward, Amity dismounted, then cast a woeful glance up at Talon.

"What vile thing have you brought upon us?" the pastor accused of the young Scaleskin man.

Red Fang rode up next to his brother and raised his chin, daring Amity's father to elaborate.

"This is one of Magnus Kane's reptiles," Talon told him. "Check what's left of its flesh for the brand if you don't believe me. It came to our village and slaughtered six people—consumed their entrails and fled. We followed its tracks into town and caught up just in time. Seems like it was drawn to the lights."

"Looks like some type of mania," said a miner.

"That describes the behavior," said Amity, "but it doesn't explain why we couldn't kill it before. Between all of us, we must have shot that thing damn near fifty times."

"It's because it was already dead," said Red Fang.

An older man frowned. "Is that some of your Indigenous soothsaying? I wouldn't be surprised if your people were somehow involved in—"

"The reptiles were fine before Anglons came spreading disease here," Talon said. "First the bluetongue, then the swine fevers and the therovirus. Whatever possessed that baryonyx had nothing to do with us. It's like something destroyed its soul ... and left this shell of a monster to terrorize everything in its path."

"You all saw its eyes," Amity reminded them. "They were red like blood. It wasn't ... natural."

"Our medicine woman," Red Fang added, "says she sensed no spirit in the body. We've never seen sickness like this."

Amity wondered if Magnus Kane's large herds and varied dinosaur species had somehow encouraged new sickness in their numbers. And he was tough on them, so much that his ranch hands often quit within weeks of employment, insisting that the man knew nothing about reptiles and had no business owning them. That's why he'd been shipping in sky rock—abundant meteorites from an ancient meteor fall on the southern continent—because for whatever reason, those rocks caused some internal sensation that the reptiles would do anything to avoid.

"We don't believe there's such a thing as 'undead,'" said Amity's father. "Our Lords would not permit an abomination like that."

The saloonkeeper scratched his chin. "Now wait a minute. I think the native boy's onto somethin'. I heard tell of another dinosaur the other day, from the likes of a snake oil salesman or some such. He'd had a lot of whiskey, so I didn't think much of it, but he said he stopped by an outpost that'd been attacked by two velociraptors with bloodred eyes—just like this here baryonyx had— and the boss took off the dinos' heads with a butcher blade. But here's the kicker: The heads kept right on movin' ... snappin' them jaws like they didn't know they'd been cut clean off. Finally the boss poured kerosene on 'em and lit 'em up. That was the only thing that finally stopped 'em."

For only in the fire can we be cleansed.

"Tall tales," said Pastor Pike.

"Believe what you wish," said Talon. "This likely won't be the last of it."

"Well, let's get this mess cleaned up for now," said the sheriff, surveying the damage. "Everybody ought to shelter in place until we have more information."

The deputy turned to Amity and Talon. "My mega's had the therovirus for about a week. Do you think I ought to be concerned for her?"

"Therovirus is harmless," Amity reminded him. "Mainly digestive issues. Chills if it gets bad. Make sure she gets plenty of water—and feed her some garlic to ease the symptoms. Whatever happened to the baryonyx, it's not related. It can't be."

"What about the foot warts?" The deputy gestured to the soles of the dinosaur's feet, which were covered in tiny bumps. "That baryonyx had therovirus. No mistaking it."

The deputy wasn't wrong, but every other dinosaur seemed to be going through a bout of therovirus, and in about fourteen days it was over. Although maybe somehow the virus made dinosaurs more susceptible to ... whatever *this* was.

As Amity wiped a drop of baryonyx blood off her face, another screeching roar in the distance set her back at attention.

Overlapping reptilian cries rang out.

The deputy aimed his ear toward the sound. "That's got to be at least two more. Maybe three."

"All who are willing to fight," said the sheriff, "stand over here. We'll divide into teams, and everyone gets a bundle of dynamite." She looked to the miner, who nodded vigorously. If incendiary power was the only way, there could be no objection. "The rest of you, get somewhere safe for the night—and *no lights.*"

Townsfolk murmured among themselves until they'd all figured out places to stay—above storehouses or filling up the spare rooms at the inn. All mounts went to the closest livery.

Pastor Pike refused to stay at the inn because it was so close to the saloon and the Crimson Crest, so the owner of the general store agreed to host him.

The pastor seemed to assume Amity would go with him, but her firm stance beside the Scaleskin brothers turned his confidence into scorn.

"Your soul is in grave danger, Amity Pike."

"So's your body, Pa. We can't all hide and hope the gods have mercy on us. Maybe our good Lords want to know we can do something for ourselves once in a while."

He tried to argue, but the storekeeper ushered him inside as the distant sounds of roaring reptiles and human screams grew louder.

Soon only twenty people remained outside.

Among the townsfolk, Amity noticed Cailey Westbrook, a girl with whom she'd attended the schoolhouse. Cailey worked at the Crimson Crest now, wearing a dinobone-corseted dress with ruffles that bared most of her legs.

"What's *she* doin' here?" asked a wrangler named Korbin Mackley. He worked for Magnus Kane now, or so Amity had heard from one of the members of the congregation last month.

Cailey raised her skirt to reveal a garter holster around her thigh, which secured a small revolver. "I'm used to defending myself against ravenous reptiles—even if most of 'em are so-called 'men.' Don't let the lace fool you; I'm not gonna let monsters of *any* kind destroy my town."

Korbin scoffed. "Ain't you have eyes, sweetheart? Guns don't do no good."

"Who says it's for a dinosaur?" Cailey asked.

Amity smiled.

"All right," said the sheriff. "We'll break into teams of five. Everyone covers a different zone."

Somehow Amity ended up with both Cailey *and* Korbin, but, to her relief, Talon and Red Fang too. The sheriff stationed them at the Saurian, the saloon that also housed the town theater; its big windows and upper landing would provide a clear view of the street. The team could remain indoors for safety while also keeping watch over everything that went on below.

Other teams got set up at the schoolhouse, the town square, the train station, and the water tower.

Inside the saloon, Amity gazed up at the high ceiling of the main floor, where an enormous iron chandelier hung with its oil lamps extinguished. By now, the chandelier should have been fully lit, its glow spilling onto the small stage while saloon girls danced.

Half-empty glasses and piles of playing cards cluttered the round wooden tables throughout the space. Several stools at the bar were overturned, along with a bottle of whiskey whose contents streamed along the bar's surface and dripped onto the floor.

Scents of cigar smoke, perfume, and alcohol lingered in the air.

A staircase led up to a gallery balcony that wrapped around the room at about the same height as the chandelier.

Amity and the rest of the team strolled that landing.

Korbin brandished a sort of dinocattle goad, although instead of a metal point at the end it displayed a stone.

"You really think that's going to protect you?" Cailey asked.

The wrangler chuckled. "You haven't seen the sky rock in action at Kane Ranch. Really keeps the little devils in line."

"You wouldn't need it if you'd treat and train the reptiles right," Amity told him. "Constant punishment is no way to handle living things."

"It's effective," he argued. "That's what matters."

"It's lazy," Amity said.

Korbin took an aggressive step forward. Amity drew and cocked her revolver—which she had reloaded since her encounter with the baryonyx outside the meetinghouse—but Talon came between them.

The wrangler flared his nostrils. "You don't know what you're talking about. With that amount of dinocattle, it's the only way. The southern continent has sworn by it for centuries." He looked between Amity and Talon, then added, "What's with you two, anyway? Why are *you* protecting *her*?"

"You just worry about protecting *yourself*," Talon said.

The group kept a couple of lamps burning dimly but otherwise remained in darkness as they spread out on different levels. Amity sat with Cailey, while Korbin polished off some of the abandoned whiskey glasses, and the Scaleskin brothers kept watch at the upper windows.

Distant gunshots, screams, and screeches sounded periodically over the next half hour, growing louder. Dynamite blasts shook the town. There was nothing happening along the dusty strip, however, that the group could see.

A while later, Talon caught Amity's eye, then disappeared backstage.

"I'll be right back," Amity told Cailey.

Cailey winked. "Sure, sugar."

Amity glanced around to ensure that nobody else was looking, then slipped behind the red wool curtains. Without sufficient light, she stumbled right into Talon.

He caught her by the elbows and steadied her.

How good it was to feel his touch in private. But despite wanting to relish it, her eyes welled. She said his name in his own language. "I'm so sorry. Your village ..."

The hitch in Talon's breath was audible.

The village had some five hundred Scaleskins in it, but this dinosaur attack was only the tip of all the destruction his land and people had suffered. Dinosaurs going maniacal on them was salt in an already-festering wound.

He thumbed away a tear that had broken loose onto her cheek, then pressed his lips gently to hers.

For an instant, alone with him, she felt peace.

"I'm glad you're all right, Wild Fire," he said.

Amity brushed her fingers up his dark bare chest but stopped at the string of dinosaur teeth that hung around his neck. Similar teeth had come so close to piercing him before he'd thrown that stick of dynamite.

"We have to find out what's causing the dinosaurs to go feral," she told him.

"Your father might say it's punishment from the Lords for all the sins in this town, or demons my people have set upon yours."

Amity's hands curled into fists at such ridiculous accusations. It wasn't anything she hadn't heard before—but that was the problem, wasn't it? She'd heard it too often. Some part of her hoped this *was* a punishment, for enmity like that. But, of course, it couldn't be; the baryonyx didn't seem to have had any sense of purpose in its attacks.

"Do you think the effect is something ... supernatural?" Amity knew Scaleskins believed in spirits, good and bad. She wasn't sure what she thought about all that, no matter what sort of faith it came from, but Talon's opinion mattered to her.

"If the circumstances were different," he said, "I might say yes. But after what I've seen ..."

She knew he'd seen too many Anglons sprawl across the west like a storm of locusts, disrupting the rest of nature in new and terrible ways. Amity's blood felt like sludge in her veins, reminding her of her heritage, that she was a locust too.

From the front of the saloon, Korbin shouted, "We've got a situation!"

A burst of gunfire busted one of the windows.

Amity and Talon rushed out onto the stage.

A carnotaurus appeared in the jagged window frame, while several men with shotguns—and one with a rifle—approached it from outside.

It reared its two-horned head, eyes red, fangs dripping with blood and saliva, and twisted its near-armless body before lunging at one of the men and clamping its jaws down on him.

Korbin grimaced.

"Those aren't any of our recruits," Cailey said.

"No, they're not," Amity agreed. *Those men must have tracked it from the outskirts.* Even without lights, affected dinosaurs might still be drawn to town because of storehouse food or from so many bodies gathered in one place.

Spurred by the sight of their mutilated friend, the men continued to shoot, shattering the rest of the windows when their buckshot pellets went wide.

Two of the men dashed into the saloon for cover, shooting behind them as they ran.

The carnotaurus roared.

"Everybody get up high!" Amity shouted as the dinosaur turned on the saloon.

Korbin, mere feet from the chaos, ignored her, waving his goad, but the sky rock seemed to have no effect on the undead carnotaurus. Amity shook her head. If bullets and arrows caused no pain, the sky rock wouldn't either. Korbin grunted, then followed as the team spread out along the upstairs landing, each taking a stick of dynamite and a pack of matches with them.

In seconds, the carnotaurus got its jaws around another one of the men on the main floor, while the man's companions rushed in, guns blazing.

Already halfway across the saloon and overturning tables, the carnotaurus chomped down, and the man screamed out his last breaths.

Korbin struck a match.

"No!" said Amity. "There are three more guys down there!"

The wrangler held his flame an inch from the dynamite's fuse. "We'll *all* be dead if we don't blow that thing right now!"

Cailey hesitated with her own match ready to strike.

The Scaleskin brothers exchanged a glance but held back.

Amity looked up at the chandelier, its heavy iron frame dangling from four chains connected to a hook bolted into the support beam.

Directly below it, the carnotaurus finished its work and roared out bloody spittle. It stretched toward another man, who worked his lever-action rifle. He flicked the lever forward and back. *Click, click, BOOM! Click, click, BOOM!* He cried out amid the noise, smoke curling around his face, spent cases clattering around his boots.

Drawing her revolver, Amity aimed at the chandelier hook and fired.

The beam splintered around the hook.

She fired again.

Chunks of wood spewed over the carnotaurus. The men scrambled up onto the stage.

She fired a third time and—

The chandelier crashed.

Its harsh, iron edges cracked and split the dinosaur's skull down the middle.

Everyone above froze at the sight.

The men below cowered as the dust settled, then slowly rose to take it in.

Cailey clutched the pendant on her choker.

"What in the gods' names ..." Korbin whispered.

Amity gaped at the dinosaur, which, despite its mortal wounds, began to twitch. But that wasn't what kept her gaze fixed downward.

The exposed brain was black as night, slick with dark fluid ... as though something had consumed it bit by bit and replaced it with this murk.

"You were right," Amity said to Talon. "Whatever this creature was before ... It's gone now."

The brain controlled the body, Amity recalled. Doc Beauregard had explained it at the schoolhouse once when Miss Millie had invited him to speak to the class.

If you wanted to move your arm, your brain sent a message to it —like a telegraph system—to flex and make it so. There was consciousness, too, but that tended to get tangled up with spirituality, and even centuries of philosophy still couldn't figure it out.

But the point was, whatever had killed this dinosaur's rational thought, maybe even its natural instincts, seemed to still be able to control the mechanics of the body—like pushing buttons or pulling levers on a soulless machine.

Amity eased down the stairs.

Talon caught up and grasped her by the wrist as she approached the heap under the fallen chandelier. She didn't take another step forward, but she also didn't shy away from what she saw.

The carnotaurus twitched again, muscles contracting in a wave along its hindquarters.

Sure enough, Magnus Kane's brand was burned into the hip.

Its jaws parted. A gurgle erupted from its throat.

The black brain matter shone in the tiny flicker of a dim—but still lit—oil lamp on the bar.

For only in the fire can we be cleansed.

Amity grabbed the lamp and smashed it on the dinosaur's head.

The glass shattered, spilling oil, and the whole thing went up in flames.

An odd sound, like a million infinitesimally small and distant cries of anguish were lost among the sizzle. And then finally, as the baryonyx had done, the carnotaurus, too, went still—and silent but for the crackling fire that consumed its flesh.

When the sheriff had determined that all immediate dinosaur threats had been extinguished—for now—and it was safe to go home, Amity found Fangor lapping water from a trough in the livery. The Scaleskins' mounts were there, too, and so was Korbin's.

Korbin kept a tight fist around the sky-rock goad, waving it at his own megaraptor, who snarled in response. "Don't test my patience. Not after the night I've had."

His raptor bore Magnus Kane's brand, which came as no surprise to Amity. A loyal wrangler would be expected to ride something from the boss's collection for the advertising. Although, Amity recalled, the baryonyx and the carnotaurus had both come from Kane Ranch.

She stepped back, drawing Fangor away with her. Talon met her with his own mount, taking her hand.

Korbin scowled at her. "What's your trouble now?"

"Your raptor's got therovirus." Amity nodded at the warts visible between the megaraptor's toe-claws.

"And?"

It reared its head.

Korbin struck it with his goad.

A growl rumbled in the raptor's chest.

Amity's heart pounded. "How long have you been carrying that thing?"

"A few days." Korbin held up the goad again in a warning move, but the raptor stood still, staring him down. He narrowed his eyes, then looked at the sky rock. "What the hell?"

"You told us sky rock was effective," said Talon.

"It was. I should hope the reptiles don't adapt to it. Mr. Kane just shipped in a hundred crates of the stuff."

A hundred crates?

All that dinocattle, all those mounts, and all that sky rock ... together on one ranch ... with therovirus running rampant.

People here barely knew what a virus was, and only because Doc Beauregard had brought his big-city science from the east. Viruses weren't living things, the doc had said, but they could infiltrate the smallest *parts* of living things and run them like a bandit driving a stolen stagecoach.

But could a virus turn from a petty thief to a full-on killer?

Perhaps under the right influence ...

Korbin shoved the sky rock up against the megaraptor's snout. "One way or another, this beast is gonna *listen*—"

The megaraptor snapped its jaws over the wrangler's arm, goad and all.

Amity covered her mouth.

Korbin shrieked like a horde of tortured souls in the pits of damnation.

The raptor gnawed twice before it ripped Korbin's arm from the shoulder.

Talon dragged Amity backward.

As fluids gushed down Korbin's side, Amity squinched her eyes shut.

This nightmare wasn't over. Of course it wasn't.

It was like that old folk ballad her mama used to sing before she'd died: "The Dust Won't Settle 'Til the Bones Do." It was a lamentation of war, of the way men would never stop fighting until they were all dead, how greed and vengeance went bone-deep—but tonight the words took on new meaning.

What would it take to settle the bones of these vicious dinosaurs, now that they kept on moving even after death?

When Amity finally had the courage to look again, the megaraptor lunged at her.

And its eyes were red as blood.

About the Author

Victoria is originally from the Pacific Northwest but currently lives in Utah, where she works remotely as a graphic designer. She recently completed her indie-published YA dinosaur fantasy trilogy, The Mystical Bones, to which this story serves as a companion (set in a different corner of the same world). She has a bachelor's degree in English and has filled multiple roles at newspapers and magazines. Aside from writing, she loves doing DIY projects, wrangling her two kiddos, and reading (of course).

A Hunger for Revenge
Jason P. Crawford

The gunshot that punctured Liam's chest matched perfectly with the drumbeat.

Liam didn't realize he'd been shot at first; the fury of battle had him, the order to charge still sounding in his ears. His service to his mercenary squadron would see his family fed for years, so when he felt the ball's impact, he let it roll off his mind, water on a duck's back. He took another two steps toward the fortified line, lifting his pike high.

The second round hit Liam in the stomach, stopping him short. Blood poured from both wounds, from his mouth. He staggered, falling to one knee and dropping his spear as his life ran into the ground, soaking into the dirt. White mushrooms swayed under the flow, turning red as the mycelium drank up the spilled fluid. His vision wavered, and he reached out to keep himself steady.

"No." Liam's muscles shook as he struggled back to his feet only to collapse again. "Dorothea. Michele. Please."

He clutched the silver locket dangling from his neck. It held locks of hair from both his wife and daughter, good luck charms for safety in battle. As his breath quickened and shallowed, Liam knew that his luck had failed him, that he would die on this muddy causeway.

More arquebus shots rang out above him, slamming wetly into the standing pikemen. Steel clanged and screams pierced the air. Warriors drove into one another as cannons blasted from inside the fortress.

"Fall back!"

Liam's eyes widened as his commander called the retreat. His brothers-in-arms began the withdrawal, guarding against the Spanish firearms and the German Landsknecht. The French behind the mercenaries broke and ran, pursued by cavalry and cut down as they fled.

Some would have been proud to watch the Swiss hold together, presenting a united front even as they quit the field.

Not Liam.

"Please!" He gasped, a feeble, threadbare cry unnoticed as his fellows left him behind. "I can't ..." His cold limbs refused to obey his commands.

His vision tunneled as his consciousness fled, blackness creeping in, shrinking until all he saw was the cluster of blood-spattered mushrooms, speckled red, gleaming in the sunlight.

"I can't die here."

Sound returned first, the dim throbbing of something that could have been a heartbeat, then an accompaniment of lute strings, a cascade of repeating chords. Liam strained to listen, but the harmony retreated from his attention, instead surrounding his awareness from unseen angles.

He felt no pain, no fear, but he needed to *see*. If he'd reached heaven, he'd meet his parents, his younger brother. He'd wait for his daughter for however long it took.

His eyes opened, but the impulse came with another strumming of strings, as if his muscles played the instrument rather than lifting his eyelids. The clouded night sky cast judgment over the fields of the dead.

He hadn't passed to heaven. But why not?

Liam's movements seemed divorced from his thoughts, as though a puppeteer guided his limbs with sticks rather than by his own decisions. Every action came with a delay. Sitting took at least two seconds, standing another four. Every motion carried with it the thrumming of sound deep in his head, a heavy drumbeat or lute strings climbing the scales.

His eyes scanned the horizon, falling on the forest of upturned pikes and blades, the slain horses, the dead men. Behind him stood the castle of Cerignola, with the victorious Spaniards garrisoned inside. He heard the revelry, the sounds of cheering and singing wafting on the breeze. The stench of battlefield blood flooded Liam's nose, but it didn't repel him.

It made him hungry.

"I should be dead." His tongue dragged against his lips, dry and scratchy. "I ... they shot me."

His hand came up to his silver locket, sending a cloud of flies buzzing away from him. The insects swirled, diving around his head and whining in his ears, an annoying distraction that disrupted his focus.

His fingertips brushed against his chest wound. The dual sensation surprised him, the strings now mixing with a haunting horn of the kind shepherds used to call to one another across the mountains. He looked down.

Blood clotted around the injury, thick and congealed. Two flies had been caught in the ichor and flapped weakly in their attempts to escape. Inside the wound, a gold-tinged, spongy substance, solid but soft, filled the hole which should have exposed his heart to the air.

What is that? He extended a finger to poke at the strange substance. *Why—?*

The horn crescendoed, louder than before, and his whole arm

stopped moving. His mind commanded, but his muscles locked, his fingertip hovering a few inches away from his chest.

"God in heaven, what's happening to me?"

Liam quit trying to touch the sponge and immediately regained control of his arm. He flexed his fingers and noticed that each movement brought a unique strum of the lute strings.

"Where is that music coming from?" His exclamation echoed in the night air, bouncing around the battlefield. "Who's playing it?"

Quiet.

The word sounded like someone had whispered it in his ear, but someone with lungs full of water and on the verge of drowning in it.

He spun, staggering under the combined surprise and the sudden drumbeat that hammered in time with his limbs' movement.

"Who's there?" Liam peered into the darkness, but the clouds obscured enough of the moon's light that he saw only vague shapes in the distance. "Who are you?"

We are hunted. Again the strings, again the horns underlying the words. **You were food. We made you move.**

Something inside the words, or around them, gave him pause, made him duck. Whatever was happening to him, the voice had one thing right: The Spaniards watching the castle gates might spot him, and if they did, he'd be killed.

But they killed me before. Liam brought his hand up again but stopped before it got too close to the hole in his chest. *I was dead.*

Yes. Food. The confirmation came with a heavy horn thrum, a call of danger that sounded if an avalanche threatened. **Now move. Need food or you stop moving.**

His eyes fell, roaming as he processed what the voice had told him, until they landed on the mushroom patch he'd fallen next to. While he'd ... slept ... the fungus had soaked up the spilled blood and grown, multiplied until they surrounded his resting place. His shape made a void in the cluster, a gap among the fungal bloom.

Is that ... Is that you?

We aren't there now. We're new, moving.

Liam's right leg twitched, kicking out like it'd been struck in the knee. He narrowed his eyes and ran his hands over the limb.

Move. We need food. The voice grew more confident, stronger, as it spoke to him. ***Or you become food.***

Liam understood. He had to find the fungus something to eat, or it would eat *him* for lack of anything better. He licked his lips again—still so dry—and reached for the dagger at his side.

The coppery aroma of blood reached his nose again. Hunger stirred in his chest, and he knew it wasn't his own.

Who are you?

We are we.

Liam brought his weapon up. *All right. What do you eat?*

You fed us before. We need more.

Blood. That made sense. However it had happened, Liam's blood had awoken this creature, spurred it to crawl into his body and reanimate it.

What about ...? He gestured to one of the corpses, but a discordant series of notes immediately dug into his brain. His free hand covered his ear.

"All right, all right!"

The horrid, jagged whine ceased, returning to the background sounds of lute, drum, and horn. He shook his head to clear it, turning his attention to the castle.

Warm. Fresh. Like you gave us. The hunger increased. ***Soon.***

Liam swallowed, but no saliva moved. "That's where the living people are. If ..." Finally, he found his locket and closed his hand around it. "If I bring you to ... food, can you help me get home?"

The strings tickled their way into the major scale, rising in pitch.

Yes. Home. Food.

He nodded. "All right. Let's go."

The guards didn't expect to be infiltrated by a single man after the great battle. Liam kept low, moving through clouds of insects and crawling past piles of bodies, until he passed the Spanish ditches and spiked barricades.

He feared being caught, but the emotion tasted different. It lacked the same rising potency, the inevitable collapse that panic carried, and the sinking feeling of worry.

I'm not breathing. This drove another spike of fear into him, followed by a horn blast in his mind. He pressed his back against a wall, minimizing his silhouette, and his grip on the dagger shook. *Why aren't I breathing?*

We breathe for you. We move messages from meat to meat, like trees. We provide for you, if you provide for us.

An image appeared in his mind of a great web stretching. Liam's thoughts became fingers that caressed the web, traveled along it, and knew everything that crossed it. He knew need and response, call and reply, a million million times over.

But now it is us and it is you. We need you and you need us. The imagery drifted away, leaving Liam against the castle wall again. **We need food.**

"Yes." Liam nodded and stepped around the corner. In the castle's main courtyard, more than a hundred Spaniards celebrated, tossing bottles and knives, singing and dancing, lit by flickering torches lining the inner walls. The stench of alcohol filled the space, repellant and acrid. Against a side wall, several rows of barrels rested, likely loaded with powder.

There's too many. Liam glanced from one man to the next. *Even if they're drunk. I can't kill that many.*

We will provide for you.

Liam's eyes moved without his command, pointed toward an arquebus, leaning against an outcropping next to one of the exits.

He couldn't kill all of them, no, but he might find one, isolated from his fellows, and murder him. Then the fungus would feed.

Feed.

Nodding, Liam picked up the dagger and stalked to the side. He crept toward the indicated exit. The drunken songs clashed horribly with the music playing with his every movement, making him want to close his eyes and cover his ears to block out the din.

Closer, closer. He stepped slowly and carefully, despite the aggravation, because getting caught would end him faster than the arquebus shot had. The drum in his head had replaced his heartbeat, quickening as his nerves rose.

Can you be quieter? It's hard to concentrate.

Liam winced at a pulse in his chest and his gut.

That is how we move your thoughts to your meat. You hear it. We cannot change it.

Oh.

Liam didn't understand, but no matter. He'd reached the exit gate just in time for his target to come stumbling back in, tucking himself into his trousers. The Spaniard blinked at Liam, bleary and very drunk.

He muttered something in slurred Spanish.

Liam said nothing.

In a burst of motion that sounded like four drums beating together, Liam lunged at the Spaniard and thrust his dagger into the soldier's exposed throat.

The drunken man's reflexes failed him. His hand came up far too late to block the attack. Dark eyes bulged, and a choking sound, wet and bloody, burbled from his lips.

As the man fell, Liam caught him and moved him to the side, out of sight of the other soldiers, laying him on the ground.

The Spaniard twitched and spasmed; his breath came in uneven hitches.

Liam knelt beside the dying man, and as a crescendo of lute strings filled his mind, the fungus leapt out of Liam's chest—a red-gold clot of tendrils and strands with bulging protrusions. The mass was the size of a malformed infant, and it landed on the Spaniard with a revolting squelch, but it remained attached to Liam by cables of the same fibrous material.

The tendrils spread and crawled their way over the Spaniard's body. They sought out the wound in his throat like fingers, peeling the flesh back, prying it open so the mass could reach inside. It sent spears of itself into the man's windpipe.

Liam's hand moved in the sign of the cross as the Spaniard began to dry up. His cheeks hollowed, and his eyes sank into his head. Skin tightened over bone and highlighted the curvature of every muscle.

God above. A wave of nausea rose into Liam's throat.

As it drained its victim, the fungal mass grew, swelling until it had doubled in size. Then it *broke*, fracturing itself down the middle. The half attached to the Spaniard forced itself into the dead man's neck, compressing to fit through the small opening, while the other piece pulled itself along the anchoring tendrils back to Liam's body. He closed his eyes but couldn't escape the sliding sensations as it reentered him, the swelling against his rib cage and pelvis, the slowing drumbeat as it settled in.

We are fed. Its voice sang in Liam's mind.

He pressed a hand to his forehead and leaned against the wall, trying to collect himself. Now that he'd fed the creature, he'd be able to go home—

A sliding sound below him made Liam's eyes snap open. The Spanish soldier twitched, his limbs moving in jerky spasms. Shape and definition returned to his flesh as the fungus crawled beneath his skin.

Liam watched in horror. *Is that ... Is that what you did to me?*

We made you move again. Triumphant strings. **You are strong. We will provide for you. You will provide for us.**

The Spaniard's twitching slowed and turned into more even movements. The body bent at the waist, sitting up, and his eyelids opened to reveal gleaming, bloodred orbs.

"You will provide for us." The Spaniard's throat wound shook, and Liam saw the fungal tendrils threading through, vibrating to replace the vocal cords severed by his attack. "We will provide for you."

Liam's muscles gave way, and he thought he would collapse, but the creature in him seized control, stiffening his limbs until the dizziness passed.

"I'm sorry." Liam shook his head. "I can't do this."

If we do not feed, you will become food. Like the one you killed.

Liam stared into those crimson orbs and imagined what that must have felt like, this thing draining every fluid, every ounce of blood and water to feed itself. He shuddered, shaking his head without meaning to.

"We must feed." The Spaniard's mouth moved as if someone had their hand in his skull, thumbs controlling the mandible and fingers behind his face. "More. Feed us more."

When will it stop? He directed the question to the fungus in his own chest. *How many do you need?*

There is no stopping. We must feed, and we must grow, and then we feed again.

The music that accompanied the words reminded Liam of the folk ballads sung in his village, the songs of comfort and warmth and home. He imagined these creatures bursting into his village, his home.

Finding his wife and daughter.

Liam clutched the locket in his fist. He wouldn't make it home, but he also couldn't let this *thing* get to the people he loved. But it would read his thoughts if he wasn't careful.

"We'll get more food for you." *Keep quiet.* "Out there."

"Many there." The possessed Spaniard swayed on his feet. "Much food. Many hosts."

"But it'll be dangerous." Liam waved his hand to indicate the Spaniard's body. "They'll fight back. We have to be clever."

We will provide. You will provide.

Liam nodded. "I'll provide."

Liam returned to the courtyard. Several of the Spanish soldiers had either retired to bed or were passed out, snoring loudly through the continued celebration. Only about twenty or thirty soldiers remained, most of them gathered into isolated groups.

Isolated means easier to feed. Liam scanned the area. *Remember that. No one to see you feed.*

No one to see us feed. The presence in his mind agreed with him, sending pleasant tones into his thoughts. **Alone meat.**

"Right."

Liam's eyes danced toward the barrels of powder and away. Lingering on that idea wouldn't help. He didn't know how much control the fungus could exert over him, but it had felt substantial before, and he couldn't risk—

Risk? Where is the risk?

His eyes moved again, but this time not by his will. The fungus searched the area, hunting for the risk Liam had been thinking of, and so he quieted his mind and focused on the torches that lit the courtyard.

If we're seen, we're in danger.

The possessed Spaniard moved behind Liam, its movements much less smooth than his own. The poor bastard must have well and fully died, leaving the fungal growth to control him completely, rather than ... whatever this one had done to Liam.

"I'll get the torches so they can't see us. Put out the fire."

In his mind, he projected the image of dousing each torch, leaving the courtyard in darkness.

"Once it's dark, they won't be able to find us until you've fed and made more of you." He tried to swallow but had no saliva. "You need to follow closely. We don't want to get caught."

"You provide for us." The Spaniard's voice croaked its response. "We provide for you."

Yes. You provide for me.

Liam clutched his pendant tightly, then released it as he approached the nearest torch, about five feet from the barrels of powder. A sleeping soldier slumped against the wall, his head cocked to one side, an empty bottle next to him.

Liam steeled himself and knelt next to the Spaniard, slicing across the man's throat. The alcohol had him so deeply that he didn't awaken even as his blood poured down his coat.

The aroma made Liam ravenous. "Go on. Take him."

"You provide for us."

The possessed soldier stumbled forward, throwing himself onto the newly slain one. Liam heard a wet slurping that indicated the fungus had begun feeding, and he turned away.

I'll grab the torch. He reached out, the heat growing as he took hold of it. *Then we'll—*

The drumbeats and strings stopped.

No.

Liam's heart dropped, and his muscles froze. He had the torch in his hand, but he could move no closer to the barrels.

We know what you want. You cannot. We must feed.

Let me go. He struggled against the creature's control, but the impulses simply didn't reach from his brain to his muscles anymore. *I don't want to do this! Let me go!*

The slurping, fleshy sounds from behind reached Liam's ears. How much longer until there were two of them? Four?

We must—

No! I won't let you!

Then you become food.

The creature presented it as a choice, vivid in Liam's imagination. Which did he prefer: spreading the creature to others, or allowing it to feast on him and kill him for good?

Liam watched in his mind's eye as the possessed Spaniard pulled the fungal mass from his own desiccated chest.

Now we are many. We will feed, and we will grow. We will be many many many.

"No!" Liam forced the word from his lips as loudly as he could. "Someone! Help me!"

His cry caught the attention of a group of soldiers, who shouted in turn, calling others to the scene.

Frozen in place, holding the torch in a locked grip, Liam watched them assemble—then point, gasp, and cry out when they noticed the fungus-possessed man in the middle of its feeding. They began priming their weapons, readying to fire.

How do we flee? The fungus felt fear; Liam sensed it. ***You must provide for us. We will provide for you.***

Let me go. Liam tried to master his thoughts, to say one thing while meaning another. *I'll flee. I'll provide for you. Let me go.*

Notes played, just a few strings plucked by an unseen hand. Perhaps the possessing fungus wasn't sure, was of two minds about the idea, but some part of the connection came to life, and Liam forced his command along those thin links between his still-living brain and his occupied body.

Let go!

His hand moved at the wrist, flicking the torch toward the nearest powder barrel. The Spaniards saw the motion, following the torch with their eyes, and scattered, dropping their weapons and running.

Liam felt his legs shift, the fungus preparing to make him run as well, but because its attention had focused there, he was able to throw his hand out and lock it around the torch sconce.

Let us flee! We will die!

The second Spanish soldier rose, the transformation complete. The two dead men shambled toward Liam, their arms outstretched.

He looked toward the barrels.

Smiled. Closed his eyes. Imagined Dorothea and Michele, safe and warm in their beds, heated by the hearth.

"Yes. Yes, we will."

The odor of burning wood reached his nose just before the explosion.

A musical scream burned through his mind as the flames burned his flesh, but he welcomed it.

Maybe now ...

The pain stopped. The fear vanished.

Liam opened his eyes again.

His mother and father, younger than he remembered them ever being, stood in front of him. Green fields and flowers stretched to the horizon, and the wonderful aroma of alpine roses and edelweiss warmed his heart.

Liam's mother embraced him, her skin warm against his own, and his father clapped him on the shoulder. He grinned broadly and gestured toward the great fields.

"Welcome home, son. Welcome home."

About the Author

Jason P. Crawford is a high school science teacher and writer living in Lancaster, California. He spends his time playing tabletop RPGs with his four kids and working with his wonderful wife on their shared dream of publishing success. He has short stories published in *Once Upon a Future Time, Vol. 4* by the Brothers Uber, *The Vampire Survival Guide* by Wonderbird Press, and in Starspun Lit magazine. He was also a top-ten Finalist in the Baen Fantasy Adventure Awards for 2024, won third place in the Jim Baen Memorial Short Story Awards for 2025, and attended the 2025 Superstars Writing Seminars under the David Farland scholarship opportunity.

MUSIC IN MY BONES
GABBIE GIBSON

Year 193 of the Lyrian Empire

*B*a-dum.

The drumbeat resonates something within me I can't name. My bones creak in tune with the old wooden oar I'm pulling as it strains against the ocean's current.

Ba-dum.

Another beat, another pull. The ship lifts with the roaring sea, crashing down, water spraying onto me from my left. I can't smell the brine in the air; there's a strange void as I fail to inhale through my nose.

Ba-dum.

My rowing mate pulls in time with the drum, keeping me on the beat. I look to my right to see the skeleton beside me. What's a Bones doing here? What am I doing here? I look down and see my skinless hands on the oar, my finger bones wrapped around the wood as I pull it back again to the beat of the drum. My hands feel dry even as water drips from them.

Ba-dum.

A loud laugh draws my attention to the people on the ship. Dozens of Bones man ten oars on each side, twice as many human soldiers stand on the center deck. They talk between drumbeats, glorifying the battles to come, the victory they're sure of, and the riches to be won. We sail for war.

Ba-dum.

Am I as dead as my neighbor? I know the answer before I look. No clothes, no flesh, just a naked skeleton. I'm a Bones—made to do what our necromancers command, mindless labor and nothing else. Just the commands, the duty beyond death, the service to the kingdom. Was I normal? Did all Bones think and see and hear? I look at my benchmate, nudging them slightly. They don't respond, their glowing eyes staring at the oar, focused only on rowing to the beat.

Ba-dum.

The gem at my throat urges me to obey. Row. Row. Row. As constant as the drum, the command pushes against the sliver of my will. I don't have any choice, I'm just another Bones, just another piece in the divine plan. I don't feel fatigue, nor can I feel the oar beneath my hands or the water in the air. All I feel is the call, the drums, and the magic compelling me to row.

Ba-dum.

I think of my past, but there is nothing. A void empty of memories. It feels appropriate. If I can't feel the world around me, what place do I have in it?

Ba-dum.

Who am I? What kind of person had I been in life? Had I given my corpse over willingly to serve? Had I been conscripted? Convicted? I have no idea.

Ba-dum.

If I had a heart, I knew it would be beating double time. Magic crackles from the gem in my neck all the way to my toes, and I curl them against the edge of a rotting deck beam. The magic fades, and my will reasserts itself. I might not know who I am, but I had been someone. That thought scares me somehow, but it's not visceral fear, not something I can feel. It's a logical progression, a new perspective on a worldview I can't remember or understand. What does being a thinking Bones mean? Am I trapped like this forever?

Ba-dum.

I release the oar as I lose myself in thought, trying to make sense of everything around me.

Ba ...

The human drummer steps away from the drum, walking toward me with a rod in his hand.

He points the shaft of dark walnut, a glowing amethyst embedded in the end, toward my face. My thoughts fade to darkness.

Year 207 of the Lyrian Empire

"Freedom ain't free if justice ain't just," a redheaded woman belts out a line of a work song with fierce determination.

"Freedom ain't free if justice ain't just," a group of farmers working the fields reply in chorus all around me as they swing their tools in time to the beat.

The music awakes something in me as I swing a hoe down, a solid *thunk* accentuating the beat between the next call-and-response. I pull the hoe back to break up the soil at my feet as I prepare a row of the field for the spring planting. The midday sun bears down on me and bleaches my already dry white bones. Humans move parallel to me down the rest of the field, several empty rows separating each of us.

"Fight for your life, and fight for your love," the woman calls and the group responds.

I vaguely recall bits and pieces of memories since the ship. Of rowing, of fighting, of working, of being sold. Those thoughts depress me, so I turn to the music in this moment and try to sing along, but no sound comes. The gem where my throat used to be as still as the earth that bore it.

As I watch the farm laborers around me happily work and sing, unbidden memories dance back to me.

I was a small boy again, a middle child of five. My parents were ... I couldn't see them, their faces hidden in a haze of lost memories. However, I remember their voices, remember singing with them around campfires, in the house, on the road, as I fell asleep. I loved their voices, but I hated my own. The screeching as my voice broke, then the deep pitch it settled into caused a dissonance that filled my soul. My sisters insisted it was sultry and would attract the ladies if I would accept it, but I couldn't.

My father gave me a lute when I came of age. Even if I wouldn't sing, I could still play, and I wanted to be a part of the family. I remembered playing along, becoming the foundation for their voices, the notes that anchored their words.

I adjust my grip on the hoe, my finger bones twisting around the shaft like the neck of the lute.

"*With one another, we can all rise above,*" the humans sing as one.

My fingers remember before I do. I start with the major chords, then the minor chords, each shift as natural as breathing. Well, what I remember breathing had been like. I listen to the humans singing and think about what chords would support their untrained voices.

I am so focused that I don't realize I've fallen behind the humans in my work until a little girl comes up to me.

"Mama, the Bones is being funny!" She points at me as I pretend to strum the tool.

The woman leading the group looks over. The workers stop, turning to see me awkwardly holding the hoe mid-strum.

I shrug my shoulders in embarrassment. I attempt to hide in the work, to fall into a groove, and to still my mind with each swing of the hoe.

Later, I find myself sitting in a wicker chair on the deck of the house that overlooks the fields. A crackling brazier fills the center of a circle of chairs and benches on which the family rests, singing folk songs. A mandolin lies on my lap.

The curious young girl from earlier stares up at me expectantly. Her hair is as red as her mother's.

I look at her, at the instrument, and back to her.

She grins and pushes the mandolin into my empty chest cavity as she bounces up and down. I pick it up and pluck the strings. Terribly out of tune. Still, I strum a G-major chord. Something stirs within me.

The family continues to sing as I play a tuning jig, adjusting the pegs and strumming to the beat. Once the soft thrum of the strings resonates with each other, I join the set.

Across the fire, a young boy sits on the lap of an old man. "Holy smokes. Annie was right, it's playing. Gramps, how'd you get a Bones like that?"

"I guess I got lucky, Jones," the old man says. He smiles at me knowingly as he gently rubs a small bone locket around his neck. His lips quiver as he looks into my glowing eye sockets. "After the war, they didn't have enough necromancers to maintain the Undying Army, so they sold off the beaten and broken ones. I got her for a pittance compared to the market price for a Bones. Had to fix up her arms, but she's worth it."

"Can they all do that?" Jones points at my fingers jumping around the neck of the mandolin from chord to chord as I throw in improvised grace notes to add depth to the piece.

"I ain't ever heard of any other Bones that could play music," Tobias says. His name comes to me suddenly, though I don't know from where. I don't think anyone else has called him anything but Gramps, but I know that's his name.

I try to smile, but I lack the skin to express anything.

The old man smiles for me. "She's one of a kind."

I don't know how I can do what I'm doing, but I know he's right. Whoever I'd been in life, whoever I am now, I'm special.

"It's a darn shame we can't hear her sing."

"How d'you know Boney is a she?" the girl asks.

"Look at the gem in her throat. You can tell by the color."

I'm curious about this, so I look down. I can't see my own throat, but there's a faint blue reflection off the mandolin. "Boy Bones glow red, girls glow blue."

Memories of the lute I once loved flare to life as my dead hands lovingly play the family's mandolin. The children dance to the music late into the night.

Years pass, but this pattern persists. I work with them in the fields during the day as they sing and play for them around the campfire at night. Even though I'm dead, somehow, I know I'm happy to be here, to be a strange part of my little family.

Year 223 of the Lyrian Empire

The brook to the right of the cobblestone road babbles. The water rhythmically laps against rocks, meandering toward the inevitable return to the ocean. Clouds of silt dance as ripples on the surface bob to the beat, little oscillations like a slow vibrato.

A man walks to my left. There is something familiar about him, but I can't place it. I tilt my head to get a better look at him and then glance around to try to get my bearings. A thick canopy of leaves stretches overhead. I see small bursts of colors of flowers blooming on vines and bushes scattered beneath thick deciduous trees. There is a flicker of motion from an animal I can't identify.

"You awake, Bonnie?" he asks.

I know that wasn't my name in life, but can't correct him. Though, as far as names for the dead went, I suppose it isn't bad. It's better than the childish nickname "Boney" the little boy on the farm called me.

What was his name? Jones. He isn't little anymore; he's a grown man with a bushy red beard and muscles earned from years of hard labor.

I'm jostled forward as I start to slow down. I barely catch myself by the thick leather harness strapped to my chest. I turn my head, realizing that I lead a team of sixteen Bones that pull an open-topped wagon. Their steps clatter in a consistent staccato that encourages me back into the ensemble.

"How long has it been since you last woke up?" Jones asks. "It's been a year at least, hasn't it? Do you know, we've got our third kid on the way?" He smiles back at his wife.

A pregnant woman with a face made from sharp angles and disappointment sits in the driver's seat, humming a soft tune.

A young girl, no more than three, pops her head up from the back of the wagon. She ducks back down and hides, bouncing up and down around the wagon's edge, giggling.

"You only saw him the once, but you should know our second didn't make it through last winter ..." Jones stares ahead with a blank expression for a moment, then sighs. "I miss him, but I know he's at peace with the gods. Here's to hoping our luck turns around with this trip," he says nervously.

I nod to indicate I understand.

"The farm's been doing well. My sister Daisy has been expanding the south fields, and we've got a new crop of beans to sell."

I realize my hand's been tapping on the shoulder of my harness along with the serenely comforting beat of the waters. The rhythm is somehow comforting.

"The king's been good too; he's been building roads all across the kingdom. This one's only two years old. Can you believe it? How quickly the world changes."

He seems relieved to have someone to talk to, and I'm happy to listen.

More memories of him flow back to me. The young redhead had grown over the years from a curious boy into a confident man. He'd decided to become a traveling merchant and had left the farm to Daisy. He sold their vegetables across the land and brought exotic fabrics and spices back to the village. Eventually, he'd married a merchant's daughter who'd wanted him to settle down with a shop in a city, but he was a strong and proud man who loved his little caravan and life on the road.

The girl jumps out of the wagon and runs up to us. "Daddy, Daddy. Are you talking to Bonnie?"

"Sure am, sweet bean."

She raises her arms, a pleading look on her face.

Jones obliges her unspoken request and puts her on his broad shoulders.

"Is she talking? You said she could talk!" The girl waves at me. "Hi, Bonnie!"

I wave back.

The girl starts talking rapidly, and I can barely understand one word in three, but I smile and nod along. Just like her father, she seems happy to talk with me.

I reach out and muss her hair. She giggles.

The girl's mother stops humming.

I look behind to see her sneering at me. "Sweet bean," she addresses the girl, "come back to the wagon. You shouldn't be talking to that creature."

The mother says it sweetly, but I hear the venom laced in her words. I guess she doesn't like that her husband is friendly with me.

Jones holds onto his baby girl, walking alongside me as the awkward silence grows.

I prepare for the inevitable darkness that comes with silence.

But it doesn't come, because there is sound all around us. The forest sings to us. Birds call back and forth in the trees, creating an ever-changing melody, the river harmonizes like nature's cello, and our footsteps become the constant beat of drums. Wind rustles the leaves to add trills and accent notes. The music plays so long as we listen.

We continue along for some time, but eventually the caravan calls for a break. Bones might be able to walk without rest, but not our minders. I try to maintain my focus on the sounds of nature around us; I don't want to go back to sleep just yet. I notice that Jones has gone back to his wife, and they seem to be having an argument.

"Don't be like that, Agatha," Jones says with the exhaustion of an argument he'd clearly had too many times. "She's just a Bones."

"It ain't right for a Bones to be acting like that. I'll stop being like this when you finally agree to sell her," Agatha says.

"I can't do that. She was Pa's before me, and my gramp's before that. She's our family's good luck charm."

Agatha turns her head and ignores him.

I should pay attention to their discussion. It involves me, but there's nothing I can say. Rather than worry, I let my attention wander to the woods.

I remember traveling through woods like this when I was a teenager. We were wandering minstrels traveling from city to city, letting the whims of nature and the road guide and inspire us. Those were happy times in a peaceful world.

We weren't beholden to society's standards, we played what we wanted, and we cared for and looked out for each other. Of course we had disagreements, even arguments, but we always worked through them. So when I told my family I wished I'd been born a girl, they accepted it. They understood it as little as I did, but they didn't care, they loved me all the same. That was the moment it registered for all of us why I hated my deep baritone voice.

I couldn't live as I liked in the towns, but on the road, I could always be myself. My family had my back. Eventually, we found an apothecary who could help me. In addition to the monthly brews for my sisters, she concocted me a daily potion to fix the ravages of puberty—not everything, but enough. After a few years of treatment, I could live true to myself no matter where we went, no one the wiser about my awkward history.

Slowly, my family drifted apart. It started when my youngest sister settled in a town as one of the local lordling's consorts. My older brother tired of the roving life and decided to study necromancy. What had happened to them? Not that it mattered now, it was so long ago that they were certainly deceased. After my father died, we had to sell the wagon. My mother, my two remaining sisters, and I found work playing at a tavern, and the carefree life of wandering from town to town became a relic of the past.

Water runs down my cheek, breaking my reverie. For a moment, I wonder if I'm actually crying as I mourn my past life. But that doesn't make sense. I look up to see a gray sky and rain starts to fall, drowning out the sounds of the forest.

I reach my bony hand to touch where I'd felt water on my cheek. The tiniest sensation, but there all the same.

I ponder what it means to start to feel again.

Year 258 of the Lyrian Empire

The orchestra crescendos. The brass section blares as four percussionists pound out the beat on timpani.

As consciousness floods back to me, I catch my balance barely in time to avoid spilling a tray full of empty glasses. I'm in a massive opulent ballroom. Three great glass chandeliers hang from the vaulted ceiling, casting a pale-yellow pallor across a room full of nobles. They are dressed in extravagant fashions, gowns that flare out in a bell and form-fitting suits embroidered with family crests. There are scores of Bones dressed in black-and-white finery. One side is a wall of open doors leading to balconies, most of which are occupied by small groups engaging in private conversation.

I'm wearing a maid's uniform, black dress under a white smock, the form filled out with padding in all the places one would expect from a living person. The idea that a Bones would need such things is absurd to me, but I twirl around, enjoying the feel of fabric against my body.

I laugh. I actually laugh! The sound comes out as a faint croak from the gem in my throat.

Fortunately, no one hears me.

I snap back to reality to pay attention to the people in the room. No one looks familiar. Where was Jones?

Out of the fog, a memory returns to me. The day after Jones died of old age, Agatha did what she'd wanted to do for decades. She sold me, swearing she would take her and her daughter's family across the border to a new life and escape her husband's legacy.

This wasn't the only time I'd been betrayed, but it still hurt.

I thought about when I'd been alive. After my mother died, it was too hard to perform for audiences, but by then I'd married a wonderful man, Marcus. He regularly came to the tavern to see me play and relax after his shift in the guard. Over time we fell for each other. He was as kind as he was strong. We got married and adopted three kids who'd lost their parents in recent border skirmishes.

Our life wasn't easy, but it was ours, and we were happy. Unfortunately, good things don't last forever. One evening, the tavern keeper's son knocked at the door of our small cottage. He and the uniformed men with him had come to conscript able-bodied men for the king's army.

My oldest son, Tobias, had just turned sixteen, but he'd never been a fighter. He'd been training to be a carpenter, finding beauty in wood before anyone else could see it. He was my precious son, and they wanted to turn him into a soulless killer.

I cried out against it, but there was nothing I could do.

My husband, bless his soul, volunteered to take our son's place. But they didn't want a washed-up old man. They wanted young blood.

Tempers flared as our argument escalated. I don't know who threw the first punch, but a brawl broke out. It all happened so fast —angry yells, punches thrown, steel drawn.

I didn't see the blade coming until it plunged through my abdomen.

My husband cried out, and they knocked him down, stabbing him.

The tavern keeper's son leaned close to me. "That's what you get for leaving the tavern, for leaving me. I'll take everything you took from me." He grinned, full of himself, full of pride as he tore my family apart.

But I'd never taken anything from him. Had he assumed there were things he was entitled to? Probably.

They left with my son clapped in irons. Around his neck hung a bone locket containing a drawing of my husband and me.

My husband lay next to me on the ground, bleeding out. He held my hand as we faded from the world together.

So was that how I had become a Bones? My body sold to the Necromancer Corps for a little extra gold?

I never agreed to live on like this. I'd been killed, my corpse sold off to the highest bidder. Everything had been taken from me in a single night. What had become of my children? Tobias had bought me, so he must have survived, but what of the other two? I can't remember their faces anymore, and I feel worse. Had my husband also been turned into a Bones? The thought of him living as a husk haunts me.

Fingers snap in my face.

"Hey, Bones. Take this!" A man scowls at me as he holds out a glass.

I suppress the agony of my past, and carefully take the glass. I can't be careless; these people have expectations of Bones. If I display emotions and thoughts, I know without a shadow of a doubt I will be thrown to the boneyard.

Maybe that wouldn't be so bad. Maybe I could finally rest.

I wander through the room and think of what it would be like finally having peace.

The partygoers don't notice me most of the time. I'm just a Bones. They don't worry I might repeat their gossip. All around I hear hushed whispers that the country has grown soft, we've grown complacent, the king is a coward for not taking on his grandfather's great legacy of conquest.

I'm glad I don't have blood, otherwise it would be boiling. But what could I do? I'm just a Bones.

Year 293 of the Lyrian Empire

Bagpipes howl indicating the order to march forward into battle. *Ba-da-da-dum.* Drums echo across the battlefield to set our tempo.

I stand in one of a dozen battalions of Bones at the fore. Behind us, necromancers hold our strings. Behind them, the human army waits. We are the fodder, just replaceable Bones to be reanimated after we fall. Forced to serve again and again. Across from us, a hodgepodge of warriors in mismatched armor stand at the base of the hill.

A breeze blows across the valley, and I smell the grass torn up by the opposing force's hasty retreat to the hills. My bones shiver as the cool air flows through me. I feel a song in my heart. I begin to feel alive.

My eyes are drawn across the scraggy grasslands by a mop of crimson hair on a scrawny kid. He can't be more than fifteen. I think of Jones, his daughter, sweet bean—who probably had grandchildren of her own by now—and my beautiful son Tobias, who was stolen from me.

The redhead's hauberk shifts uneasily to one side as he struggles to hold a sword and shield. He shifts it back, but it only unbalances him in the other direction. As he tries to balance himself, I see a familiar bone locket hanging around his neck.

They expect me to kill this child. A distant progeny of my lost son. How many greats of a grandson is he to me? I have no idea.

Ba-da-da-dum.

Behind us, on a skeletal horse, our necromancer points his rod, channeling the command for us to march. My feet move. I try to fight it, but they keep going. One foot in front of the other. The magic subverts my will. The kingdom wants me to follow their orders, to be a monster in their endless desire for expansion, conquest, and profit. To be only a Bones, killing without fear or remorse.

I refuse to let the kingdom have him. I will die again before I let them take another one of my children!

My instincts drive me to do what I'd done in life—make music.

Ba-da-da-dum.

I reject their rhythm and find my own.

I don't have a throat, but the vibration in my ear tells me I'm *humming*. The gem in my throat is thrumming to my will.

I hum one of my mother's favorite songs—a song of freedom for those who'd lost it, of those who'd had it stolen from them. In life, I'd never really come to terms with my deep voice, but I'm no longer limited by the constraints of the flesh.

I am my soul given form. I am the minstrel returned, and I sing. Like birdsong, my voice soars. The high notes rise above the din of the drums.

My soul asserts itself over the necromancer's magic.

The rest of the Bones in my battalion slow as I stop and sing.

The necromancer behind us shouts orders again, the amethyst in his rod growing brighter and brighter.

But I sing louder and louder, drowning out his magic. I put every emotion I'd felt in this life and the last into each and every word. To the tune of my mother's favorite melody, I sing about the Bones' ability to make choices for themselves. With each verse, more Bones stop and turn to face me.

We don't have to be what they made us to be. There is something left of us in our old bones, some piece of the soul long forgotten.

I remember the words my father told us when we performed: "There's a soul in the music, and there's music in the soul."

It's time for the dead to sing. It's time for our souls to sing.

Ba-da-da—Our voices drown out the drums, the bagpipes, and the necromancer shouting at us.

"Freedom ain't free if justice ain't just," I cry out, echoing the words of the granddaughter I'd met long ago on that farm.

Other Bones croak out only sounds, but I feel the intention, the desire, the emotions behind them.

I sing loud enough for all of us. We turn on our keepers. The only blood that will be spilled today is blood from those who demanded we spill it.

They will no longer control me or the music in my bones.

About the Author

Gabbie Gibson is a game developer who decided to transition from creating fantastical worlds on the computer to on the page. In addition to writing, she also enjoys teaching aerial circus, a myriad of crafting projects, larping, and cuddling with her two cats. You can learn more about her and her other projects at GabbieGibson.com.

A SAXOPHONE, SILENCED
LOU J BERGER

My saxophone's brass keys hold memories like water holds light.

Seventy years of neglect can't erase the way my fingers once played, creating a musical dialect of smoke, sweat, and defiance.

I drift through the basement of what used to be the Spotlight Club, watching a kid with green hair adjust microphone stands. His tattoos writhe under overhead lights as he pulls cable across the concrete floor. The modern equipment looks alien against the old walls. Walls that remember a time, long past, with different music and different souls.

The kid—Rick, according to his name tag—glances at the stairs. His fingers tremble slightly as he works, and I recognize the signs of someone fighting panic. Stage fright. Lord, how many young musicians had I seen wrestle with these same demons?

I focus hard, letting my memories spill into the room. The present dims. Like watercolors bleeding through paper, the past soaks through and becomes the now.

Red velvet curtains materialize along stark white walls. The LED track lights soften to old incandescent bulbs, amber light bathing the space. Modern speakers fade into shadow, replaced by the ghost-memory of our battered piano, its scratched mahogany still regal in the smoky light.

Rick strides through a table that isn't there anymore—not in his time—but I remember how many drinks had been spilled on its scarred surface. How many deals were made. How many threats were whispered across it.

"Check one, check two." Rick's voice cracks. He swallows hard, tries again. The sound system squeals feedback, and he curses. Behind him, a guitar case lies open, the strings gleaming. His hands shake worse now as he reaches for it.

I drift closer, remembering *my* first night on stage. How my teacher, Miss Adelaide, had shown me a trick for steady hands. I focus on letting a whisper of my old warm-up song filter through. Not ghost-music exactly, but a faint memory of it. Something soft and sweet, like a mother's lullaby.

Rick pauses, head tilted. His breathing slows. His hands steady as the melody wraps around him, though he probably thinks it's his imagination. He picks up the guitar, fingers finding their place.

I smile, though he can't see me. Modern musicians and their electronics. In my day, you didn't need amplification. You played until the notes were loud enough to reach the back row, until your lungs burned and your fingers blistered and the music controlled every soul in the room.

A new figure appears at the bottom of the stairs. Tall, dark-skinned, with careful movements and observant eyes. He carries a tablet, but there's something in the way he touches the old walls—reverent, curious. Like he can feel the echoes.

"How's the setup going?" he asks.

"Better now, Mr. Wallace." Rick strums a chord, his guitar perfectly in tune. "Something about this place ... the acoustics pop."

Mr. Wallace—Marcus, according to his name tag—walks the

perimeter of the room. He pauses at my favorite spot, where the stage used to be. His hand rests against the wall, fingers unintentionally tracing the wall where Reynolds's office door had been, now replaced by a blank wall. Something shifts in his expression. "My grandmother played piano here in '49," he murmurs, more to himself than Rick. "Said this place was where real music happened, or it was before they shut it down. Before that musician was killed."

He's talking about me.

I drift closer. Most people sense my approach as a cold breath, a shiver down their spine. When I hover near him, though, his eyes snap directly to where I stand. He blinks hard, like someone trying to clear their vision.

He sees me.

Not just feels my presence. *Sees* me.

I let the past bleed through stronger now. The walls groan, as if they're being stretched across time. A whisper of my saxophone's signature wail lingers in the air, threading into the modern silence. The old stage doesn't just appear—it remembers itself into reality, piece by piece.

Marcus stumbles back, his tablet clattering to the floor. Rick doesn't notice, head bowed over his guitar, his earlier nervousness forgotten.

"You're new here," I say, my voice husky from the smoke of a thousand cigarettes, the bite of aged whiskey. "But these walls? They know me."

He swallows hard. "This isn't possible," he whispers. Only I can hear him.

"Sugar, ain't nothing impossible in Nawlins." I gesture, and the room shifts again. Ghostly patrons fill phantom tables. A spectral band tunes up on the stage. "Especially not here. Not in *this* room."

"Who—" he starts.

"Cecile Marshall. Saxophone, Spotlight Club. 1952." I move close, letting him see me clearly. The red dress I died in. The way the stage lights caught the brass of my saxophone. "At least, until the night somebody decided I'd played my last note."

Rick's voice cuts through the vision. "Mr. Wallace? You okay?"

The past recedes like a wave pulling back from shore. The modern basement snaps into focus, but Marcus's eyes stay locked on me.

"I'm fine," he answers, but his voice quavers. "Just ... thought I saw something."

I laugh, the sound rippling through decades. "Oh, sugar, you did more than just see something. You saw *me*!"

His hand trembles as he picks up his tablet. "Why can I see you?"

"That's the wrong question."

I drift toward where the stage used to be, my red dress flickering. Behind me, Rick plays another chord, his confidence growing with each note. "The right question is: Why did they *kill* me?"

The sound system squeals feedback again and, this time, beneath the electronic shriek, I let them both hear a bit of my last original song. The one I performed just before I was killed.

Rick's fingers freeze on his guitar strings. Then he plays something in a new chord progression that echoes my old song, though he couldn't know that. Each note he plays stirs the air differently, as if he is unconsciously tapping into the building's musical memory. The ghost-sounds of my saxophone harmonize with his guitar, past and present blending into something new.

This basement holds more than just memories. It holds secrets. And that blank wall where Reynolds's office door used to be? That's just the first one waiting to be uncovered.

Marcus sits on an empty equipment case, his tablet, now forgotten, beside him. Rick has disappeared upstairs, but the ghost of his guitar practice lingers. Hesitant notes float down the stairwell, reminding me of other young musicians who'd found their courage in this basement.

"Show me," Marcus says, his voice steady. Professional curiosity triumphant over fear. "Show me everything."

I drift closer, letting my ghostly fingers trail along the modern walls without touching them. "You sure about that, sugar? Some memories bite."

He nods, and I let the past bleed through again, stronger this time. The transformation starts slowly, like honey oozing down glass. Modern lights dim and soften. White walls are shadowed with burgundy velvet curtains. The concrete floor ripples, hardwood leaping from underneath like fish roiling in a silent pond. Even the air changes, clouding with phantom cigarette smoke and the stench of spilled whiskey.

"August 15, 1952," I say. "A Friday. Hot enough to make even the devil sweat. I'd arrived early that night. Two hours before showtime. Told myself I needed to practice, but the truth was, I'd been watching Reynolds. Waiting for my chance."

The ghost-memory shifts. I show Marcus an empty club, just me slipping through the kitchen door with my saxophone case. Moving like smoke toward that office.

"The safe was behind that ugly painting—dogs playing poker. Reynolds thought he was so clever. But I'd watched him open it a dozen times, memorizing the combination."

I let Marcus see it: my ghostly fingers working the dial, the safe clicking open, my face changing as I read page after page of corruption. Names. Bribes. Murders.

"That's what helped fuel my performance that night," I say. "Every note was rage."

Marcus can see the fire in my eyes, the way my hands shake—not with nerves, but with fury.

The scene shifts back to the club, now full as ghost-patrons materialize at tables: men in sharp suits, women in cocktail dresses.

White faces mostly, clustered near the stage. Black faces in the back, near the kitchen door, where the help was supposed to stay.

My memory recreates every detail: the way ice clinks in glasses, how the waitresses balance trays with practiced grace, the subtle nods between musicians as we prepare to take our places.

"Jesus," Marcus whispers. His eyes are wide, drinking in every detail. "The segregation—it's so obvious."

"That's how they wanted it," I say. "Clear lines. Clear boundaries. Until the music started, of course."

A spectral band takes shape on the stage. Willie at the piano, his fingers dancing across keys that responded to his touch better than his wife did. Jerome on drums, keeping time like his ever-lovin' heart would stop if he missed a beat. Maxwell's trumpet, sweet as summer rain. Thomas on bass, laying down a foundation solid as bedrock.

And me, in that same red dress, my alto sax gleaming through the blue haze. We play "Strange Fruit" that night, but with a twist— my own arrangement, mixing Billie Holiday's pain with bebop's defiance. I wrote it after seeing a lynch mob celebrating at the bar, their laughter poison to my ears.

My new arrangement has my alto sax weaving chromatic runs through the melody, each diminished chord progression a challenge to their authority. I mix bebop's syncopated rhythms with a classical counterpoint, my staccato attacks precise as gunshots.

"Listen to what I gave them," I command, and Marcus leans forward, his face alight with wonder, drinking in my musical stylings like they were from a faded newsreel.

The ghost-music swells. Not just a memory of sound, but the full force of my anger fueling that night's performance. The bass thrums, rumbling the floorboards. The trumpet cuts like a blade, sharp notes letting you know what's what.

And my saxophone ... I'd studied classical music in secret, learning techniques that no self-taught jazz musician was supposed to know. That night, I'd stitched Mozart into the melody, braided

Bach into the blues, created something that didn't just cross boundaries—it erased them.

My saxophone is a weapon against injustice and the casual hatred of lynch mobs.

Marcus's breath catches. "I've never heard anything like this."

"Nobody had." I watch myself play, remembering the fire burning in my bones. "Classical training meets gut-bucket blues. The kind of sound that made people forget what color I was. Made them forget everything ... except how music is supposed to *feel*."

I point at Tommy Reynolds, who stands at the bar and listens to my saxophone, his face twisting with something darker than mere hatred. His hand strays now and again to his jacket pocket. His eyes track every movement of my fingers on the keys.

"He owned the club?" Marcus asks.

"He owned half of Nawlins. Or *thought* he did." The memory overlay flickers as anger ripples through me. "Owned the police. The politicians. Thought he owned me too."

"But he didn't."

"Child, nobody owns Cecile Marshall. That was his problem." I let Marcus watch the rest of that night's first set. The way the crowd falls silent when I play. The mix of awe and fear I bring out on the white faces. The pride and terror on the Black ones. Everyone in that room knew something was changing. My music was redrawing the lines of what was possible.

Through my memory overlay, I see Marcus glancing toward that blank wall again, where Reynolds's office had once been. Smart boy. He was putting pieces together.

"After this song," I say, watching myself build to the finale, "I had fifteen minutes left to live."

The ghost-music reaches its crescendo. I hold that last note—high, pure, and defiant—until the walls themselves seemed to vibrate with its power. In the back of the club, a young Black busboy stops wiping tables to listen, his eyes shine with emotion.

I remember his name—Daniel. He'd wanted to learn saxophone. He had disappeared too.

Daniel would polish the brass rails every night, humming along with our rehearsals. He'd saved up three months' tips to buy a used saxophone, then hidden it under the kitchen floorboards.

"Gonna play here someday, Miss Cecile," he'd told me. "Gonna make music like you do."

He had the talent too. I'd heard him practicing in the alley on his breaks.

The scene dissolves, past and present merging like waves hitting shore.

Marcus's hands tremble. "Why did you show me this?"

"Because you're going to help me find justice." I drift closer, letting him feel the cold that marks my presence. "The music never dies, sugar. But I did. And somebody needs to answer for that."

He picks up his tablet, fingers moving across its surface. "There must be records. Police reports. Newspaper articles."

"Oh, there are. But the truth?" I laugh, the sound sharp as broken glass. "That's buried deeper than my body."

"Then we'll dig deeper." He stands, determination replacing fear in his eyes. "Where do we start?"

Upstairs, Rick's guitar finds its rhythm, playing something eerily familiar, echoes of my last song. Almost, but not quite. The past is still here, waiting to be uncovered. Behind that wall is the truth.

"Meet me tonight," I say. "After closing. Bring something to take notes." I gesture at his tablet. "And, baby? Leave the electronics upstairs. Some conversations shouldn't be recorded."

The modern band finishes their set upstairs, their bass beat thumping through the ceiling. Marcus sits cross-legged on the basement floor, a leatherbound notebook open on his knee. The pages are already filled with his cramped handwriting—names, dates, connections he's found in old newspapers.

"You ready?" I hover near the spot where the stage had been. The basement feels different at night, as if the walls of time are thinner in the dark hours.

He clicks his pen. "Show me."

The walls ripple, and 1952 lights up the basement. This time, the club is darker, smokier. The ghost-patrons move slower, their faces tense. Even the band members watch the door, as if expecting trouble. Tommy Reynolds stands at the bar, a half-empty whiskey glass in his hand, his bow tie loosened and stained with sweat.

I see myself walk through the kitchen door, saxophone case held tight against my chest, protecting me like armor. My red dress catches the light as I cross to the stage.

Mama had sewn that dress herself, staying up three nights running to finish it. "You wear this proud," she'd told me. "You wear it like you belong there."

"Reynolds had been drinking that night," I say. "More than usual. The mayor had shut down two of his competitors that afternoon—health code violations, he claimed. Tommy was celebrating."

Marcus watches Reynolds drain his glass, then signal for another. "Did you know what was coming?"

"Sugar, every Black musician knew what might come at the hands of the Whites. We played anyway."

I let him see the whole room. The way the white waitresses avoided Reynolds's grabbing hands. How the Black busboys kept their eyes down, moving like ghosts through the crowd, picking up empty glasses and full ashtrays. The bartender's bruised face from the last time he'd "disappointed" the boss.

The ghost-band assembles on stage. Willie at the piano, his fingers shaking as he adjusts the bench. Then Thomas with his bass, the neck scarred where Reynolds had once smashed it for playing too loud. Jerome's drums, Maxwell's trumpet. Each of us doing our best to survive.

I open the saxophone case, the horn's brass gleaming under the lights.

I'd spent my morning tips on having it professionally polished, wanting it to be perfect for that night. For what I'd planned.

"This was a new arrangement," I say so Marcus can hear. "Something I'd been working on for months. Classical structure, but with teeth. The kind of music that brings truth to power."

The music starts soft. Willie and Thomas laying down the foundation, a rhythm like a heartbeat, like a warning. Then my saxophone soars into life, reworking familiar melodies—songs of protest disguised as love songs, slave spirituals buried in dance tunes.

The audience shifts in their seats, worried because the familiarity had been stained by my intrusion. By my anger.

Tommy Reynolds's face darkens. He sets down his glass and moves toward the stage, weaving slightly. The crowd parts for him and then closes behind him, like a bait ball surrounded by sharks.

"Here," I tell Marcus. "Watch."

Reynolds reaches into his jacket. Someone bumps his arm—Daniel, the busboy, no accident in his timing. Something metal glints and disappears back into Reynolds's pocket.

The music grows louder. I watch myself, lost in the performance, my eyes closed, body swaying, lips clamped to the reed as if it provided oxygen to my soul.

The saxophone's wail rises higher, fiercer. I play every forbidden note, every rhythm that white folks claimed we'd stolen from *them*. Playing the truth about where jazz was born, in the hearts of the oppressed, in the bodies of the beaten. The music, in that moment, showed exactly who had really paid the price of the birth of jazz.

"Miss Marshall." Reynolds's voice carries over the music. "A word."

I keep playing, deliberately ignoring him. The band falters, but I urge them on with a nod. This song *has* to finish. Has to be *heard*.

"Now."

The last note hangs in the air as I lower the saxophone. The band falls silent, but the silence feels alive, dangerous. Like the sizzling tension in the air just moments before lightning strikes.

Lightning always rises from the ground, leaping to the clouds above.

"In my office," Reynolds says. Behind him, two of his security men appear, their suit jackets bulging over shoulder holsters.

Marcus scribbles in his notebook. "What happened in there?"

"I remember the knife. The look in his eyes when he saw what I'd found in that safe. The way he—" The walls shudder, past and present intermingling.

Modern lights flicker. Even now, seventy years gone, the terror of that moment shakes the foundations of this place.

Marcus stands, his notebook falling, forgotten. "Cecile?"

"Check the newspapers," I say. "August 16, 1952. They called it a robbery gone wrong. Said I was in the wrong place at the wrong time. But, sugar, ain't nothing wrong about standing up for your art. About telling the truth."

The ghost-memory of my own scream echoes through the basement.

Marcus flinches.

Above us, Rick's guitar practice falters, as if he had felt something ... shift.

"There's more," Marcus says. "Isn't there?"

"Check city records. Property deeds. Follow the money. Reynolds didn't act alone that night. Power protects power, sugar. Always has. Always will."

"I'll find it. I promise."

The basement door opens. Rick clomps down the stairs, his earlier confidence replaced by exhaustion. "Mr. Wallace? They need you upstairs. Something about tomorrow's permits."

Marcus gathers his notebook and whispers to me, "Tomorrow, I'll bring what I find."

I watch him climb the stairs, the weight of seventy years pressing down against my ghostly shoulders. The truth is out there, buried in yellowed papers and forgotten files. In that walled-off office.

Marcus spreads the copies of newspaper articles he's brought across the basement floor. The headlines tell lurid stories of jazz and violence, of lines crossed and prices paid. August heat presses down through the floorboards, making the pages curl at the edges despite the modern air-conditioning.

I drift above the papers, watching him work. His fingers trace headlines, dates, names. The modern band upstairs had finished hours ago, leaving us alone with history and dust.

"Reynolds owned more than the Spotlight," Marcus says. "Look at this." He points to a property listing. "Three clubs, two restaurants, a hotel. All bought within five years."

"All built on blood money." The walls ripple with my anger. "He ran protection rackets. Smuggling. Anything that made a profit, legal or not. The clubs were just a front, a way to launder the illicit income."

Marcus pulls out another article, this one from 1949. "There were others like you. Musicians who disappeared. Women who 'left town' suddenly." His finger traces a familiar name. "Daniel Martinez. Busboy at the Spotlight Club, aspiring saxophone player. Reported missing August 17, 1952."

The day after I died. The temperature in the basement drops ten degrees.

"Daniel saw something that night," I say. "Through the office doorway, maybe. Or heard something. Reynolds never left witnesses alive."

A cold wind sweeps through the basement, scattering papers. Marcus grabs for them, then stops. His eyes fix on something in the corner.

Marcus stands, then approaches the wall. His hand presses

against it, and I let him see what I remember. The wall dissolves in my overlay. A heavy wooden door materializes. Inside the office, Reynolds's desk. Filing cabinets. The safe behind a cheap print of Cassius Coolidge's dogs playing poker—Reynolds's idea of high culture.

"The room's still there," Marcus whispers.

He grabs a multi-tool from his pocket, flicks open the blade. Drywall crumbles under his careful cuts. Behind it, dark wood emerges. Brass hinges, green with age.

Marcus presses his ear against it, as if listening for echoes. The basement's temperature drops another five degrees.

"The door's been locked for decades," Marcus whispers. He runs his fingers along the drywall's surface, finding a seam that doesn't quite match the others. "But this drywall's newer. Maybe five years old."

"Reynolds's grandson took over then," I say. "Started renovating. Must have found the old room and decided it needed to disappear entirely."

Marcus works faster, clearing the drywall, uncovering the mahogany door one bite at a time. When he finally pushes the door, it groans open on ancient hinges. Dust billows. He turns on his phone's flashlight.

The office is a time capsule. Reynolds's desk, warped by decades. Empty bottles in the trash, labels long faded. The painting hangs crookedly, hiding the safe. The air feels old, thick with secrets, musky with memories.

Marcus moves to the desk, opens drawers. Papers spill out, brown with age. His fingers move faster, sorting. The beam of his flashlight catches cobwebs, rat droppings, the accumulated detritus of stagnant decades.

"Here." He holds up a ledger. "Names. Dates. Payments."

As Marcus turns the pages, I peer over his shoulder, careful not to let my cold presence touch him. The handwriting is neat, precise. Each entry a record of corruption. Of ownership. Of death.

"Stop," I say, and then point. "That page."

August 16, 1952. My name. A number. And beside it, three sets of initials.

"Police captain," Marcus said. "District judge. And ..."

"The mayor. Reynolds had them all in his pocket. Every one of them profited from his empire."

Marcus photographs the pages with his phone, hands trembling. A receipt slips from between the pages. He picks it up, squints at the faded ink.

"A knife," he says. "Purchased the day before. From Chen's Hardware on Canal Street."

"Premeditated," I whisper. The walls ripple with my rage.

He turns, facing the spot where I hover. "We can prove it, now. Show what really happened. Who was involved."

A door slams upstairs. Footsteps cross the modern club floor. Heavy steps, purposeful.

I stretch my senses upward, memories gathered 'round me like a thick fleece blanket.

Three men. The night manager. And ...

"Reynolds," I said. "His grandson. He owns the building now."

Marcus shoves the ledger in his jacket. More footsteps sound from the top of the basement stairs. A voice calls out.

"Mr. Wallace? You down there?"

Boot heels strike wooden stairs, each step deliberate, as the three men enter the basement.

Marcus stands in the open doorway of Reynolds's office, his phone flashlight illuminating decades-old dust.

"Inspecting the walls," he says, his voice steady. "Found some water damage."

Tommy Reynolds III steps into view, his suit as expensive as his grandfather's had been, a blued-steel semiautomatic in his hand. Same eyes, same sharp nose, same way of looking at people like they are property. The night manager's flashlight sweeps the basement, catching Marcus in its glare.

"At midnight?" Reynolds moves closer, each step precise. "Behind drywall in a sealed room?"

The night manager circles left. The third man, thick-necked and silent, blocks the stairs. Their movements are choreographed, practiced. Like they've done this before.

I gather myself, focus on the past and summon the ghost-overlay one more time.

Reynolds stops. His eyes track the changes, widening slightly as he finds me in the dim light. "So, it's true. The ghost of the Spotlight Club."

"You knew?" Marcus's voice cracks.

"Family legend," Reynolds says, his smile tight. "Grandfather wrote about it in his private journals. Said he could hear saxophone music some nights, coming from an empty room. Said it drove him to drink, hearing those same songs over and over."

The gun in his hand looks too modern against the phantom backdrop of 1952. But it will kill.

Behind Reynolds, the thick-necked man draws his own weapon.

"The ledger," Reynolds says. "Please."

Marcus's hands move toward his jacket.

I surge forward, pushing through him. The temperature plunges. Ice crystals form on the walls, on the ancient desk, on the painting that hides the safe.

"You want to know how it happened?" My voice echoes with rage. "How your grandfather killed me? Killed Daniel? Killed anyone who threatened his worldview?"

The ghost-memory of that night slams into the room.

Earlier that evening: I am at the safe, discovering the ledger. My hands tremble as I photograph pages with a small camera I'd borrowed. Daniel appears in the doorway. He'd followed me, worried about my safety.

"Miss Cecile, what you doing in here?"

"Documenting the truth, sugar. Every bribe, every murder, every—"

Footsteps in the hallway. We freeze. I shove the ledger back, close the safe, grab Daniel's hand. We slip out through the kitchen just as Reynolds's voice echoes from upstairs.

Later: the performance. My saxophone wailing with righteous anger. Reynolds watching, his face darkening as he realizes something has changed in my playing. Something dangerous.

"Miss Marshall. A word."

The confrontation. Reynolds with the knife he'd bought the previous day. Daniel bursting through the door, trying to save me.

"Cecile," Marcus whispers.

"Watch," I tell him. "Watch what power does to protect itself."

Reynolds's grandfather grabs my wrist. The blade catches the light before slicing into my throat. Daniel runs, making it halfway up the stairs before they catch him.

The knife slashes again, a final time. My saxophone clatters to the floor from nerveless fingers.

But, this time, the memory continues. Beyond the knife slash.

Beyond the blood.

To the safe. To my memories of what I'd seen inside. To what Daniel had witnessed me photographing.

Reynolds's gun hand trembles. "Stop."

"Pictures," I say. "Documents. Proof of every crime your grandfather ever committed. Every bribe. Every murder. Daniel tried to save me. That's why he had to die too."

The night manager raises his phone to call someone. The thick-necked man moves toward Marcus.

I reach deep, pull every bit of strength I can. The walls shake. Music rises from below—not ghost-music, but the powerful notes of early jazz, whose echoes had lain dormant in the walls, pushing up through the foundations. Through the floorboards. Through time itself. Every note ever played at the Spotlight Club, every song of defiance, every cry of pain and pride.

I watch myself stand from the floor, bloodstained and defiant. It's me, becoming myself back then, not dying as I had, but finding new life through joyful redemption. The air turns icy, and my breath frosts as I pick up my saxophone and press it to my hungry lips, letting it wail out my pain of betrayal, of hatred, of subjugation now rectified. I'm free for the first time in my life, decades after I shuffled off my mortal coil.

The music swells—Maxwell's trumpet, Willie's piano, Thomas's bass, Jerome's drums. And, through it all, my saxophone speaking truth to power in 4/4 time.

Marcus bolts for the stairs.

The thick-necked man grabs for him, passing through a ghost-table, and stumbles.

Upstairs, Rick's guitar joins the music, though he's probably wondering why he suddenly felt the need to play.

"The ledger stays here," I say as the music grows louder. "But your *secrets* don't."

Reynolds fires at me. The bullet passes through my past self, through Daniel's ghost, through history itself. It strikes the safe, sparking.

Marcus reaches the top of the stairs as police sirens wail to a halt outside.

Reynolds's gun hits the floor as blue and red lights flash through the windows.

The thick-necked man tries to run but slips on an icy floor that shouldn't exist in August.

The past fades. The music softens. The modern basement returns, looking the same yet changed forever.

As police boots thunder down the stairs, Reynolds raises his hands in surrender, as do his henchmen. Justice arrives, finally.

I feel Daniel's presence beside me. I look down at his beautiful face.

He smiles and nods at me. He is holding the saxophone he's retrieved from beneath the floorboards. The one he'd buried so long ago. The one Reynolds would never allow him to play.

I lift my saxophone and grin, and Daniel raises his. Together, we play a single, pure note that soars through the walls, through years, through death itself.

A pure note, without guile and full of hope.

A note of truth.

A note of freedom.

Above us, Rick's guitar answers in melodic agreement.

***

About the Author

Lou J Berger lives near Ocala, Florida, with his high school crush and three rescue dogs. A member of SFWA, he has been published in *Clarkesworld* magazine, *Galaxy's Edge* magazine, and a host of anthologies. He is *still* working on his first novel.

His author website is LouJBerger.com.

Follow him on the following social media platforms:

Bluesky: bsky.app/profile/loujberger.bsky.social

Facebook: facebook.com/AuthorLouJBerger/

Substack: loujberger.substack.com/

GRAVE'S GRAMOPHONE
ELIZABETH LOWHAM

I crank the gramophone. It's the original, crafted by my great-great-grandmother, Marie-Louise, the last witch of the Somme, who saw the German advance coming in the First World War, saw the death that would sweep her beloved French countryside, and gave her response in magic. Magic conducted by steel needle and brass horn. Magic that compounds with each twist of the handle. Twisted once, twice, three times—three circles start a spiral continuing into eternity, and eternity contains those we've lost. Through the music of a gramophone, the last witch of the Somme brought peace to the dead.

These are the things we believe in our family.

My song is "When I Lost You." To discover the magic, you must first discover your song. My mother didn't have the patience, and she told me not to bother, not to waste my life searching for a song I might never hear and one that might make my life worse by the hearing. But I believed, and for six summers in a row, I sat with my grandmother in the open garage at twilight, fanning mosquitoes in the dry air and listening to the static and crackle of sound grooves in old shellac records.

"Listen," my grandmother told me, "for what sings in your bones."

In the sixth summer, I decided to surrender. My sister had a college degree and a new internship in a newsroom, and, as she so often reminded me, the world was passing me by. So although my soul sighed at the disappointment of it, I was going to take a grant and take exams and take a degree I didn't want to pay bills I wanted even less, and I—like most of the world—would never hear what sang in my bones.

But when I told my grandmother, she laughed.

"I'm going," I said crossly.

"Then go." She kept her blue eyes on the gramophone's circling turntable while her reverent hand brushed the plinth, and her lips trembled as they always did when she remembered her mother and her mother's mother and the faraway French countryside where the last witch of the Somme found her purpose.

I didn't go anywhere.

Ten days later, I heard it. In the crackle of my song, I heard a hum that went beyond hearing, that sank like water into the pores of my skin and quenched a thirst deep in my skeleton. I came alive, and for the briefest moment, I saw beyond the grave. Grandmother said it was a lavender field for her, with the purple turning red when someone passed the rows. For me, it was a tree with too many branches, hung with the stars themselves and bowing beneath the weight yet still stretching relentlessly upward to conquer a black sky.

Your glimpse into eternity is both a truth and a warning. That is what we believe in my family.

The hospital morgue is silent while I crank the gramophone. For morticians, it's always that way. Silence. The dead not talking. Just an empty space of white paint and cold metal where they have to make their own conversation and company. I am not a mortician, and they prefer not to be around me. They leave me alone with my gramophone to work, only a security camera in the far corner standing guard to be certain I do only what I've been hired to do.

On paper, I'm a translator, accurately enough. Rather than speaking Spanish, Russian, or Arabic, I speak the grave. I speak the death rattle. I am the steel needle tracing the grooves of a lost life to give it sound.

The gramophone shivers with vibrations through brass that bring it to life and open a lost era inside a sterile, modern morgue. Static and white noise, a pleasant crackle infusing the air with all the decades between myself and the singer, Henry Burr, who is in the grave just like everyone our shared song will connect me to. Cradled in the melody, I breathe more deeply.

> *I lost the angel who gave me*
> *Summer, the whole winter through.*
> *I lost the gladness that turned into sadness,*
> *When I lost you.*

You would think I'd be tired of it by now, but you can't get tired of your song. It would be like getting tired of the sound of your own heartbeat.

I sit beside the examination table, where a body is arranged beneath a sheet. It's always best if I can speak to them before an autopsy or embalming. The dead grow testy once they've been cut open or filled with chemicals, and can we blame them? Quickly, I scan the chart left for me by the head mortician: Janice, female; mid-thirties; car accident, died of resulting injuries.

The questions submitted by her family have been transposed for me, typed into the chart along with all the other information, so I can't see if the writer's hand was shaking, if tears of grief marked the page. I can only assume.

I wait a full play-through of my song, gathering my thoughts and my nerves—a meditation attended by myself and the dead and an heirloom gramophone—until we reach the end and begin again.

> *The roses, each one,*

> *Met with the sun,*
> *Sweetheart, when I met you.*

Janice opens her eyes. She won't ask any questions of her own, won't speak except to answer me. Her gaze is glazed and distant, like a coma patient with eyes open.

Three questions and she'll be gone forever. We can never speak twice.

Janice, Janice, gone too soon.

If you could ask three final questions of your mother, what would they be? Three final questions of your wife, your daughter, your sister, your friend. That's what families face when they hire me. They face a form with three empty lines that can't hope to cover an entire life, and I've never blamed the ones who change their minds, who leave the lines blank. Sometimes nothing is better than the overwhelming possibilities of everything that can't fit.

> *The sunshine had fled,*
> *The roses were dead,*
> *Sweetheart, when I lost you.*

First question.

"Janice, who do you want to leave your belongings to?"

That's common—detached questions about estates and wills, to solve family disputes or to cover what was never discussed in life. I understand detached. There's no need to even acknowledge magic at work; we can all just pretend the dead left this behind in writing.

Janice speaks slowly, cataloging a list, and I take careful note of each word using shorthand in a notebook, because typing on even the quietest of keyboards interferes with the sound of the gramophone. She lists a cedar chest from her grandmother, a set of Thanksgiving china never used, a car she doesn't know has been totaled. The dead don't comprehend dying. In that, they're no different from the living.

The birds ceased their song,
Right turned to wrong,
Sweetheart, when I lost you.

Second question.

"Janice, what last words would you leave your daughter?"

Last words—I've heard a spectrum. One man said to me, "Nothing," and that shocked me into a laugh that sat heavily in my stomach all night. I'm privy to too much intimacy. This is the real reason my mother has never searched out her song. She sat beside my grandmother three times and listened to the dead and thought it was better to let them die than to trespass on their lives and their deaths.

I didn't deduce that on my own: She screamed it at me during my grandmother's viewing three years ago. The last time I spoke to my grandmother. The last time my mother and sister spoke to me.

I clear my throat. A mistake—the needle skips on the shellac, warbling the song. I let it play all the way through again to stabilize.

My family doesn't like to speculate about theology, but we all wonder. We can't help it. When you can touch the afterlife but can't define it, it increases the torture of not knowing. What waits for us beyond? Does our work please or offend an eternal being? Do we offer peace to families or interfere with the natural order of the dead? Are we hurting or helping?

Hurting, said my mother.

Helping, said my grandmother.

Helping, said my great-grandmother.

Helping, said Marie-Louise, the last witch of the Somme.

For me, I can't escape the knowledge that a record is on the turntable. If I don't act as the needle to translate it, it will go unheard, but it's still playing, playing, playing. And what if there's no peace for the dead if that song goes unheard?

These are the things we believe in my family.

I write Janice's last words to her daughter, trying to capture each one precisely while not seeing them at all, while offering the thinnest curtain of privacy. It never really works.

> *I lost the sunshine and roses,*
> *I lost the heavens of blue,*
> *I lost the beautiful rainbow,*
> *I lost the morning dew—*

Third question.
Final question.
"Janice, you know that I love you, right?"
A cheat question. Those are familiar too. The people who want to speak one last time—or, perhaps, are too afraid to hear any more answers. They could leave a line blank, but no one ever does. If they commit to questions, they always fill all three lines. Even for people who don't understand what I do, there's an unspoken superstition about beginning things and leaving them unfinished.
If I never asked a third question, would Janice never close her eyes? I don't know. That's not the sort of thing I want to test.
In response to the question, Janice nods, and I wonder if she knows who the unnamed "I" belongs to. A spouse? A parent? I can't tell, and I can't tell if she can.

> *I lost the gladness that turned into sadness,*
> *When I lost you.*

She closes her eyes.
She's gone, never to be returned again.
And I wait for the next body.

I'm not at the morgue when my sister calls. I'm at the library, using their Wi-Fi to stream crime dramas, because I can barely afford my apartment much less add amenities like internet and air-conditioning. While my phone buzzes in my hand, I stare at the screen, and the only reason I don't let it go to voicemail is because I'm certain if I have to call her back, she won't answer.

But after three years of silence, there's only one reason she would call to begin with.

"Mom's dead," Sophie says with detached bluntness. "She suffered a ruptured aortic aneurysm and died before reaching the hospital." Her newscaster voice is showing. *We now go live to our correspondent on the scene.* "I'm letting you know because it's a courtesy."

"She's my mother too," I say numbly.

"Which is why you're invited to the funeral. But the witch relic isn't."

Witch relic. That's what Mom called the gramophone after I used it to speak to my grandmother. Three small questions that gave me three silent years that have now turned into eternity.

"I want to talk to her." The words spill from me without control, like a leg bucking beneath a reflex hammer.

"You're too late," Sophie snaps. "Talking is for the living."

She gives me the details—*Saturday, 11:00 AM, luncheon afterward at the funeral home*—and emphasizes that everything has been arranged. There's no need for me to help. No need for me at all.

It's Tuesday.

It's Tuesday at 2:00 PM and I'm watching a muted crime drama play on a cracked laptop screen and I haven't eaten lunch and my mother is dead and my sister hangs up the phone.

I wish for a body in the morgue, but there's no body on Tuesday, and there's no body on Wednesday. There's no body until Thursday, when I crank the gramophone, and I speak to the dead. In my dreams that night, I see a star-laden tree with branches directly overhead but still unreachable.

Somehow, even living between its fingers, the touch of death manages to be a shock.

On Friday, I go to the funeral home. *Sneak* to the funeral home might be more accurate, though I'm walking in broad daylight. Walking in the open and feeling like a thief.

I speak to the front-desk assistant, tell her I'm here to see my mother. She eyes the cumbersome wooden briefcase weighing me down on one side, but I don't bother explaining a magical gramophone disassembled for transportation.

"Please," I say instead.

After checking to confirm my mother's body is here, she leads me to a room filled with sample caskets.

"Wait here," she says, "and the funeral director will take you down to the fridge."

The room is no doubt meant to be comforting with its warm lighting, plush carpet, and gentle elevator music filtering through overhead speakers. I prefer the silence of the morgue. Each moment of waiting aches more than the arm carrying my gramophone, and the waiting goes on for far too many moments. I fiddle absently with the brass pendant at my neck, but even that fails to offer comfort.

Finally, I make my way back to the front. "Excuse me—"

Just then, a familiar figure blows through the door like one of the dangerous storms covered by her newsroom.

"I knew it." Sophie points at me in accusation. "I told them to call me when they saw you. I *knew* you would do something like this, after you promised to leave the witch relic out of it."

"I never promised that," I say uncomfortably. I *should* have promised something like that to make the sneaking more effective. But lying has never been a skill of mine, which is why I spent years suffering punishments for things Sophie blamed convincingly on me while I was never able to exact revenge.

My mother finally caught on, and one Saturday afternoon, she sent Sophie to play with friends while the two of us went downtown to a little boutique where she bought me the necklace I'm wearing today. A fleur-de-lis pendant on a chain, because fleur-de-lis stands for virtue.

My Lou never lies, Mother said.

"Get out," Sophie orders.

"I have a right," I say.

"A *right?*" Sophie looks to the front-desk assistant for support, and the woman suddenly becomes very busy at her computer, clearly wishing we'd hold our family disputes in private. "Lou, you don't have a *right* to ignore how Mom felt about what you do. You didn't have a right to talk to Grandma without asking the rest of us."

The gramophone's box feels unbearably heavy, trembling my arm.

"You have to let the relic go and live in reality. Get a real job that supports a real life. I've seen your apartment, if we can call it that."

I set the box by my feet, trying to work feeling back into my fingers. "You don't want to hear Mom's last words to you?"

Sophie's lips thin. "I've had a lifetime of words, and that's all anyone gets. What you want is unnatural. It isn't how life works."

"This is what our family believes."

"Not everyone in our family! Go home, Lou, or I'm calling the police, and then you won't even be at the funeral."

My hand is tingling and my heart is shrinking in my chest, but I shake my head. "I'm not leaving."

She stands silent, and I realize silence is worse. Her eyes dart to the box at my feet. Before I can stop her, she snatches it, crouches, and unsnaps the fasteners.

"Sophie, don't!" I wrench the box away, but not before she grabs my record in its sleeve.

With a decisive movement, she pulls the record free and hurls it to the floor, where shellac fractures against tile. I clutch the gramophone's box, and I stare at the broken black pieces, the ones that held my song.

Sophie breathes heavily. "I'm sure you can find a replacement, but not by tomorrow. If I was stronger, I'd break the whole thing. I should."

With tears in my eyes, I give her what she wants—I leave.

It's the last night before the funeral, and my dreams are all nightmares.

I'm trying to glue a record that can't be glued.

I'm standing beneath a tree, trying to glue a star back on a branch because I didn't mean to pick it, because I think I might have hurt it, and I didn't mean to.

If you pick an apple from a tree, it can never be returned. You could tape it or glue it or nail it to the wood, but the connection is severed and can never be replaced. The apple can only wither and die. Is that the warning of my glimpse into eternity? Have I been pulling people from trees?

If so, then my grandmother has been pulled and my great-grandmother and great-great-grandmother. Where will they go?

Where goes the fallen fruit?

Maybe Sophie saved our mother's soul by keeping her away from me. Or maybe all she did was ruin my last chance for peace.

I dream again, but this time, I'm a bystander. I'm a shadow in a canvas tent, breathing stale air tinged with rot while a nurse in a white uniform tends to wounded soldiers. No, not wounded. Dead. The nurse sits beside a gramophone and turns the handle once, twice, three times, before the last witch of the Somme asks her three questions.

"Who are you?" Men without identity bracelets, without their names embroidered into their clothing, give her the answer that will keep them from the Tomb of the Unknown Soldier.

"How do I find your family?" They give commanding officer names and childhood addresses, anything to direct their bodies back home.

I wait for the final question.

"You fought to defend us, and I am grateful. Will you remember that?"

I frown. Not last words but a cheat question. I considered them cheats. *The last witch of the Somme brought peace to the dead.* That is what my family believes. Last words are left behind, and that's peace to the living.

One last chance to speak to the dead, I realize, is not one-sided. Their final chance to speak is also their final chance to hear, and it matters what is said. Not just what my mother would say to me, but what I would say to her.

But the record is broken, and our last chance to hear broke with it.

Though I consider not attending the funeral, it's all I have left. The service is held at the graveside, next to a closed wooden casket, and the cemetery is beautiful and peaceful and green. A far different place of death from a morgue. Trees line the fence, casting shade across the manicured grass. We stand in oak shadow. From the corner of my eye, I see the branches multiplying, twinkling with sparks of light against a black sky, but it isn't real.

What is real?

I can't be a translator today. I have to forget the gramophone sitting at home, because the ache is too sharp if I can't. The knowing is too sharp. Knowing I *could have* spoken but can't now. I have to be an ordinary person, not the descendant of a witch. At my own mother's funeral, I have to pretend I'm not of this family.

We stand beneath a white canopy, pointless shade that seems an impostor next to the trees. Sophie and I take opposite sides of the shelter, piling between us as many people as possible—our mother's coworkers, friends, neighbors, extended family.

Extended branches.

Stop it.

The funeral director begins the service by reading a quote from classic literature. He offers platitudes about peace, gentle and soothing. They're meant for us, of course, not my mother, because he can't speak to the dead. No one can.

I watch my sister on the other side of the canopy, and I hate her for taking this away from me. It's a sad hatred, dull and throbbing, fueled by frustration, because I don't think either of us *wants* to hate the other, but we are face-to-face while both trying to walk forward. One of us had to move, to lose, because we are diametrically opposed.

Hurting.

Helping.

We can't both be right about magic's effect on the dead. We might both be wrong together, but we can't both be right.

I stepped aside, and Sophie walks forward. Why can't I accept that?

Because I didn't step. I was pushed. And I still want to walk.

I want to talk.

I want to talk to my mom.

My uncle reads a poem. I think he spoke to my mother even less than I did, not out of anger but just out of the distance of life. Poetry and platitudes. Condolences. A sea of words swirling around me without meaning and around her without hearing.

A bird rustles the overhead branches, dislodging a leaf that twirls down to rest on the canopy, separated from the tree.

Before the funeral director can speak again, I step forward. I'm not on the program, but no one stops me. I'm the daughter of the dead.

"In harvest season," I say, "the unharvested fruit falls to the ground. In autumn, the leaves abandon the trees. Leaves and apples, they fall down."

My heart is hammering in my chest. People are staring with polite expressions meant to veil their confusion.

"But stars are meant for the sky. Maybe after plucking, they fall up."

That oppressive sky bearing down on all the branches. Maybe after life, that's the next battle. Maybe that's the truth of my glimpse into eternity.

"In order to shine against a black sky, a star needs a little light. I can give a little light. This is what *I* believe."

My hand is on my necklace, my thumb caressing the fleur-de-lis like a worry stone.

I turn the brass pendant between my fingers, twist the chain. Once, twice, three times. Three circles start a spiral continuing into eternity, and eternity contains those we've lost.

My song is "When I Lost You," and I may have lost it, but my mother's record is on the turntable, and the music is in my bones, and I am the needle.

So I sing.

> *I lost the sunshine and roses,*
> *I lost the heavens of blue,*
> *I lost the beautiful rainbow,*
> *I lost the morning dew—*

Most of the listeners wear faint smiles or tearful eyes. It's just a sad song at a funeral.

But Sophie's expression darkens. "Lou, what are you doing?"

I am the translator. I speak the grave. I am the daughter of the dead, and I am the daughter of magic. Both meet in me.

My voice strengthens with feeling.

> *I lost the angel who gave me*
> *Summer, the whole winter through.*
> *I lost the gladness that turned into sadness,*
> *When I lost you.*

"Stop it, Louise!" shouts Sophie.

I am the needle.

I am the needle.

I am the needle.

As I stride toward the casket, Sophie leaps to stop me. We wrestle like we did as little girls, sending gasps rippling through the audience and an embarrassed plea from our uncle—"Now, girls, let's be calm"—all while I'm still singing. The whole thing must be uncanny for the funeral director, who openly stares and will no doubt tell his own family this evening, "You'll never believe the funeral I directed today."

Despite being my older sister, Sophie almost never won our fights as children. She fights too cleanly, unwilling to fully sacrifice her composure, while I embrace anything that gives advantage.

Even at thirty-one, I'm not above hair pulling.

"Charlotte Louise!" Sophie shrieks, like she's my mother. But she isn't. My mother is in an oak casket in the shadow of an oak tree, and I won't let her go without knowing one more thing.

While Sophie's off-balance and cradling her scalp, I dart past her and heave the casket lid up. Everyone's in turmoil now, yelling or reaching to stop me. My uncle pulls at my arm, but I clamp my hands around the pallbearer's bar, and I dig my feet into the ground like roots. The music is singing in my bones, singing and singing even without my voice.

> *The birds ceased their song,*
> *Right turned to wrong,*
> *A day turned to years,*
> *The world seemed in tears,*
> *Mother, when I lost you.*

"I am talking to my mother!" I scream, giving awkward pause to the reaching hands.

She's laid out in the casket, dressed in a beautiful navy skirt suit but looking stiff and cold and unlike herself. As if in response to my voice, she opens her eyes, a distant gaze aimed toward a distant sky.

The graveyard falls still, as if everyone is afraid to move, afraid to speak. There's no sound beyond the song in my soul.

> *I lost the sunshine and roses,*
> *I lost the heavens of blue.*

First question.

"I don't know where you're going"—my voice is raspy and terrified, and I'm still clinging to the bar as if my hold alone can keep my mother from leaving—"and I hate that I don't know, but wherever it is, will you be at peace?"

"No," she says without looking at me, without looking at anything. Just a ghost with her voice, just an echo.

My uncle draws back, his hand pressed to his mouth. I don't turn to see anyone else.

> *I lost the beautiful rainbow,*
> *I lost the morning dew.*

Second question.

"Why not?" I choke out.

"My girls," she says, like I should know what that means, like it means everything.

I turn to look at my sister. Sophie's on her knees, grass stains streaking her Ralph Lauren skirt and tears streaking her cheeks.

"I hate you," she whispers, but I hear it.

I hate her, too, but that's a problem for another time. We *have* time. My mother has one question left.

And I don't know the right question to ask.

In my mind, I see Marie-Louise in a canvas tent with fallen soldiers. Bringing peace to the dead. I do know what to ask; I just don't want to ask it. One question, and my mother is gone forever. If I never ask, will she stay?

But she won't be herself. Most of her is gone already. All that remains is the answering machine, the mailbox, the courier waiting for one last message, and I can either give it or withhold it, but I can't bring her back.

All I can do is shelter one pinprick of hope that we'll meet again as stars.

> *I lost the mother who gave me*
> *Summer, the whole winter through.*
> *I lost the gladness that turned into sadness,*
> *When I lost you.*

Final question.

"I forgive you, Mom, and I love you, and Sophie loves you, and we'll manage. We'll work it out. You leaving would always be too soon, and we're a mess right now, but we'll manage. Do you believe me?"

I hold my breath. This was my only chance to bring us both peace. She could say no.

She says, "My Lou never lies."

It's my imagination, but for just an instant, there's a spark of her previous self in her eyes, like a star catching light. I let go of the casket's bar, my hands numb and bloodless.

My mother closes her eyes.

She's gone, taking with her the song in my bones, leaving behind silence and unspoken questions, the difficulties of death for everyone who survives.

But we'll manage.

That's what I believe.

About the Author

Elizabeth Lowham is the multi-award-winning author of *Casters and Crowns*, as well as other YA fantasy novels. Her short stories have been included in the anthologies *Once Upon a Future Time, vol. 4* and *Once Upon a Moonless Night*. When not writing, she enjoys taking train rides with her family, listening to crackly old music, and sleeping when her baby sleeps (or not).

About the Editors

Lisa Mangum has worked in publishing for more than twenty-five years. She has been the managing editor for Shadow Mountain since 2014 and has worked with several award-winning and *New York Times* best-selling authors.

Lisa is also the author of four national best-selling YA novels (The Hourglass Door trilogy and *After Hello*), several short stories and novellas, and a nonfiction book about the craft of writing based on the TV show *Supernatural*. Her most recent book, *Write Fearless. Edit Smart. Get Published.: A Master Class for Fiction Writers*, was awarded Utah's Best of State for nonfiction in 2024.

She regularly teaches at writing conferences across the country as well as hosts a writing weekend twice a year in Capitol Reef National Park.

Wendy Christensen is a certified word nerd who knows how to help authors turn a good story into a great one and the difference between a gerund and a present participle. A freelance editor and a writer of fiction and poetry, Wendy lives in a picturesque valley nestled in the Rocky Mountains with her husband and six children. She is fond of carousels and eating ice cream straight from the carton.

Wendy has a BA in English from the University of Utah and professional certificates in Copyediting and Creative Writing from UC San Diego Extension. She is a member of ACES, Editorial

Freelancers Association, and serves on the board of Utah Freelance Editors. She is also a Plottr-Certified Editor. Find her at CarouselEditorial.com.

IF YOU LIKED ...
IF YOU LIKED REQUIEM,
YOU MIGHT ALSO ENJOY:

Other WordFire Press Anthologies

<u>Edited by Lisa Mangum</u>
One Horn to Rule Them All (2014)
A Game of Horns (2015)
Dragon Writers (2016)
Undercurrents (2018)
X Marks the Spot (2020)
Hold Your Fire (2021)
Eat, Drink, and Be Wary (2022)
Of Wizards and Wolves (2023)
A Bit of Luck (2024)
Weird Wilderness (2025).

<u>Edited by Jonathan Maberry</u>
Shadows & Verse (2025).

Visit us at:
wordfirepress.com